The Short Cut

By the same author, translated into English,
and published by The Marlboro Press

THE VIA VENETO PAPERS

Ennio Flaiano

The Short Cut

Translated from Italian by Stuart Hood

The Marlboro Press

Published in the United States
by the Marlboro Press, Marlboro, Vermont
through arrangement with Quartet Books Limited, London

Originally published in Italian under the title
TEMPO DI UCCIDERE
Copyright © Longanesi, Milano, 1947
Copyright © Rosetta Flaiano, 1992

This translation first published in 1950
by Pellegrini & Cudahy, New York

The publication of the present volume is made possible in part
by a grant from the National Endowment for the Arts.

Library of Congress Catalog Card Number 93-80761

ISBN 1-56897-019-6

"A time to kill and a time to heal;
and a time to . . ."

ECCLESIASTES III 3

Contents

The Short Cut

THE SHORT CUT

1

I WAS AMAZED to be alive, but tired of waiting for help. Tired above all of the trees which grew along the ravine wherever there was room for a seed which happened to have finished up there. The heat, that clinging quality in the atmosphere which not even the morning breeze was able to temper, made the trees look like stuffed animals.

Ever since the truck had overturned just at the bend on the first hill the tooth had begun to hurt again, and now an irresistible impulse—perhaps impatience brought on by the neuralgia—impelled me to leave the spot. "I'm going off," I said, getting up. The private, who was smoking contentedly and by this time prepared to share the surprises of this latest adventure with me, became gloomy. "Where to?" he asked.

"Down to the river." We were not yet in sight of the river, but it was down there in its valley, hollowed out by the centuries and guarded by a few lazy crocodiles, hunters of the native washerwomen. I thought I might find a lorry, so as to climb up the other side. I had to get there before evening or waste one of the four days they had given me to find a dentist.

Yes, I had to go. Beyond the valley, in the white sky, there rose the opposite rim of the table-land. The river had dug its way round the mountains, leaving them as dry as bones. The two rims were kilometres apart—how many I don't know because distances deceive in that light which brings out the most distant details; maybe five, maybe six. And beyond the rim, the calm life of the mines. Farther on still and the word Sunday would acquire meaning again. I would find the first bed with sheets, the first newspaper stall. And a dentist.

The soldier did not want to give in. "Wait," he said, "someone will pass." I looked at the truck lying with its wheels against the bank, and shook my head. No one passed. Only a colonel had passed, as bad-tempered as a general. And the soldier's petulance began to annoy me. The fact that we had escaped together no longer seemed to me a good reason for showing each other photographs, telling each other about our affairs, making the usual forecasts about our return to Italy. And yet I was sorry to leave him.

"So you've going to leave me alone?"

I began to gather up my things; my pack, my belt with the revolver. To make my flight less brutal I looked for a pretext, but it was a bad one. I told him that if I found a truck down at the river—the drivers often stopped to bathe—I could come back and help him. The soldier pretended to believe me and this unexpected and unfriendly act of acquiescence on his part made me blush. He shook my hand without warmth; he was really disappointed. After I had gone fifty yards a bend in the road hid him from me, him and his truck, and from that day I never saw him again.

Was it still very far to the bridge? I could have taken a short cut, but I have not much faith in African short cuts. Yet every so often the road—on the side towards the river—gave on to a path which after a few short twists and turns led steeply down towards the bush.

So I disregarded the short cuts and after two hours—the heat had increased and the trees grown terrifyingly tall, but more and more like pieces of cardboard, more and more old and greasy, like the saints of an abandoned cult—saw that the bush was growing thicker and that the road was becoming hot and sandy. Suddenly the river appeared in front of me. They were building a bridge.

There was still a cross or two among the great trees, and under the hot sand; in packing-cases for bully beef and ration biscuits, there was still a corpse or two. Some soldier who had halted saying: "I'm finished," and had even taken the trouble to convince the sergeant and then the lieutenant and then the captain to let him rest. And something in the surroundings—perhaps the grey sand, perhaps the buds on the trees—had told him that he was indeed about to rest. The people who pack the ration biscuits and the bully beef all those thousands of kilometres away have no idea that the wood is precious. Such fragile wood. A packing case is always useful, and you need only have one to cheer up your tent with a wonderful piece of furniture. When things are quiet it does to put up the picture of the woman you love between a book and your tobacco pouch. And it is not so difficult to get a woman to love as to get a packing-case.

There was not even a lorry. The labourers had stopped work because of the heat and were eating. Fresh arrivals to judge by the large sun-glasses which they had not yet thrown away. They were sitting in front of their tents chatting with the carabiniere from the check post, still surprised to have landed up here, in a country so different from the Africa they had imagined.

So there wasn't even a lorry. They said that the section lorry had just left, and indeed you could hear its engine, a long way off already, on the first hills. "And when does it come back?"

"Tomorrow morning," said a workman, really astonished that I did not know this detail. "It comes back tomorrow morning with the rations and the mail."

That was a nice word. Through the stuff of my pocket I touched her last letter. It had arrived the day before. A long letter, closely written in a regular, round but slender hand, the pages full right up to the margin without a white space: a letter to read and read again. But if a lorry didn't turn up I would have to stay there. I began to get excited, my trip was being wrecked. Then I explained where I came from, how important it was for me to reach the table-land at once, and told the story of the accident. I certainly did not expect to arouse much interest, but these workmen neither made any comment nor proposed a solution to the problem. Africa is full of trucks overturning.

"There's not much chance of a car passing at this time of day," the carabiniere said at last. He advanced various hypotheses, talked of convoys that might pass and on the other hand might not; and meantime he looked at me, stretched out on the ground, with his helmet leaning on his brow.

"If I walk up, where will I find the first lorries?"

"There's a command post twelve kilometres away, right on the edge of the plateau," said the carabiniere, and gave a long yawn. Twelve kilometres would be three hours' marching if the heat didn't make it four. And it was the worst moment to start an undertaking like that; but I had to make up my mind. "How long do you think it will take me?"

From the first answers I gathered how useless my question was, but I had asked it because I hated to go away and was looking for excuses. The workmen were calling each other names good-humouredly in dialect, making even this topic a regional matter. They were accusing each other of bad judgment of distances they, too, had found an excuse, but one for amusing themselves—and finally agreed that I would take four hours.

"You won't take long if you walk quickly," called a voice behind my back. I looked to see who had spoken; it was a young fellow with fair hair. Rather a shy person; when I looked at him he became flustered as he repeated his opinion which he had not at all meant to be ironical. On the way down, the tablets for my toothache had taken away my appetite completely. Down here the heat was unbearable. I turned my face to the first hill, but had not gone a hundred yards when I heard someone calling to me. The fair-haired workman was running towards me, and when he was close said: "If you take the short cut you'd take half the time." He stood still looking at me, waiting for me to ask him where the short cut was.

Where had I seen this young man before? He had one of those gentle workman's faces which one has seen at least once before, looking perhaps from the window of a train. Or did I attach to its singular beauty more importance than it merited? I have often thought of that youth (he must by nature have been an attentive waiter), but I would like to dispel any doubt as to the importance of his presence in this story. He was only a workman who wanted to do me a service and to show me a good short cut. Heaven forbid that I should arouse the suspicion that he is more than a simple walker-on, and that what happened to me later owes anything to his intervention.

In a couple of minutes we reached the fork; we had to part. I offered him a cigarette, but he lit it badly, puffing like a person who does not know how to smoke. He had accepted out of nervousness, and now eyed me like an inferior whom one has just tipped. "You can't go wrong," he said almost as if to repay the debt. And he added a joking remark which he had undoubtedly heard others make; he was ashamed to mention it, but made up his mind to. "Follow the smell of the dead ones."

"I know, thank you." There had been a murrain among the supply mules, and all the paths of Africa now stank of dead mules, of the remains of mules devoured by nocturnal animals, of skulls that laughed immoderately and swarmed with ants.

"Good luck then, sir." And the workman ran off. His good wishes were the last straw which brought on my bad temper—I mean to say it seemed to me to be going too far to invoke the aid of fortune on this occasion. I was not going into battle, nor was I going to cross the Alps. I had only to follow a short cut and reach the top, the rim of the table-land. I had only to find a truck and that very evening I would cut the pages of a book in bed— the first bed for eighteen months.

However, after the workman had thrown his good wishes at me like a challenge I was tempted to turn back. Only for a moment. By way of exorcism I touched the wood of a tree; but the trees in these woods were of cardboard, the real shoddy products of the universe. "Only an unscrupulous theatrical outfitter can have stuck them in these out of the way places," I said. And with determined steps took the short cut.

2

I had been walking for perhaps an hour when I saw the chameleon—a nice beast. It was crossing the path with the caution of a thief walking along the cornice of his favourite hotel. Calm, really terrified by this Africa so full of hidden dangers, it was delicately putting one foot in front of the other. The sight of my boots could not upset it more than it was already, nor awaken any further doubts in it as to the necessity of going on. After having examined them for a long time, uncertain whether to climb over them or not, it turned its back on them. It trusted to my sense of honour. I would not dare to strike it, I would not distract it from its painstaking search for food.

"Cigarette?" I stuck the lighted cigarette in its mouth. It went off smoking like a good diplomat, even more frightened at being alive, ready to throw away the fag-end for a fly, ready for anything, but terribly lazy!

I looked at my watch, which said ten o'clock. So I had been walking an hour and twenty minutes. The path was narrow, splitting into two sometimes only to reunite suddenly later; fairly good going, too good going, with a few short ascents and long level stretches. It was this that made me think I had made a mistake. And for the last half-hour I had not come across the remains of mules rotting in the sun. But that could be explained; mules don't die at each kilometre-stone, they aren't spread out equally along a stretch of road even if they are used to military discipline. You find three of them in a hole in mysterious conversation, and then you go ten kilometres without coming across one. It was rather that it seemed to me that I had not climbed far above the level of the river. Perhaps a few hundred feet. The table-land still rose in front of me, shining more brightly, although the bush often impeded my view of it.

I went on. I knew that one has to take short cuts as they are, not argue with them. All of a sudden I would come on the edge of the table-land close to some smoking unit cook-house, perhaps at an M.T. park. That's how short cuts are.

So I put out of my head the idea that I had made a mistake and went on. I was not tired. On the contrary, the fact that I had not broken my fast loosened my legs and made my body lighter; and the pack did not have much in it. On the other hand the heavy revolver at my side annoyed me, and I was tempted to put it in the pack; but I was alone and, moreover, in unknown bush, in the midst of hidden dangers which I neither could nor would imagine so as not to spoil my walk towards four days of liberty; and then there was the tooth to take up my attention, making itself felt at intervals, dully, far away, but ready to make me start howling again. I had three tablets left.

And suppose instead of a chameleon it were an early morning hyena, tired of looking for corpses and ready to make a compromise with its tastes? But more horrible to you than the hyena is its excrement which a native points out to you on the path, laughing at your disgust.

No, no hyena. They only go about at night, and it is a pity that they don't talk about literature like the friends you left back there, otherwise I would know how to fill certain sleepless nights which instead I dedicate to her.

Yes, I had made a mistake; in every sense of the word. First, in taking a short cut at all. Secondly in taking this particular one. In fact it never crossed the road as I had naively supposed. So I could not have stopped some truck or other; the truck for instance whose noise reached me indistinctly. It was at least three kilometres away and climbing.

I followed the noise, prey to an uneasiness I could not understand. But since the track turned towards the north—that is towards the table-land—I set out again. I had made a mistake; all right, there was no need to make a drama out of it. In two hours I would arrive, since the path had now struck towards the north and was becoming rough.

I crossed a dry watercourse (there were a few pools of almost clean water and a tuft of green trees, always the same cursed trees even if they were green) and set out again along the path, which made its way through thick bush strewn with ant heaps. Some black bird rose as I passed and flew ahead to settle farther on, screeching. I had the feeling of being followed and observed, but perhaps it was only fatigue and the tooth, that tenacious molar. I began to whistle, and pleasant thoughts soon sprang to mind—leave above all. Then the letter which was burning in my pocket and which I should soon be able to re-read, the dear letter I had brought with me. I tried to make out a few words which were not very clear, written in haste and to which I attributed excessive importance. Perhaps those few words might have answered all my anxious questions and there was the usual disappointment when I deciphered them. They were words without any particular meaning, the sort of words fated to be written in haste even by a woman who loves you. "A pity," I said.

Now the undergrowth was becoming closer, with high bushes which blocked my view; and this fact once more made me stop and consider the situation. I was in the valley of a tributary of the river; I had therefore gone farther away from both the bridge and the table-land, because the edge of the table-land now receded until it was indistinguishable from the distant mountains. It receded, hollowed out by the tributary which rose in the north. I saw the little stream below me, almost hidden by trees.

There was a primeval peace in that spot. Everything had been left as on the first day, the day of the great inauguration. It could not be difficult to make one's way down to the stream, but what reasons could ever have led men to go there? Not the need for a crossing-place; not fishing, which is unknown here; and not even the need to quench their thirst, since even on the table-land there is abundance of water and no-one would live in that heat. The pleasure of an excursion? The natives are somewhat averse to picnic parties. If I had gone down to its banks I would have found traces of animals and nothing else. There was perhaps not even a path and I should have had to invent one. But what was the use? And yet the idea of going down to it had struck me, which shows how deeply ingrained in me is the love of useless undertakings. Perhaps I am merely an idler? I am beginning to suspect it.

At one point a light breeze ruffled the calm surface of the river. Looking closer I decided that it was a rotten trunk. But the trunk gave a whisk of its tail and disappeared; so it was a crocodile, or perhaps only an iguana. From that height I could not judge the size. "Perhaps it is waiting for me," I thought, trying to laugh. But it was difficult for me to laugh now; so I went on through the bush.

The path had come to an end.

I began to be worried, so that I went back a kilometre or perhaps two in the direction of the bridge, but attempting to climb. Too late I remembered the precautions I should have taken—leaving pieces of paper on the trees every so often. Yet how often we had laughed at one of our officers, who always went into the bush with his roll of paper, leaving a piece every fifty paces and even numbering them. To find the right road now would mean losing a lot of time. I had walked hurriedly and if I had reached even the first watercourse I would have had to walk two hours more, or not far short of it, to get back to the bridge. And be looked at ironically by the workmen. The blond workman would ask me: "Have you forgotten something?" Yes, that's what he would say.

Go back—it would certainly have been a good idea if I had found the watercourse. But it was evident that the stream rose at the very point where I had crossed it. If I did not find that point there was no use talking about it.

There was another solution—to climb up in a straight line towards the table-land. The table-land was not a mirage, but stood there, and I would have reached it after four or five hundred yards climb. So I faced the first rise and found myself on another clearing similar to the one I had left—the same trees, the same flat solitude. There now, another terrace and I would be up; I was perhaps nearer than I had dared hope. "Stick it," I said aloud. And, although I was annoyed at having got myself into this mess like a tripper, I decided to get out of it and reach the edge of the table-land at least before the sun had sunk beyond the far side. So I got my breath back and began to climb again; but on reaching the third terrace I saw that I was lost.

In front of me rose a wall of basalt. To the left the terrace fell away. I could follow the path to the right, but why add a sequel to an adventure already so ill-fated? There was no point in getting farther away from the bridge. To the left I could have tried, too, but it was equally useless since the path did not skirt the wall and lost itself in a ravine. Should I search for a way out on that roasting basalt at the risk of staying there in the sun? "Go on, make up your mind, go back," I said.

Then I smelt, but I did not want to deceive myself, I smelt the stench of a carcase, the stench of a mule. Perhaps I was safe. I cast my eyes round and my hand went rapidly to my revolver while my heart gave a leap. An Abyssinian was sitting on the ground looking at me. He was leaning against a boulder, he held up his gaunt head with one hand and looked at me, fixedly, without moving, one eye open and one half closed. "Get up," I cried.

The wall of rock sent back my cry, and the Abyssinian did not move. Only a flight of crows, like sombre fireworks, rose behind him. Suddenly the crows came back.

I moved off quickly and another corpse appeared. It was stretched out, its unmoving hand pointed to the sky. Behind it another corpse, lying face downwards, the head resting on the forearm, supremely calm. Perhaps it was listening to the words of the other who pointed to the sky. They lay there with the remains of their encampment; empty petrol tins, and the ashes of a fire between two stones; and above the stones a pot where something had stopped cooking a long time ago.

This time the squirrel that stopped to look at me, and sympathetically into the bargain, did not make me laugh. I repeated to myself that if I got flustered I would stay there. If I began to run—which I had a mad desire to do—if to overcome my fear I began to scream, what would I have gained? I had to think it over calmly, rest a little in the shade of the least unpleasant tree. But those were broken remnants of good intentions; already they were being overwhelmed in a wave of distress. And my watch had stopped.

And that noise? I strained my ear to hear the comforting noise of a truck, but now I was too far away, too far away.

I unfolded the map, looking for the village on the table-land which would have been my first stopping place. Various paths struck off from the river. I found the crossing place or the site of the bridge. Everything was extremely sketchy, the stream did not appear, and the names of the paths showed what romanticism had inspired the topographer. Being incapable of putting out a map with so many blank spaces he had added a few words according to his whim—"possible shepherds' dwelling," or "many ostriches here." Only then did I notice that the map was very old, printed half a century ago.

I got some of my courage back by laughing, and my nerves relaxed. But I must add that the sound of my voice—which in that spot seemed almost foreign to me—very soon put an end to this futile mirth and cast me once more into the blackest anxiety. "I shall never get out of here," I thought. The idea of passing the night beside these corpses, and of, in the morning, once more seeing the hand pointing to the sky was unbearable. I looked at the map again. There was a path, perhaps the very one I had left before or the short cut I had not been able to follow. It was called *Harghez*.

I began to walk again. I made my way back over the two terraces—found a path of some sort and plunged into the bush. An hour later, completely finished, I sat down on an ant-hill.

3

How on earth had I not seen that clump of green trees before. If there were such leafy trees there was also water, and where there is water there is always a path. To think of finding a path, a shepherd's path, an ostrich path or a crocodile path, or a path without a name, with its good old rotten supply train mules—or a soldier reading a month-old paper! My calm restored by the sight of his uneasiness I would say: "Is this the right way?"

I gathered up my things and ran towards the trees with a new and sudden lease of life, but stopped after a few steps. There it was on the ground, the envelope which I had pulled out of my pocket and which must have fallen when I was reading the letter.

My name stood out, written by her hand, and then I remembered that these two words distinguished me from all other human beings, and in this sinister bush proclaimed the fact of my existence—it was the most welcome letter I could have received at that moment. It further told me that I was near "my" path, indeed that the path was there, at the other side of the trees and the pools of water. Among these blessed trees life began again and everything took on its proper proportion once more—even my fear. And those Abyssinians up there were only three dead men. Or perhaps the letter was trying to give me some other help which I could not understand.

I started to run again and let my legs move automatically; but once more I had to halt. Among the trees there was a woman washing herself.

The woman did not notice my presence. She was naked and was washing herself at one of the pools, squatting down like a well-trained domestic animal. I thought as I watched her that she would show me the way and so I would not have to go back to the bridge. A woman washing herself is a very common sight in these parts and shows that a village is near. "There are all sorts of things in this bush," I said. And went on looking at the woman. In fact I sat down, noticing now that I was really tired after the morning's useless march.

The woman lifted her hands lazily, raising the water to her breast and letting it fall on it; she seemed rapt in her game. Perhaps she had been there a long time and would stay there a long time still, determined to wash without haste for the pleasure of feeling the water run over her skin, and letting the time run by the same way. She did not notice my presence and I stayed to watch her. It was a very common sight, but better than any others that had come my way up till then. Since the game showed no signs of stopping, I lit a cigarette and meantime decided to rest.

She was raising her hands and letting the water fall, repeating the gesture with sad monotony. It was her way of amusing herself and perhaps of taking pleasure in herself. Her way of washing herself was different; she scrubbed herself like a housewife, almost as if her body were not her own. But these were brief interludes in her ennui. When a raven came down to drink at a neighbouring pool, the woman threw a stone at it, shouting, and struck it full in the body. The crow fluttered up vertically and reached the tree, where it squatted among the branches. The woman went on shouting, then fell silent and began to wash herself again with the utmost indolence.

Why disturb her? She had a very light skin, but I did not pay much attention to what was in this bush a surprising detail. Only on the Gondar hills had I come across women with such light skins; there I suppose Portuguese rule has given a new quality to the skins and the desires of the women. I remembered the woman I had met among wonderful grassy meadows, who had come up to me to say one word only: "Brother." And had added a smile which had not yet lost its timidity; then she stayed looking at me as if she were not implicated in the affair. She left me the whole burden of almost unavoidable responsibility.

For washing, the woman had gathered her hair up in a sort of white turban. Let me think: that white turban affirmed her existence, for otherwise I would have thought of her as one aspect of the landscape to be looked at before the train goes into the tunnel. That cotton handkerchief defined everything; I did not then know that it would define all that was to follow. I could not know it, and admired the instinctive grace of the woman, who by means of a single handkerchief managed to remain dressed and to offer a link with me, with her spectator.

When she rose to her feet and began to wash her belly and legs I saw that she was very young, yet she moved with the slowness of a mature woman, which I could attribute only to the languor of the hot day. Then I noticed that she was pretty, in fact she seemed to me to be too pretty, or perhaps the solitude made me come involuntarily to this conclusion. No, she was really one of those types of beauty that one accepts with fear; beauty that takes one back to far-off times, times not wholly lost to memory, or re-discovered in our sleep; and then we do not know if they belong to the past or the future; because prudence urges us not to exclude the second possibility. This was no dream. I was awake and she stood washing herself a few paces away with a piece of army soap. I saw her light and shining skin stirred by her thick blood—"blood which is innured to the sadness of this land," I thought.

Perhaps she knew nothing of her beauty. Her mirror was that pool or else a mirror costing a few lire, which gave back a broken image. And no man had yet fought for her, the men here steer clear of jealousy and set a proper price on things. Since they are forced to live in the midst of somewhat dramatic surroundings, their desire does not need the stimulus of drama. Perhaps she had a husband and even children. But no, she was too young. And if she had had children she would not have left them in the village, they would have been there making a noise, asking me for money or something to eat.

When she caught sight of me through the trees she went on washing furiously without bothering about me and perhaps really not caring. I almost felt like laughing, and thought that one of us could be a mirage, but that I myself could not be. As for her, was she not too much like that kind of beauty the soldiers look for to photograph or for other purposes?

I had finished the cigarette and approached her, I had to pass that way to reach the path. She re-entered the pool and resumed her monotonous amusement. She watched the water run down the skin and that was enough. Her thoughts, if she had any, moved slothfully and did not concern me. The woman had no idea that at that moment the valley seemed to me to be extremely unreal, created by a desire to which I had never dared to confess. She really had no idea that I desired her; or else she did not move, so that I would respect her calm. A woman who flees attracts her pursuer, indeed creates him. She must have thought this instinctively and therefore kept still, waiting for me to go on. Or else she thought I could tell her clearly.

I was a "signore" and could even express my will. In fact if I had taken into my head to follow her to her hut and had said: "I want to marry you for a month or two," she would have followed me without question. Her father would have taken the few coins in his hand and the woman would have followed me, taking things as they came. But it was an absurd idea because one doesn't go back to camp and go into the mess tent shouting: "Another blanket." After a couple of nights, tired of having to hide her, I would have started to look for ways of getting rid of her, relinquishing her to some blasé quartermaster. And we would have seen her walking along with an umbrella and a pair of nailed shoes, a little too broad for her, and yet keeping her balance. No, the kind of beauty one finds in dreams is best left on one's plllow—or in the bush—and not carried around with one. Or I would have sent her back to her village. And she would have remained faithful to me without any effort for whatever period was agreed on.

I went up to her and said:

"Is this the right way?"

She smiled, but it was clear that she did not understand. I pointed to the table-land and she made a sign in the affirmative. But it was meaningless affirmative. It meant only that she saw what I was pointing to. There was no way of making her say anything but "yes." For her everything had a positive sense— whether I went to the right or the left, this way or that. And she watched me with half-closed eyes.

"*Adi*" (*adi* means village—one of the few words I knew).

"*Adi?*" she repeated in a voice which made her seem less young, but more desirable. Then she made a sign in the affirmative, always in the affirmative. It was not easy to make her understand that I wanted her to point out the direction of the village. She rose, not worrying about her naked body, came up to me and stretched her arm over my shoulder. I saw nothing but the jagged mountains, the river. Then looking again, I saw a tree-clad hill. Perhaps the village was there. A few huts, I suppose, the "possible shepherds' dwelling." In any case there was no point in going there now that I had found my path again and could go back to the bridge and find the truck. And the village, if there were one, was not on the road to the table-land, but in the direction of the river. And it was strange that there should be huts there. Or else they were new huts, built by refugees from the table-land who had been frightened by the war's advance into their country.

I did not see her naked body but felt her indifferent breast close to my shoulder. I touched it. She put my hand from her breast almost with terror and went back into the pool. Perhaps my hand had trembled, in any case she was sitting in the pool and if I had asked her to show me some other place—the river, for example—she would not have risen. She no longer smiled.

"I must go," I thought; "there is nothing to keep me here; certainly not the extremely common sight of a woman washing herself." But although I attempted to deny it, the exact road to take was no longer uppermost in my mind. At that moment the wind brought the sound of a truck. It rebuked me sharply for not having reached the bridge; by this time I would have been on the table-land. It was the second truck I had heard climbing and who knows how many had passed in the hours I had spent there tiring myself out. I looked at the palm of my hand—it was still wet— and decided to wash myself. There was another pool of clean water; I took off my shirt and thought: "It will do me good. I won't get sunstroke."

She became interested at the sight of the new piece of soap. She was excited now and could not make up her mind whether to ask me for it. I threw it to her—I had another—and she soaped herself over again, laughing and sniffing at the soap; she was even ashamed of herself for having given way to the lure of something that belonged to me. She began to recognise that I had certain rights. Perhaps because the people down here look upon our machines as supernatural beings who function by divine intervention and, since they accept metaphysics, do not marvel at them over much—at least until they drop bombs and fire at them. But a bottle, soap—oh, these things are made by men. God has nothing to do with them, they are made by the "signori" and are a mark of their superiority.

I looked at her and her glance had lost nothing of its purity. I asked myself how she could make such a pretence of innocence and thought again that she was a mirage, a photographer's mirage. Yet my hand preserved the impress of that form, and unfortunately does so still.

I began to dress, it was really time to go. Reality was different, the woman must know by now the hasty demands of the soldiers, of the workers on the bridge, and their exact recompense. A pity, I thought. And without taking my eyes off the woman I also thought of the letter in my pocket.

She would have laughed. We had always laughed together at certain possibilities, considering them to be imaginary. Can one prevent a man from satisfying his desires when they leave no trace, so futile are they? When I came back she would ask me: "Well, are the women down there really pretty?" and would not have waited for a reply, as if it were a subject already discussed and of no importance. It was not even betrayal, but homage to the long boredom of exile.

I gathered up my things and gave her a wonderful salute. She smiled at me gratefully because I was leaving her that incomparable soap. I had taken only a few steps when the woman began to dress. The operation was very simple; first she had to slip on a tunic and then wrap herself in a wide cotton toga. She still dressed like the Roman ladies who had reached here or the borders of the Sudan, following the lion-hunters and the proconsuls. "A pity," I said, "to live in such different ages." She perhaps still knew all the secrets which I had rejected without even examining them, like a paltry legacy, in order to content myself with boring trite truths. I looked for knowledge in books and she had it in her eyes, which looked at me from two thousand years away like the light of certain stars which take that time to be picked out by us. It was this thought, I think, that made me stay. And then I could not distrust an image.

I watched her. She was putting on her tunic, and for a second her head disappeared in the cotton and there remained that naked body, that breast which had difficulty in passing through the belt and had to be gathered up in her hands. I turned back, took the toga which she was wrapping about herself, laid it on the ground and made the woman sit down on it.

When I touched her she pushed me away and made to rise. Her face had darkened. I made her sit down again brusquely; the same fever as before had gripped me again; and she repelled me with firmness, but my desire, so ill expressed, did not offend her—she did not make it a matter of good manners and of a fitting occasion. She repelled my hands because thus Eve had repelled the hands of Adam in such a thicket. Or perhaps so as to give greater value to the adventure, because to repel is a phase in the game, or perhaps because she was afraid. But afraid of what? It was certainly not fear of being raped, but the more profound fear of the slave who yields to her master. She had to pay her part of the war which her menfolk were losing. Or was I being too subtle? That army soap. Wasn't it merely fear that I wouldn't pay her?

In my pocket I had two silver coins. I laid them on the palm of her hand. That wasn't it. She seemed very tempted to take them, but she gave them back to me. There was something I didn't understand. Hatred for the "signori" who had destroyed her hut, killed her husband? The fear of being surprised there by some inhabitant of the village she had pointed out to me? I made her get up and led her to where the trees were thickest. She followed me tamely, but as soon as I tried to take hold of her again she once more began her slow and tenacious resistance. She defended herself courteously, without believing in her defence, and—I might almost say—thinking of something else all the time.

I asked her if she were married, I knew how to ask her that. She shook her head violently. Then what obstacle was there to my most justifiable desire? "Come on, sister, cheer up, this scene from the Bible has gone on long enough," I said. But I could not make head or tail of it any longer and left her alone. She made the mistake of smiling and I took hold of her again. And once more she defended herself.

Perhaps, like all the conquering soldiers of this world, I was presuming to know the psychology of the conquered. I felt myself too different from them to admit that they might have any thoughts other than those suggested by the most elementary of natures. Perhaps I thought that these people were too simple. But I must stress that her eyes looked at me across two thousand years and that there was in them the mute reproach of a neglected heritage. And I noticed that in her indolent defence there was also the hope of succumbing.

Why did I not understand these people? They were poor creatures, grown old in a country from which there was no way out; they were great walkers; great experts on short cuts; but ancient and uncultured. None of them shaved listening to the morning news, nor were their breakfasts made more exciting by pages on which the ink was still damp. They could live knowing only a hundred words. On the one side there was the Beautiful and the Good, on the other the Ugly and Bad. They had forgotten their times of splendour, and only a superstitious faith now gave their souls the power to resist in a world full of surprises. In my eyes there were another two thousand years, and she felt it.

They were perhaps like prehistoric animals which have landed in an armoured corps depot and discover that they have had their day, and for that reason feel an insuperable melancholy. No, that was too simple; I would never understand it.

The struggle still went on and could have continued; I too was thinking of something else. And instead it finished as suddenly as it had begun. But she avoided looking at me.

4

Something had been born within me which would never die. Looking at the wood I saw it shake as if it were the victim of a harmless earthquake. The ravens had not stopped their disorderly flights and came one after the other to the pools a little way off; in fact one of them—rendered curious by our immobility—flew down upon us and stayed there a second, beating its wings. Then it resumed its gawky flight.

I thought that something had been born in me that would never die. It had been born from the contact of this dark-skinned woman. Or had I rediscovered something? I asked myself why she should lie without opening her eyes and, when she opened them, avoided looking at me; and meantime her hands—strangers to me a little while ago—now sought my skin and held me tight, terrified that I might go away, leave her as one does in such cases, when one has brought oneself to consider, with disgust, one's own error.

I heard far off the noise of a truck and decided that I would leave at once, but I could not move, perhaps I was tired, and the woman lay there, silent and indolent. When I realised that it might be she that kept me back, I undertook to leave before it was too late, before I let myself be led to her hut and spent the four days of my leave there and perhaps more, before I accepted that incalculable defeat. I rose and she scarcely looked at me through her half-shut lashes and put her forearm across her face. In a second—I told myself that I was too tired and that I had to rest—I was beside her again. She held me in her arms with indolent sweetness. It was warm and I fell asleep.

I slept a most uneasy sort of sleep. I was afraid of it and yet did not want to abandon it and hoped it would continue. I found deep rivers, banks I had never seen and from which it would have been difficult for me to return to reality. Did a table-land exist and a truck to reach it? Did anything else exist? I went down to the bank of the tributary, and the crocodile seemed to welcome me and disappeared like the trunk of a tree, leaving me pleased with a welcome which at the same time absolved me.

I had not slept much—twenty minutes. The woman had meantime slipped on her dress and was watching over my sleep. I looked at her with disgust, and besides she was immersed in her own thoughts which once again were not concerned with my person. I went to wash myself at the pool, and from the other pool took water to drink—it was lukewarm but I drank a lot all the same. I was hungry too, now, and took from my haversack a ration biscuit and a tin of meat; but the meat had melted in the heat so I opened a tin of fruit. The woman watched me, following my movements as if she were watching a conjuring act. She would not accept the meat, but ate the peach—it was something new of which she was not sure. Perhaps she would have preferred one of these terrible Abyssinian stews of sun-dried meat. Here I reassumed control of the situation. Memory united us, but the tin put a high unscalable wall between us. I wanted to go now; I had had enough. I wanted a book and a chat in the mess at a post on the road, where you can even meet a friend who doesn't want to know when your story is going to end and doesn't inflict on you the story of his own adventures.

I had to go and gathered up the pack. The woman said nothing. She knew it would not have lasted and was not surprised at my sudden decision, nor did she deplore it. Perhaps everything was a matter of indifference to her, although her hands had sought my skin with such ferocity. And I could not imagine the reason for that fury. There, the woman was looking at me as she had a short time before when I asked her if the right way was in this direction or that. It was all over. Her disappointment appeared only when I said goodbye, and I remembered that for the second time that day I was leaving someone and at the same time trying to overcome a sense of guilt. First, I had left the soldier with his truck—and perhaps he was still waiting for help—now I was leaving her, two thousand years.

"Yes, two thousand years," I thought, "but they're past. Aren't four days worth more?" And I laughed while the woman, leaning her chin on her knees, which she held clasped in her arms, seemed sunk in thought. "It's late," I concluded, "and there's nothing to keep me here now." The woman herself had become a poor thing in my eyes, and my sin insignificant. Even the surroundings were the same as before: hostile but old, decadent, blinded by a sun, which no longer allowed of equivocation. The woman was only a woman, had a name, a bed, and those pools of water were her miserable sea. Everything became ludicrous, and when I thought that two hours away there was a carabiniere I actually smiled.

I took the two coins out of my pocket again and put them back in the palm of her hand. She looked at them again, tempted to take them, and once more gave them back to me. She did not want anything and I was only too proud of it.

Then I sat down beside her—only a minute, the time to say goodbye to her—and opened the pack. Was there anything in the pack that would please her? I took everything out, and every time made a sign that she could take what I showed her. Did she want a pair of drawers? a shirt? A towel—nothing short of a wedding gift? Did she want this little Bible printed in Oxford? It lacks only a blank page which unfortunately ended up in a cigarette tin. But you don't really notice it. Or this woollen jersey? Well then, the toilet articles? the toothpaste perhaps, or lily of the valley? But no, the smile which at intervals breaks the gravity of your face is like the moon among storm-clouds. No toothpaste? Well then . . . No, not this, let's leave this packet of letters. Perhaps this pair of shorts? Yes?

"Too little," I thought; I showed her the watch. It was a very bad watch which always stopped at critical moments; I had found that out that very day. I had been thinking about buying another for a long time, and this time I would buy one at Asmara. What better chance of getting rid of a watch with a muddled sense of time? I would have left it in the bush, it deserved it.

The woman looked at the watch fascinated. It was too much, the offer was proving too much for any real power of refusal and her sorrow at my unexpected departure disappeared before this unexpected sacrifice. It was a cheapjack watch which stopped punctully when I had most need of it. There was one night when I should have been up, and it let me down. Tell me, was there ever a better chance of getting rid of it?

I fastened it round her wrist and her breast heaved with profound joy, shook with emotion. Now, I think I have come to understand that woman's nature. On that day, to be precise during these hours, she was crossing the threshold of adolescence and of youth, leaving adolescence behind her, and her gestures partook of both ages. Sometimes indolent, then suddenly vivacious again, full of unsatisfied curiosity. And an instant later, far far off, two thousand years off and amazed to find herself alive beside a man clad in brown cloth. While I was fastening on the watch she looked long into my eyes, bending her head; and I had the pleasant feeling that I was slipping on the wedding ring.

She didn't want anything else. Then I could go.

But I was mistaken. The woman had not even for a moment believed in the possibllity of my so rewarding her. Instead she had thought—I noticed it too late—that these things were a pledge to reassure her that I would not go away. And when she saw that I really was going she uttered a cry that pierced me to the core. She had run up to me and held me back by the arm and leant against me with her whole body, and once more I felt her breast—unhampered by her tunic—press against my arm. She was speaking now, although I did not catch a single word of her passionate discourse. To make her stop I gave a sign in the affirmative—I would stay a little longer; the sun was high, and after all it was sufficient if I reached the bridge before dusk.

I went back to the trees, allowing her to lead me, and it started over again. Once again there was the terror of falling into that age-old river, again the joy of falling and the certainty that it was useless to emerge from it. Afterwards I fell asleep once more. And once more, above my head, was her watchful breast.

5

When I awoke the woman had gone away. My first act was a mean one—I searched in the pack to see if she had taken anything, and everything was there.

The air had changed, it was not hot as it had been before, but as if the earth was relaxing under the first breath of evening; the sun was approaching the horizon and the noises of the valley were becoming muffled. I was exhausted; that sleep, instead of refreshing me, had given full rein to my fatigue, I felt my eyelids heavy, my mouth bitter, my body racked. I ran to wash, and changed my shirt which was a muck of sweat and dust. I was in a hurry to get away, but now the woman's departure left me unsatisfied, as if all that had happened had been a product of my fantasy, a dream to be set down to my prolonged chastity.

But I had to go away, there were too many ravens in the branches. I would finish my sleep at the section post, and I was already thinking up an excuse to give to the workmen. That was it—I had lost my pocket book and had gone up and down the short cut a couple of times. At dawn the truck would take me to the table-land, from there another truck to Axum, to Adua and then to the old colony where there was a bed, a restaurant, a book. And a woman, perhaps? No, my leave was over as far as that was concerned, in fact I felt a certain dislike for myself, and feeling in the haversack the beloved packet of letters I caressed it and was reassured. That day would be cancelled from my memory more quickly than many others because I wanted it to be. Yet if the woman had reappeared among the trees and had said: "Stay here," I would have stayed. It was this certainty that annoyed me. Not that the woman had assumed any importance in my eyes; but I was beginning to fear that she hid some unpleasant design and felt myself incapable of coping with it, in fact did not want to. But what design? There was no use asking the trees and the ravens, or nature which constantly tells of your ancient victory and shares the spoils.

The woman crossed the torrent in haste. So noble in her Roman mantle and yet with bare feet. She was coming towards me and was carrying something, I could not make out properly what. When she was near me she sat down and opened a straw basket; there were eggs and unleavened bread, the bread the natives cook by putting a red-hot stone among the dough. It was still hot.

I did not even doubt that I would sit down beside her. It was tacitly understood that I would do honour to her offering, and while I sucked the eggs—I don't think there is a more depressing operation when you are being watched—she held her hands in her lap; just as some parents watch with satisfaction their little boy eating up his lunch. She was still looking at me with her half-closed eyes, and it was then that I noticed that she had very light pupils, grey-green in colour, at all events not of that bold hazel colour common to all the women in these parts. Her Portuguese forebears had left their mark—unless it was the proconsul or the lion-hunter. And I wondered more and more that a princess like her should have descended to live in this low-lying territory, when in the city some general or some driver would have been happy to protect her. Wisps of hair protruded from under her turban; so she did not have her hair done up in braids. "Let me see," I said, and tried to take off the turban. She pushed back my hand brusquely, and took off the turban herself, scarcely giving me time to see that her hair was almost smooth and not braided. Then she wound her turban again as if it were not her own head, clumsily.

Our enforced silence was beginning to make me uncomfortable. And then I did what every soldier does in a foreign country; I took out my notebook and drew a dog. I showed the woman the drawing and she said: *"Kelbi."*

Excellent, *kelbi.* Then I drew a hen and she said: *"Doro."* Fine, let's go on. I drew a naked woman and pointed to her hair, her nose, her neck, her mouth. When I pointed to other parts, she laughed, hiding her mouth in her hand and did not answer. I drew a fish and the moon, I drew a crocodile. *"Harghez!"* she exclaimed with fear in her voice, almost as if my drawing could have come alive and the crocodile fall on to the ground and assume its true proportions.

I turned over the page. She enjoyed seeing me draw so quickly and scarcely had I sketched a new drawing than she interrupted to save me the trouble of finishing it by saying the name of the thing it was meant to represent. So I filed a few more pages. Every time I attempted to push the game beyond the limits of decency she laughed, hiding her mouth with her hand and did not answer. And as the game progressed I felt her draw nearer to me, felt her warm and heavy body lean on me to allow her to see better what I was drawing; but she was not interested in what the things were called in my language. At last she took the pencil from my hand and drew something herself. She drew a scrawl that could have been a cross, a Coptic cross. She wanted to tell me that she was Christian. "That's fine," I said, "but who isn't in war-time?" But she didn't understand and it was useless my try-ing to make her understand my foolishness. And then I was tired.

From the moment when she came back—this last ignoble vanity having been satisfied—I could have gone away. But imag-ine a jet of water trying to go back into the crack from which it emerged, and that after long efforts you have managed to make it fall—so at that moment the sun fell to the horizon, tired of continuing the comedy of an African sunset. Soon the air grew dark, the noises multiplied and the first cry of the obliging jackals was heard in the distance: in these parts it takes the place of the whistling of the trains in the night and even the desire to leave on them. And only then did I notice that the pocket lamp was broken, perhaps by the fall from the truck.

I was in a fix. I could never reach the bridge unless the woman agreed to lead me there. I drew a sketch of the bridge and showed it to her. I pointed to my chest with my finger and showed her that I and the bridge were one; we must meet, I must go there. She nodded her head several times to show that she had understood. But she made no sign of getting up. The matter did not concern her at all.

Irritated, I took her by the hand and explained to her by signs that she must accompany me at least to the point where I had lost the road, but probably she thought I wanted to take her to the bridge to spend the night in my tent, and the idea must have seemed absurd to her because she refused to follow me. She remained immovable as when I had first known her, stubborn, impregnable.

I lost my temper. I pushed her on in front of me and for a few steps all went well. Then she stopped, looking at me with half-shut eyes, with that unbearable look of hers that I shall never forget. There was nothing to be done. It was dark now and it was going to be a moonless night. I sat down to smoke a cigarette; after all it had been my idea and I mustn't put the blame on the woman. Seeing that I was calmer she came up to me and pointed to the village again beyond the trees. I shook my head—I wasn't as stupid as to get involved in such an unhealthy adventure; it is easy to get rid of an officer's body, you only need to carry it in procession to the crocodiles. And no one would ever have asked these natives if they had seen me passing there. Was the woman trying to carry me into the very den of some unsated warrior? I put my hand on my revolver and reassured myself, I still had my seven rounds and the reserve magazine as well—well greased rounds, a clean revolver which never jammed even if you covered it with sand.

Very far off the din of the jackals started again. "It's still too early," I thought. But there are nights when the jackals are in a hurry to finish their work.

Meantime the woman had risen and made a sign to me to follow her; and since she did not make towards the village I fell in with her wishes. After a hundred yards we found ourselves among the high boulders still warm from the sun they had absorbed. One of these boulders was concave on one side and smooth and could give shelter to two or three people under its dome. The woman gave me to understand that I would sleep there.

It was a stupid suggestion and I rebelled. "The bridge," I repeated several times and pushed her again, but she set herself free, smiling, and set about gathering twigs and dry branches which she piled up a little way from the boulder; she wanted to light a fire, perhaps to set my mind at rest, perhaps because women have a genius for domestic intimacy. I gave her the match-box and let her carry on. The flame flared up and I took the opportunity to make some coffee, boiling it in my dixie. I gave her some which she drank. I had now to resign myself and must add that this resignation began to be too pleasant; indeed, from the way the woman behaved I gathered that she was going to stay and keep me company. She kept going off to collect dry branches and every time she dropped her load she smiled to me.

Yet I could not get rid of a growing feeling of uneasiness, but it was compounded of so many elements in themselves of no importance—the night, my tooth, the unpleasant noises of the bush and the discomfort of an adventure which was going beyond its prescribed limits—that I quickly decided to set my mind at rest. After all, there was no great difference between sleeping at the post on the road and sleeping in the open. Perhaps at the river the mosquitoes would have devoured me. Here instead there was the advantage of feeling oneself in virgin country—an idea which does have a certain fascination for men who in their own country have to use the tram four times a day. Here you are a man, you find out what it means to be a man, an heir of the dinosaur's conqueror. You think, you move, you kill, you eat the animal you surprised alive an hour before, you make a brief gesture and you are obeyed. You pass by unarmed, and nature itself fears you. Everything is clear and you have no other spectator than yourself. Your vanity emerges flattered.

You approve of yourself, you see yourself living and see yourself life size, your own master—you would do anything not to delude yourself. The others are a nuisance, oblige you to share a glory you wish to keep intact; you are happy in your solitude. And you finish up by staying.

Perhaps they would accuse me of excessive imagination. I proposed to tell my adventure to my friends in the mess. And they would laugh. The M.O. would laugh more than the others, he always laughed more than the others when someone told stories that went beyond his own modest imagination. He was a great slugabed and took medical parade in his pyjamas, cursing the soldiers who snatched him from his dreams of home. And Lieutenant B. would take from his wallet one of his cards, offering it to me with a smile. The card he had had a hundred or so printed in Naples—said: "Although that is a very tall story, it is considered that it was told in good faith; you are therefore presented with this certificate in the conviction that you will derive pleasure from it."

I burst out laughing and the woman looked at me. Lit up by the fire her beauty grew. "You can't understand," I thought, "you will provide an evening's fun." And the memory of the friends I had left behind almost moved me; good comrades whose names I would one day forget perhaps, but not their gaiety and their disinterested friendship, nor its absolute gratuitousness, which would make that time seem, in memory, the prologue to another life to which I could no longer attain.

But perhaps I would keep quiet, and the next day, at dawn, would begin to live again as if the preceding day had never existed, because secret holidays are the best, and, after all, I had satisfied my curiosity. And even if desire for the woman took hold of me again—and I knew that that might be inevitable—never mind. She wasn't the only woman on the table-land and perhaps one was as good as another.

I was hungry. Hesitatingly, with a little distaste, I took the bread she had brought me; we ate it together. I had no more food and I sucked another egg. She ate modestly, raising crumbs of bread to her mouth with a calm movement that never varied.

Afterwards I stretched myself out under the enormous shell, made a sign to her to join me and soon we were laughingly entwined. Then we fed the fire and sleep took us. She was the first to fall asleep and to look at her I had to turn my back to the fire. The light, reflected from the rock, lit up her face and breast which rose with the slow rhythm of her breath. Only then, watching her sleep so calmly and trustingly, did I remember that I had not asked her name. "It's better that way," I thought, "let's live incognito." But she could only be called Mariam (they are all called Mariam in these parts), at least that is what I call her sometimes when I cannot sleep. In fact it was her name.

6

There was a profound beauty about her when she slept. Only in sleep did her beauty reveal itself fully, as if sleep were her real mode of existence and her waking time some sort of torture. She slept, just like Africa, the warm and heavy sleep of decadence, the sleep of the great unrealised empires that will never arise until the "signore" has been worn out by his own imagination and the things he invents turn against him. Poor "signore." Then this land will find itself again as always; and her sleep will seem the most logical answer.

She held one arm on her belly and what little light there was in the night was concentrated on the silver of the watch I had fastened to her wrist. What would she do with this stubborn and damaged gadget, she who did not know how to read? Even if she had known how to read, what sadness there would be on the not far distant day when the marvellous ticking stopped; perhaps it would seem a bad omen to her. Certainly a watch was the most absurd thing possible to see on the skin of that round arm which shortly before I had had round my neck. Time, like a feeling, is indivisible. What is the sense of a year, a month, an hour, when the true measure is in myself? I am very old and consider myself immortal, not to conquer the fear of death, but because I see proof of it in these mountains and in these trees, in the eyes of this woman which find mine again as if after a long absence.

Her lips were barely parted by her breathing and the eyes rested like two quiet cats; and now I discovered the perfection of their line, the unexpected tremor of the lids and the long lashes which, when open, made the eyes seem half shut.

Another sleep came to mind and I put it away. Then another, and that too I put away, only the sleep of this woman confused me—because like all extremely simple things it was impossible for it not to conceal a secret. Once master of that secret, and I, too, would sleep as one sleeps the first night in the grave, in the certainty that it could not have been otherwise, and snapping one's fingers at the sleeplessness of others which the poets sing so well.

I remembered the first time I had sat a horse and had felt between my knees a force that obeyed while awaiting better times. Or the waters of the sea far from the shore which push you and keep you, and are yet ready to engulf you if you show yourself the least bit indiscreet and lay claim to too much knowl-edge; I remembered all the things for which I had felt an unjustified attraction. Well, let's let her sleep, poor princess, with no other thoughts than to procure herself wretched unleavened bread and to wash herself—but not too much—and only for fun. I, on the other hand, could not sleep. My fatigue had gone beyond all limits and now the nerves were laid bare, sensitive to every rustle, to every cry the night amplified. Farther and farther off the jackals bayed to tell the hyena that there was need of his aid to dig up some carrion. And the hyena, the terrifying walker by night, would arrive, making his allies mad with joy; digging, tugging, excavating for all and helping himself first. And what gorgings there would be with so many dead left scattered there. If men make friends it will be the end. We will go back to the lean repasts of the old days, to the dogs—those traitors—to the skinned camels: but we will always have the mules of the good old thoughtful supply columns.

The other animals slept, huddled up here and there, and did not make a nuisance of themselves. Sated with mosquitoes, the chameleon, now in evening dress, thought over that stinking cigarette which they had tried to tell him was good. The squirrel, too good for this world, rested in the hollow of his tree. Thus the wild cat hoped to surprise him at dawn. Everything, then, was in order, and her sleep made part of the picture.

I saw a shadow twenty yards away and instinctively touched my revolver. I slipped it cautiously from the holster, holding my breath, and put forward the safety catch; I knew there was a round in the breech and that I could not miss. But the shadow had already disappeared. And as if this had removed the danger I felt easier. But thinking over it again it seemed more serious, precisely because the shadow had disappeared—a sign that even the most cautious movements had not escaped it and that it felt that I was awake. Or so I thought.

Should I stir up the fire or put it out altogether? If it were an animal the fire would be sufficient to keep it off, but if it were a man, the jealous custodian of the woman or a disbanded warrior, there was no need to give him the chance of a good aim.

But it could be an animal, because the shadow I had seen was low and long. I do not believe that a man can go on all fours like that and disappear all of a sudden without making too much noise and without feeling the impulse to stand up. If it were a man, so much the worse for him. But a native would not have faced the bush without even a burning brand to act as torch. It could, I repeat, have been a disbanded enemy soldier—but it seemed to me that this hypothesis must be set aside. It was many weeks since the war had passed that way. And yet, these corpses up there beside the basalt wall. . . . No, I could account for that too; the three Abyssinians had died from machine-gunning by an aeroplane, and in the gesture of the one pointing to the sky there was no need to read any hope or certainty beyond that which death had brought him. And if they had been from the village they would have buried them. No one in the village suspected that there were three corpses up there.

So it was an animal. But what animal is so cautious as to hide when it feels that it is being watched? What animal is not tempted to howl when it smells a suspicious odour—the odour of man?

I stirred the fire. The woman went on sleeping and there was no need to waken her. Perhaps she would have misunderstood my intentions and would have offered herself again before I could explain what it was about. And even if I had managed to explain to her that there was a shadow she would have laughed. "What a frightened 'signore' I've found. There are shadows everywhere, but shadows don't hurt you."

Prey to a fear which was all the more subtle because I saw its weak points, I lay back beside the woman with my revolver in my hands. And waited. I heard the ticking of the watch.

The shadow did not reappear nor did I hear any sounds which I could consider to be signs of its presence. It was possible that the large animal had hidden itself and that, far from awaiting the opportune moment to attack us, it was terrified by the fire which flamed up merrily. If I had remained awake everything would have come out right. Dawn could not be far off and would come unexpectedly, like the turning on of a switch; then the noises would cease, all the shadows disappear and what worried me now would reveal itself as a bush moved by the night breeze. I had to have the strength to wait and—such adventures don't happen every night—the strength to say goodbye to sleep. For I confess that now I would willingly have slept if my anxiety had not urged me to keep awake.

The woman went on sleeping, and, seized by a sudden tenderness for this inexplicable being who entrusted herself to me with such simple acquiescence, I caressed her with my hand. Love is made of too many other things, among others of letters written and received. I had stooped to this woman more in error, I felt, than sin. She did not give to existence the value I gave it; for her everything would have come down to obeying me, always, without asking anything. Something more than a tree and something less than a woman. But these were foolish fantasies which I hazarded to pass the time; other hands were stretched out to me from the radiant distance, other smiles invited me to return; and I would be wise to forget that night.

The shadow passed again in the other direction. It really had passed, it was not an hallucination on my part, nor a joke played by the toothache which had begun to make itself felt again because of the dampness of the night. I rose to my feet. I clutched the revolver, felt it secure in my hands, it gave me courage.

The shadow had disappeared again. I could not see it, for it had gone behind a boulder and squatted there, waiting. Then I had the idea of taking it by surprise, I could not give it any more advantages; there were six or seven yards between us. It could cover them in a bound, and it is just when you are distracted and the pistol is at your side that the thing happens.

I could go round our boulder and cautiously take it in the rear. I trusted in my revolver, it wasn't the kind they carry in towns but a solid weapon with a long barrel. There was the danger of the wounded animal becoming wild, but it was a danger I had to face and there was also the chance that I would hit it in the head right away.

The woman sighed and turned, moving her arms.

Slowly, without making the least noise I rounded the boulder that sheltered us. I left the woman undefended for a moment; it was a risk I had to run—I told myself that in the meantime nothing would happen. I felt my heart beat and push up into my throat but now my hand no longer shook. I took a few steps until I had turned the boulder and looked over towards the other rock where the shadow was hiding; but I saw nothing. Then with decided step I went up to the rock and inspected it. Nothing there. I coughed to reassure myself, to hear a sound that was not hostile.

At that moment I formed an absurd theory. It was the fault of my already jangled nerves, I know, the fault of that never-ending night and of that dark that never grew thinner; I thought that the shadow was a crocodile. The fear of the woman when I had drawn that animal on the note-book, the name *Harghez* printed on the map to mark the spot, were the two factors which fed my romantic fancy, quite worthy of the cartographer. But suddenly I put it away; no crocodile would ever have ventured so far from the river. And besides, these creatures have a slow pace when they walk on terra firma. So I laughed at my fancy. No, it was a hyena, perhaps even a leopard, although they are becoming scarce even in the low-lying parts.

Suddenly the shadow passed before me at great speed. It glided along the ground, illuminated for a moment by the fire; it was like lightning. I fired twice. The shadow jostled me; I smelt the rank odour of its skin and fell as I fired at it for the third time. The beast disappeared howling and later I heard it far off in its death agony.

I went back towards the woman. I can hardly believe all that happened after that.

The woman had thrown herself down with her face to the ground and a hand pressed to her belly. A second later, still deep in an absurd sleep, she uttered a lament, long, agonising, a lament I had already heard in hospital, behind the door of the operating theatre. It was the lament of the savage, the protest which we keep in reserve for the great moment when it arrives too soon and surprises us. It was above all the lament of one who does not wish to believe in it.

I stood near her and pretended I did not understand, but I did understand. I had done it. The hand that fires knows if it hits the mark, and my right hand trembled. When the woman took her hand from her belly I saw that it gleamed with blood. I had hit her, the bullet had been deflected, perhaps by some stone, because I deny that even in the confusion of my fall I could have lost my sense of direction. I had not missed with the first two shots and the third I had tried to fire low, precisely because I did not want to make a mistake, because the kick of the revolver tends to throw up one's arm. I had fired low and there was no other explanation—a stone. However hard the skin of that beast, it could not have deflected the shot.

A stone, then, and don't let's think of it any more—one of these damned stones which, for good or ill, conceal the treachery of the scorpion.

But now the woman was there, lying face downwards, groaning. That body over which I had watched before now contorted itself because of the agony of a wound which was all the more terrible because inexplicable, and it was even painful not to be able to make her understand that it was a case of a tragic accident. When I tried to raise her and put my pack under her head, she looked at me as she had always done, with half shut eyes, trying to understand. It wasn't me, I thought. Someone had fired, but not I, it was not possible that it should have been me. I was terrified, I caressed her brow so that she should not feel that I was her enemy. A cold sweat covered her face. Her hand, decked with the watch, once more returned to her belly and withdrew full of warm blood. The tunic was already soaked and a brown stain was forming on the sand.

She continued to groan, but more softly, modestly, so as not to frighten me further. From time to time she opened her eyes and once she even smiled at me; and for some moments there remained at the corners of her mouth the wrinkles of a smile trying to reassure me, the heroic smile of the wife who faces childbirth and is suddenly extinguished because of some invisible thread which drags down from her womb.

I stirred up the fire again. In my mind rage began to rise alongside my panic. I was angry with myself, I blamed myself unreservedly for having been stupid, for having allowed myself to be overcome by fear. Now I thought that if I had merely thrown a stone the beast would have fled. And instead another part in that ill-starred comedy had been reserved for the stone. I was really angry.

At that moment the howling of the beast that I had wounded to the death began again. It howled and moaned and went on for a long time, calming down at intervals, resuming with greater violence after the silence, terrified by the night, also dying from fear. But it was very far away and I had no fear that it would come back to avenge itself.

I was really angry, but already a question was arising to torment me: what would I do? It was a question suggested by my unconfessed, inadmissible eagerness to get out of this mess. I must help her, of that there was no doubt. But how? What does one do when a woman is dying and you are lost with her in the darkest night of the year among hostile shadows in a country which has already frayed your nerves and which you hate with all your soul? I thought that I must go away and leave her.

This idea formed itself suddenly; but it had already been maturing since the moment when I had run up to the woman and had seen that I had wounded her. I tried to put the idea away from me and felt it return with increasingly irrefutable arguments. So that to put it away I determined to help the woman in some way, to do something. To plug the wound. But that really was an absurd idea. I am no doctor, but I could still understand that there was nothing to be done about that wound. From the woman's inability to move I guessed that the bullet had gone deep.

With infinite care I laid her on her back. She let me do as I pleased. I raised her tunic far enough to uncover her belly and what I saw took away my courage completely. The blood had already stained the whole belly and at one point gushed clear and thick. I took a handkerchief, bathed it in water and first of all cleaned the wound. I did it gently but felt under my fingers the little hole and the implacable slow flow of the blood which was forming a crust all round. I took another handkerchief and held it on the wound until I felt it damp. Then I lowered the tunic. Her legs were gleaming but cold.

The woman had watched my actions without groaning, perhaps a great hope was comforting her. Perhaps she had heard tell of the miracles performed by the "signori," of the mysterious stitches they can make, of mixtures so potent that no illness can withstand them. She had raised her head and was looking at me. I did not have the strength to smile and this was not the least of my villainies. She had understood. She lowered her head and began to groan again. Then she turned and said: *"Mai."*

Mai? In my language that meant "never." It was only after a few seconds when she had repeated the word looking at my water-bottle that I understood that she wanted to drink. I bathed her lips, but she wanted to drink properly, avidly. I let her drink. And when she closed her eyes I hoped that it was the end. Instead the woman was breathing, almost tranquilly; the sand had in the meantime absorbed the brown stain.

A light beyond the river announced the dawn. The last noises died away, the trees were reappearing and, although it was still indistinct, I could feel the edge of table-land up there, a dark stain against a sky barely turning pale. Then my desire to leave the spot turned into a real anguish. I began to walk to and fro beside the fire trying to rearrange my ideas. What must I do?

Well, I remember thinking that there were a lot of things to do, but all of them full of pitfalls. I could run to the village which the woman had pointed out to me—but was there a village or only her hut? All this region is full of abandoned convents where there live, a hundred and more kilometres apart, monks or merely persons who are looking for something or other—perhaps only for solitude. I had never heard tell of villages in the low-lying parts or in that valley where life is difficult. Perhaps the woman lived alone, was a widow living in penitence, witness her hair cut short and hidden by the turban. If I had found the village, what would I have gained? Would they have operated on her, done a laparotomy, these people who cannot heal a scratch and drag about sores as big as handkerchiefs?

I could send someone from there to the bridge to ask for help, and in four hours the medical orderly would come with his little box, provided there was an extraordinarily brave orderly at the post. And what a box! Epsom salts, quinine, aspirins, cognac—an empty bottle—gauze, cottonwool, two fingers of alcohol and the photograph of his girl on the lid.

We certainly could not carry the woman down merely to see her die from loss of blood on the way, even if I had found natives willing to help. Once we had arrived there would be a wait for the doctor who would arrive at eight with the mail and the rations and would take a look at the woman of that fool who plays tricks with his revolver. And after having established that she was dead would write his report. And the corpse would infest the air and we would have to bury it a long way off not to attract more hyenas than necessary.

The woman was in her death throes—don't tell me that she could have been saved, I shall always refuse to believe it—one might as well wait an hour or two till she died and then go off. There was no use setting the bureaucratic machine in motion, stirring up inquests, new circulars from Army Corps and perhaps a court-martial. In fact certainly a court-martial. The major chose his expressions with taste, releasing them from his mouth like soap bubbles: "Allow me to express my surprise"; and would walk up and down inside the tent and re-read the report, saying finally: "I do not know what to do about it. Therefore let me express my surprise." While the captain, who took things more easily, was more understanding, and my colleagues in the mess whose friendship I considered a gift of fortune, so noble and fine in itself, would they not have said the worst ones are those who display their wives' photographs on their packing-case? And my month's leave that would be cancelled? There—I could not but recognise that my arguments were petty, but there they were, petty like everything society provides for its defence. A court-martial, a leave cancelled, the scandal. But did I really have to fear the scandal?

I had not yet thought of Her. And yet the scandal would have hurt her, in fact I saw her face at its most serious, when the mouth became thin and between the brows a little wrinkle hollowed itself out to disarm my smile.

7

While I walked up and down, in uncontrollable impatience, I struck something with my foot. It was the revolver which I had dropped when I ran to the woman. I picked it up, cleaned it against my shirt and put it in my trouser pocket.

The woman had grown calmer, she still held her hand on her belly and waited, supported by that faith known only to simple souls. Certainly I would not abandon her. And as soon as the dawn had come and the bush had resumed its colours and shape, now confused, I would help her in some extraordinary way not given to her to foresee but quite certain. Since the evening before I had made towards the bridge more than once; she knew that shortly I would go there for her, bringing her one of those miraculous "signori" who cure. I am convinced she thought this because she looked at me serenely.

Her face was no longer beautiful, and round her nostrils the colour had grown darker, while her mouth was dry and showed itself to be hard. And between the brows, on her forehead, two very deep wrinkles began to darken that face which before— while she slept—had for one instant outshone the others. Only her eyes remained calm, still half closed because of those long lashes, slightly clouded. But the pupils moved following me. She had not spoken again since I had given her a drink and to spare myself the sound of her voice I offered her the water-bottle again. But there was no more water and I had to go to one of the pools, almost groping the short distance, to refill it.

Now that I did not see her the thought of leaving grew stronger. I must leave her. She would be dead in an hour, two hours at the most. This kept coming back to me. Or else I had to stay, accept all the responsibilities, give infinite explanations, and leave in people's minds the suspicion that I had killed a woman for no very clear reason. The woman had resisted and I, to threaten her, had drawn the revolver. Or, worse still, first I had taken advantage of her and then had killed her so that she would not go to some H.Q. and demand justice for the wrong suffered.

No, I would stay. To hell with respectability, the law and the rest of it. I could not leave her even if my gestures remained incomprehensible. I must run to the village, find the road to the village, get help. If, on our return, we found her dead among the inquisitive ravens, I must accept the blame for her death. The priest would come to bless the corpse, the funeral rites would take place and I—since I had asked this woman to carry me back to a time which I had repudiated but which was still present—had to pay the consequences. There is no need to add that this resolution vanished while I was giving the woman a drink and her hand touched mine.

What had I to do with this woman? And why did her hard hand linger on mine as if to signify a possession more enduring than that which we had futilely conceded to one other? It was certainly not the hand that had held me and caressed me to excite me. It was a hand that asked for other sentiments while I could give only pity. I stood and thought of finishing her off.

I must kill her. Many reasons counselled me to kill her, all equally strong. I must finish her off and hide the corpse. And, above all, not lose time—the dawn had already begun to appear. Indeed, awakened by the light, the birds were resuming their work. The usual cloud of ravens were croaking among the trees of the water-course, rising in unexpected and simultaneous flights. There came down from the valley the last cries of the beasts seeking their lairs, angered by the light.

I went away from the woman and looked round the bush which fell away to the north into a ravine to rise again towards the table-land. Fifty yards away I found what I was looking for—a fissure wide enough and long enough for a person to enter lying full length.

I went back towards the woman, smiled at her, took the pack from under her head and pretended to look for something in it, but in reality I only wanted my pack. I had decided not to leave the least trace of my passage there and did not want to take along with me a bloody pack. For, if I left it there, it would shortly be covered with blood.

I was ready. I leaned over and caressed her brow. I chased away two flies which had alit at the corners of her mouth and, still smiling, took the turban which had come loose in her sleep and spread it on her face, giving her to understand that thus the insects would not annoy her. Other flies were slaking their thirst on her hand, but that did not trouble her. When I had arranged the handkerchief I ran to the path and looked. There was no one and there was not the least noise to be heard. Down there the village—but was there a village?—must still be sunk in sleep. The table-land was beginning to be lit by a pink light.

I went back to the woman and drew the revolver from my pocket. The bullet was already in its place and I had no need to make any suspicious noise. I did not think of anything except of aiming straight. I was worried about the sound of the shot which might be heard from the village and then I picked up her dress and twisted it round the hand which held the revolver, hoping that the noise would emerge muffled. I pulled the stuff tight. At that moment I had a suspicion that the woman could see what I was doing through the turban. But no, perhaps she was falling asleep.

And that long lament escaping from her was only one of the first groans in the over-long agony that was now beginning.

I saw her turning her head under the turban. I fired.

I must not lose my presence of mind now. After all I had not killed her, I had prevented her from suffering any longer. "Come on, it's not the first time you've seen a corpse," I said, and my voice surprised me.

The turban was scarcely stained with blood, but I did not raise it, was always careful not to raise it. The woman had died without making the least sign and, only for a moment, I trembled at the suspicion that I had not hit her. But when the little stain of blood appeared on the turban and then spread, and when the hand she held on her belly slipped to the ground I understood what had happened.

I went back to the hole in the rock without knowing why, perhaps to assure myself that it was still there; it was a fissure more than a yard deep and a yard wide, four yards long; there were a few bushes in it.

I went back to the woman. The turban was now completely stained and modelled the shape of the nose and mouth. I had to carry that body to the hole. I tried to lift it but almost fell on top of it on my knees; I was so exhausted that I had to rest, stretched out, for a few interminable seconds. And I told myself to hurry, terrified at the thought that I might not be able to continue.

I carried on with the job. I laid out her cotton dress on the ground, it was fairly wide, a white Roman toga. I took the woman under the arms, taking great care not to get dirty—since it had to be done it was as well to do it properly. How heavy it was and how different from the body I had embraced. When I had put it on the dress I tried to pull it by the hem. Yes, it worked.

The turban was sticking to the face and did not even move when the corpse had to overcome the unevenness of the ground; and it did not even move when I made the woman slip into the hole and she fell there with a thud.

Now I had to find sufficient stones to cover the body, but whatever else was lacking in the bush it was not stones—that I knew too well. Before putting the stones in place—I was careful to go some distance to get them—I laid the dress on her corpse like a shroud and said a short prayer. On the dress I placed two crossed branches, thinking that I would not be able to put them on the grave mound. While I was doing it I hit a fold of the dress and her hand moved and protruded.

I bent down hastily and unfastened the watch from her wrist, putting it in my pocket. It was going. I was sorry to take away from her the gift she had accepted, but my name was engraved on the case. I must leave no traces.

With what care I chose the stones and with what care I put them, one at a time, on this body that received them so gently. I worked for a long time, perhaps for an hour, to fill the grave and put bigger stones on top to prevent the hyenas from removing them. When the stones had reached the level of the earth I took handfuls of earth and put it so that no difference could be seen. I beat down the earth with my hands and threw some bushes on the tomb.

8

The sound of a stringed instrument made me flatten myself on the ground.

Voices—guttural and childish voices—could be heard along the path from the direction of the village and shortly after there emerged—I saw it through the branches—a procession of five persons. At the head was a priest—I knew he was a priest because he wore a high brimless head-dress—accompanied by an old man who kept on his left, silent and not in the least interested in what the priest was saying in a bass voice. There followed two adolescents and a little boy, and it was they who were chatting gaily. One of the adolescents was playing a long wooden instrument, a kind of rough violin capable of producing only stridulant and reluctant notes. The player moved the bow carelessly to and fro, as if the business bored him, and the other, laughing, sketched the steps of a very simple but lively dance keeping behind the beat. He jumped here and there making the child laugh with his sudden capers and his grimaces that mimicked fear.

The priest walked on with the old man oblivious of his boisterous company; but every so often when the three forgot to follow after him he would turn round and, raising his long stick, utter a cry which had the immediate effect of stirring up the gay sluggards. With a run they rejoined the dignitary and the dance recommenced shortly after, and it seemed as if the child never wearied of wondering at it. I saw them cross the water-course, going towards the river, and for a few more minutes the sound of the violin reached me and the laughter of the boys.

When even their voices disappeared I became aware that it was hot and that the bush was losing the little humidity of the night before. The watch showed six but I could not put any trust in it because the day before I had put it on at a venture when it had stopped. With repugnance I fastened it round my wrist and my thoughts for another second turned to that woman who now lay a few paces away.

It was time to go or I would find no more trucks. In fact I had to hurry, there were so many things to do. The grave was in order, but round the boulder there were too many traces of our stay. I ran back to it and first of all concentrated on finding the cartridge cases of the rounds I had fired. I found only two of them.

The brownish mark was crowded with flies; I threw a handful of earth on to it, stamped it down and managed to make it indistinguishable from the rest of the ground. I scattered the ashes of the fire and swept everything away with a couple of branches. Every so often I had to rest. Then I took off my shirt—it was filthy with blood—and put on the one I had taken off the day before. There were no traces on my boots; and in any case the dust of the path would soon cover them up. What was there still to do?

I remained for some minutes in a stupor, asking myself that question, searching my memory and trying to obtain clues from the things around me. The handkerchiefs? In the grave. In any case they had nothing on them and could do me no harm. The watch was all right. Ah, the basket. I looked for the basket, it was behind a stone, in our alcove. I carried it a long way off and set it on fire. Now there was nothing else to do.

I went to the pool and washed my hands. I had got a cut on the right hand, perhaps from some stone; I soaped the cut too and tied a handkerchief round it. The soap I threw among the trees and at once a raven went to see what it was. They did not leave me for an instant, these sombre birds, fussing heavily round me and fleeing only if I chased them away. Now I could go. Yet I could not make up my mind, for one thought obsessed me, as it does when one is leaving for a long journey and one is afraid of forgetting something and looks round the room, lifting things, opening doors. What had I to do? I didn't have to do anything. Not even a policeman would have found traces of my passage in that spot. And that was the only consideration. Perhaps no one would look for the woman, although that party of people.... So everything was as it should be. What was lacking?

I went back as far as the grave and put some more bushes on it. And since I had my pack with me, without going back to the boulder—there everything was in order, I had even destroyed the egg-shells—I set out once more along the road to the bridge.

One last look at the grave before losing sight of it and then farewell. "Goodbye, woman," I thought. "You have taught me the value of many things in such a short time. I will not be able to forget them. And that perhaps is why I walk calmly and feel different, bigger, of greater stature, since all experiences enrich us. I look at this unpleasant bush with other eyes."

I changed the magazine of the revolver and put it in the case. It is the same sort of job as changing a blown bulb and requires as little care. I looked upon the revolver as an ornament on my uniform, cleaned it regularly, quite certain that it would never be used. I had gone to the wars certain that I would never use it. What use is it? There are so many weapons more effective for holding at bay an enemy who has none and whom you find only the next day collapsed under a bush. Who was it? Not I. I fired in the other direction.

Goodbye, woman. My throat contracted but I did not stand there weeping; there was a long way to go to reach the table-land; I walked quickly. In an hour's time I again found the path which led to the bridge; I had been retracing it for a while when I noticed that I did not need to turn downhill, that I had found the short cut again. How on earth had I not seen it the day before? Simply because the fork was hidden by a dead animal. So I took the short cut and in half an hour crossed the road at a corner. I stood on the bank a moment resting, smoking a cigarette, then stretched myself out on the ground. I did not think of anything.

When I heard the noise of a truck climbing I made an effort and rose to my feet and signed to the soldier to stop. The soldier slowed down only because it was on a hill and at a corner. I caught up with the truck all the same and jumped on to the running-board.

THE TOOTH

1

FOUR DAYS LATER I was resting in a tent at the command post at A. I had to get ready for the return journey and I had no desire to do so; instead, a far from unpleasant torpor kept me from moving my limbs; but there was nothing odd in the fact that I had not got my strength back—the tooth gave me no respite. There was no dentist at A. and my stay had been in vain. "Four wasted days," I thought. So because of a tooth I had been incapable of movement, had heard the stir of that little town reach my camp-bed and now I had to go away, go back to camp or my delay would be unjustified. Perhaps it was this very thought that took away all my energy.

Stretched out on the neighbouring bed a young man was pretending to read, but in reality he was watching me over the top of his spectacles. He was a young fellow with a round face and a pair of moustaches which gave a mock irony to his lips; he still wore his tunic, had not taken off his cap nor even his boots. He did have his eyes fixed on the page of his book, but his eyes were careful not to miss my slightest movement. He was smoking a cigar. That cigar set in his boyish face reminded me of the blots that boys invariably make on the faces in their school-books. It had been precisely the cigar smoke which had awakened me, turning my stomach. "Please," I said, "your cigar."

The young man—a second lieutenant from my own division —threw the cigar out of the tent with a flick of the two fingers that held it. By that gesture he wished to convey his disappointment. He began to read again without bestowing any further attention on me, and it was I instead who continued to watch him with half-closed eyes. A minute later he had already taken another cigar from his case and had put it between his lips, without lighting it, however, but gnawing at the tip with his teeth. Now he really was reading and he turned over a page.

My nausea choked my throat and my tooth began to hurt. They were sudden stabs of pain which set the brain on fire. For some time the image of the reader disappeared behind a veil of tears. I wanted to yell. "Excuse me," I said instead when the stabbing pain had passed.

The second lieutenant smiled. My contorted face did not induce him to stand on such ceremony as is usual between two officers who meet in a tent at a command post. He began to read again, and after a little, interpreting my interruption in the most favourable way, lit the cigar. He seemed pleased, however, that he had wakened me; perhaps he was bored. He lit the cigar and looked at my watch, which I had put on the chair, and he certainly was not looking at it in the hope of reading the time from that distance. He looked at it fixedly, then turned his attention to the cigar and the book once more.

I took the watch—the edge of the strap was stained—and turned the other way. I had to get ready and go back to camp or else go on to the nearest dentist. But where would I find a dentist, and the delay? When the second lieutenant put the book under the pillow and went away I called him and asked if he had a tablet for toothache. He had none, but if I went with him he would show me where I could get some; he spoke politely, and the unpleasant impression of the first moments disappeared. Leaving the command post we went towards a grove of eucalyptus trees. There on the threshold of a wooden hut, sunk in a deck-chair, we found an M.O. who listened to me unwillingly and went to fetch a tube of tablets from his hut. I thought I would take the opportunity to change the bandage on my wounded hand. Then he called the orderly and—deliberately ignoring us—sat down again.

He was a man of about forty, he was reading old papers, indifferent to the disorder that surrounded him. On the ground there were two coffee machines, papers in their wrappings, books, dirty boots and the various parts of a stripped motorcycle; and the orderly, instead of bothering about it, whistled. The officer seemed deep in his reading and so we left him. But how were we to spend the afternoon now that the toothache would die down yet leave a dull memory in my jaw?

Someone was calling me. It was a major. When I went up to him he said I would do well to have a shave. He raised his finger a fraction towards his shining cheeks and repeated the phrase, sharply. He looked at me with his head erect and since I continued to look him in the eye added that I could go. I saluted and the major—in a softer tone—gave an "All right" and went off. He was a tall fat man who dressed with great care and walked with his hands behind his back. I did not imagine at that moment that I would see him on quite a different occasion. No, I could not know it and went on with the second lieutenant towards the square.

It was a shapeless square; I saw it for the first time and had the shattering sensation of a place which we have imagined and which when we visit it does not disillusion us because reality surpasses imagination, indeed the latter notices that it had overlooked the way the light fell and the sounds rose, the soft quality that came into the air at dusk when the trees close up like umbrellas and the houses breathe the kind of sadness that makes us slacken our pace. There, too, there were big eucalyptus trees, and one walked noiselessly on the fallen leaves along the unpaved streets. Between the houses the granite hill appeared, and beneath it the oil-lamp of an inn sparkled. The natives sat at their food, served by a fat Ethiopian woman dressed in pink. From the streets came the noise of workmen, women passed going towards the well with empty petrol cans, and under an immense tree two men sat without talking, waiting for some passerby out of the Bible. Places, like people, achieve a happiness of their own, and that out-of-the-way and forgotten square expressed the peace of times that will never return. Almost as if guessing my thoughts the two men waiting under the tree rose to their feet and, before separating, kissed each other on the cheeks.

The man who came towards us was very old and walked looking at the ground as in the grip of some thought that prevented him from hurrying. We had sat down, the second lieutenant and I, on the steps of the telephone hut, attracted by that building through which the news came; if there had been good news—for example the news of a unit that was being posted home—the operator would have shouted it to us with an undercurrent of hope.

I felt sick, but only because of my extreme languor, and scarcely heard what the lieutenant was saying. He was telling me about something that had happened, another attack by brigands on a post on the road, there had been many wounded, luckily no dead; but the news did not interest me and I asked no questions. And then, encouraged perhaps by my silence, he asked me if I knew the story of the "lettuce plane." I did not answer. The old man was coming closer and when he passed in front of us with his gaze still fixed on the ground I recognised him as the old man who had accompanied the priest along the path in the bush. He was bare-foot, more and more deeply sunk in some thought which perhaps he could not bear and which made him slow his pace from time to time and look at things around him. Or perhaps he was merely annoyed by the pebbles hidden under the fallen leaves. As he passed before the hut I saw that he was picking something up—the butt of the cigarette I had thrown away a short time before?—and then he disappeared behind the enclosure. He appeared again and made towards the last houses. A little later he entered one of them, or rather stopped on the threshold with his back to the square.

I would willingly have left the boy, but the thought of the evening, which was already upon us, held me back and I answered drily that I did not know his story and that he should get on and tell it. He did not seem to feel my rudeness in the least, and said that it was the story of a recce plane. It came every morning from a field in the old colony and before beginning to recce beyond the river it dropped a packet of lettuce on the general's tent. It was so punctual in bringing the lettuce that the armed natives across the river set their watches when they saw it appear.

"Provided," added the second lieutenant, "that they have a watch." And having said so stopped absentmindedly for a moment before going on.

The old man was speaking to a young woman now, still with his back to the square. He remained motionless while the woman, having appeared at the door, looked round and pointed to the inn and then to the command post, speaking quickly. Finally she went in again and a little later the square of the door was brightly illuminated; the woman had lit a lamp. The old man set off towards the inn, which was now full of people and more and more brightly lit because of the onset of dusk.

"So," continued the lieutenant, "the observer never once saw an armed man on the other side of the river. Not even one? Not even one. And then the general thought it was time to send a unit to give a demonstration of force before the final offensive; and the unit went off unwillingly, they all knew that there were only too many armed men across the way. And the officer in command of the unit—a silent young fellow, said smiling before leaving: I hate lettuce. That's all. He had to go and didn't waste time."

(The old man was standing talking with the Ethiopian woman clad in pink who answered him with sweeping gestures of her arms and then invited him to sit down. The old man sat near the door and stayed, looking at the square but without seeing it, because his thoughts were certainly elsewhere; and when the Ethiopian offered him a cup he took it and bent his head but kept it in his hand and could not make up his mind to put it to his lips.)

"Well," I said, "how did it end?"

The second lieutenant shook himself. "The same evening," he answered, "we saw a soldier come back, an askari, who kept his hands on his belly. In his hands he had his guts, and he was the only one who had got away."

He burst out laughing. Yet that forced laughter imparted a

little mirth even to me. "It's not worth worrying about," I said; "war is made up of stories like that, of young men who study literature or music and in a year's time are killed because of the general's salad. No one is to blame."

"That's right, no one," said the second lieutenant, "certainly not the aeroplane."

"And not even the general," I said, "is to blame. At his age you have to watch your diet."

"Yes," said the second lieutenant thoughtfully, "no one. The only one perhaps is the soldier who resists the blows of fate and defies logic. I ask you, going about with his guts in his hands. It isn't fair. It is not fair to get better in certain cases."

I looked at the second lieutenant. Why had he wanted to tell me that story? Perhaps.... Any suspicion that he had spoken intentionally disappeared when I looked at him—his childish face, that unassuming moustache, those glasses with their one mended leg, inspired confidence. Even more confidence was inspired by the inadequate cigar which betrayed all his ambitions. I calmed down. It was the first time I had laughed for many days and the square of that little town now seemed to promise me much more than it could give me.

We strolled round it. Various streets left the square, one of which led to the church, a building which we saw at the other end of a courtyard between two huts with verandas. It was an old piece of work of the Portuguese period, grown nobly ancient, asymmetrical, standing by a miracle, and we stopped to look at it. After so many months the sight of a building constructed not by instinct but with intelligence gave me deep joy; but what to ascribe it to I did not know. When I did know, I became sad again.

I swallowed a tablet because the tooth had begun to hurt again and it melted in my mouth, very bitter.

2

Where was the old man? I could no longer see the old man on the threshold of the inn.

I was looking into the shadows of the square when I saw him coming towards the church. He was walking more quickly, the upper part of his body bent forward, and passed through the gate before us, making towards the door of the church. He disappeared, absorbed in the shadow of the trees, into the courtyard where other silent shadows wandered.

"Shall we go in?" said the second lieutenant. I replied that it was already late and that it was too dark for us to see anything. The streets were clearing of people and the thought of going back to the tent and waiting for supper-time did not appeal to us; it was better to wander about waiting for night. We stopped and the second lieutenant proposed that we should ask for the hospitality of some girl or other, of these two making eyes at us, laughing and exchanging what were certainly flattering impressions. Before my companion had finished making his proposal to me it had already been taken up at the nearest doorways, arousing suppressed laughter, slamming of doors and in short a state of excitement which we could not now disappoint. "I'm not coming," I said, but now the two girls were waiting for us at the door. They smiled.

The lieutenant—he must have been fairly well up in the local customs—threw a coin on the table and lay down on the bed which occupied one side of the room. One girl ran off to fetch two bottles of beer; I sat down and the other girl came up to me saying a few words, but I did not understand; and then she began to wind up a gramophone with proud care, because this was a miracle which could be made to repeat itself every time at her pleasure. I could not take my eyes off her and tried to find out the reason. When she had finished, the girl put on a military march; then, at random, another record, and it was the song she used to sing to herself sometimes in her bath. "Perhaps I had better write to her," I thought.

The girl came to speak to me again and I smiled at her, pretending to understand, but I scarcely saw her and only the unexpected gleam of her teeth told me that her blurred image was speaking. I saw instead the Suez Canal at sunset, with a soldier who had climbed up into the cross-trees singing despairingly to the desert and everyone listening to him, because he made us laugh and moved us—I still had her flowers in my cabin and would keep some of them between the pages of a book. The boat moved so slowly that it almost seemed to be impelled by the voice of the soldier.

It was not possible to go away. Now the two girls were drinking, astonished that we should refuse, and already there began to come into the room relatives and neighbours with their children, attracted by the exceptional munificence of the second lieutenant, who had sent for more beer. And that song—so good natured and sentimental that elsewhere it would have made me smile—one had to accept it for her sake and for the sake of the soldier who had clambered up there and was howling with melancholy to the desert. Once Suez was passed the holiday would be over—months of separation to be marked on one's belt with a pen-knife. And on one's return the woman one loved singing new songs and smiling at the other woman as one smiles at emotions one has outgrown. "Will we stay here long?" I asked the lieutenant.

He was still stretched out on the bed, this strange friend of mine, undisturbed by the little respectful crowd that listened to the gramophone, smiling and perhaps convinced that they were flattering us. "Are you bored?" he replied and began to speak to the women who were now invading the room. They were old women, heavy and wizened, but gay, and they laughed at every word my friend said. As for the two girls, they were in no haste to conclude their business and seemed to be the most amused of all, happy that their house should be the scene of a real festival. Looking round I saw that there was another room as well. I caught a glimpse of the bed and, at the far end, the door which gave on to a courtyard. The children began to play among themselves, running about the room and knocking down the stools: no one checked them.

Who had left these two girls the gramophone? All their pride was now centred on this possession; they had put it on a three-legged stand and had to climb up on to a stool to change the records. Thus I was drenched in nostalgic voices which added to my melancholy the boredom of futile memories. The petrol-lamp was lit and thick shadows formed in the corners of the room, while the women—how many were there? (I tried to count them, but had always to begin from the beginning again; perhaps there were nine, perhaps ten)—sat chattering and waiting for the coffee to boil.

How sombre the years made them, prettier than ever. One could read nothing in their eyes except the boredom of decline. Time had defeated them decisively. "Another two or three days," I thought, "and I shall go back to camp." In three days a lot happens, not everything that I had in mind before leaving, but one gets back one's elasticity; one shaves, one goes for a walk, one tries to read the book which the second lieutenant keeps under his pillow. Goodness knows what kind of reading matter—macabre stuff perhaps, because he has a taste for macabre stories and disguises his weakness under a cloak of cynicism—but the important thing is not to go back to camp tomorrow.

The major passed with studied slowness in front of the wide-open door. He was perhaps tempted to come in, but went on pretending not to have seen us, and I thought that under his veneer of paternity he nursed an unsatisfied libido. He had stopped a little way off and stood for a long time uncertain whether to enter or not, before going away. When he departed one of the girls, the one who had smiled to me before—and that smile now surprised me into desiring her—came to offer me the coffee.

She left me the cup on the palm of my hand and stood still waiting to see me drink. Smiling, she leant over towards me and in the opening of her dress I saw her breasts. Then she said something, came and sat beside me, slipping an arm under mine. "Isn't it late?" I asked the lieutenant.

"No," he replied, "we can't offend them now by running away. And remember when you drink the coffee that they use salt instead of sugar."

I balanced the cup in the palm of my hand and listened to what she was saying; I did not understand, but I wanted to listen; and when her breast touched my shoulder I tried to move away and upset the cup. They all laughed, the cup was refilled and again I felt the girl's breast, unhampered by her tunic, on my arm. I sat there like a fiance in front of a girl's approving relatives; perhaps they were waiting for a sign from me and her breast always urged me on, but very slothfully; I had only to look at her, amazed that I should dare to do so, and her face opened into a smile of innocent complicity. I wanted to go away, but I would not have reached the door, perhaps the little crowd of gossips would have prevented me from doing so, or I would have fallen to the ground, and then the second lieutenant had begun to talk to one of the children and everyone was following the conversation and laughing at the children's replies. The fat mother of the two girls—she was the mother because she was seeing to their coif-fure and admiring them with pride—was laughing more than anyone else, counting the notes the child had earned, how many I do not know.

And then, if only I had found the energy to write to her! "As a matter of fact it's settled," I thought, "I'll write this evening, there's no use putting it off." I took such comfort from this decision that everything in the room seemed pleasant and I began to laugh with the child while the girl pressed herself closer to my side, laughing too. I made the child say all the Italian he knew: and he went through his repertory at a great rate, sometimes standing on tiptoe to look at the ceiling, as if asking for help, or wrinkling his face with the effort of remembering, but always making a sign to me not to prompt him. Most of them were indecent words. "They are the ones you can't do without," said the second lieutenant, "the rest is literature."

While the boy went on, delighted to be examined in front of his own people, who could thus admire him, I was seized with a fit of laughter and the girl was just in time to take the untouched cup from my hand.

While I was taking my handkerchief from my pocket to dry my

eyes I saw the old man at the far end of the courtyard. Or it was someone very like him. No, it was he, he was looking through the open door attracted by the laughter; then he advanced to the threshold and stood watching, and finally entered the room, which was dark, and came to the entrance of the room where we sat.

No one seemed to have noticed his presence. The old man stood still on the threshold and his glance rested on all of us, one at a time, like a person searching for someone, a person who wants to be quite sure before giving up. His face already expressed the conviction that he would not succeed, yet the eyes searched, halting here and there, and I saw them appear above the heads of the women drinking the coffee. Meanwhile the girl had got up and climbing on the stool had taken off the record without putting on another.

This was the signal the other women were waiting for, and in some confusion they began to leave the room, since the celebration was over. The fat mother came to take the child away from before me, smacking it and smiling, showing it the door.

At last there remained only the two girls, and unhurriedly they tidied the table, removing the cups. The one I had had beside me turned her face towards me from time to time and smiled; then she began to sing in a low voice the same song as before. But so slowly that I had difficulty in recognising it.

All had gone away and then the old man entered the room and spoke to the girl who was singing. He spoke quickly in his own tongue with an unpleasant guttural voice. Having listened to him the girl shook her head and then turned to the other girl and repeated what the old man had said, because I heard almost the same words and a name always repeated: Mariam perhaps it was the name of one of the girls). The other girl, too, replied with something that did not satisfy the old man.

He did not go away. He stood by the table and turned his back to me, he seemed tired. Without anyone inviting him he sat down and the girl—who had begun to sing again unbearably slowly and was smiling at me from time to time—offered him a cup of coffee, one that had been left over, perhaps the very one I had refused.

The old man drank, then turned to the second lieutenant and said a few words. The second lieutenant replied.

The old man had never looked at me and no sooner did he see me than he stopped to examine me and gave a brief salute with his head. I was sitting in a corner and covered by the shadow cast by the lamp. Finally the old man rose and said in Italian: "Good evening" and went out by the street door. I followed him with my eyes through the half-open door. His figure grew smaller, and soon the white speck of his gown was lost in the shadow.

"What did he want?" I asked the lieutenant.

"Nothing," he replied. I did not insist because my jaw was already beginning to hurt and the twinge went up towards my eye and brow like a sword held firmly in a cruel insistent hand probing to reach the brain.

"Let's go," I said. But the lieutenant did not move and I was incapable of moving either. The two girls were closing the door and then I rose: I made them understand that I needed air, to breathe. They left the door open a little and I sat down on the steps. Through the glass I saw the old man pass again, going towards other houses, bent on the search which he knew to be useless.

The next morning the lieutenant and I took a truck for Asmara, he determined to enjoy himself, and I to have my tooth out.

3

It was not a good film and yet I had seen it several times. Every day, although I was beginning to be ashamed of this weakness, I left the hotel determined to have a stroll; I went as far as the gardens, looked at the valley, went into a bar to drink an aperitif and then, insensibly, there I was in front of the stills of that film I had already seen so often, in Italy too. I was afraid the cashier would recognise me that day and be amazed at such stubborn constancy, but she did not recognise me and a little later I was deep in the muffled narcotic calm of the dream.

I knew why the film made me so calm. There was something in the eyes of a supporting actress—oh, nothing special!—something which reminded me of other eyes. An overpowering peace comforted me when those eyes rolled on the screen; I gave myself up to them and tried to live with her memory, to retrace in my most forgotten memories the moments of our happiness. And I was ashamed of it.

When the lights went up I was broken-hearted because I was left alone. Now if anything could induce me to go back to the camp it was her reply to my letter. It was there that it waited for me, in the post-orderly's tent, and I was still putting it off. From that letter I expected some sort of absolution, one sentence sillier than the others that would deliver me from my fear. Perhaps she had understood, although my letter had not alluded to anything, but only repeated that I needed her, that I missed the tranquil atmosphere of the long evenings beside the fire, her unpremeditated answers. Yet I had to go back to the camp, to face the hill down to the river, to take the road once more to the country I feared.

After being a week in the city, terrified by my inertia, I decided to do something. Meanwhile I had to have my tooth out although it no longer hurt me. But if I had gone back with my tooth as well, my trip would have sounded a downright insult to those who had stayed behind.

When the dentist showed me that accursed molar in the forceps I breathed again. "You eat too many sweets," said the dentist laughingly. "Yes," I thought, "too many sweets from her parcels. I must write to her to send more books and other stuff, but not sweets." The young assistant took the molar—I wanted to look at it first, that most bitter of enemies, and search for the secret of its power: so it was to this that I owed a month of suffering—and wrapped it in a piece of cotton-wool. "Keep it," she said, smiling, "it keeps away the pain."

"Really?" But at once I smiled. Yet before leaving, seeing that the young assistant was not looking, I took the bundle of cotton-wool and put it in my pocket-book. My tongue kept touching my gum and every time the anguish of my now inevitable departure came over me.

The hill down to the river, that was the point. But perhaps I would even find time to bathe in the river if I arrived there in the heat of the day. Perhaps ghosts amuse themselves by pursuing us when we are far from their abodes, and that is why it is necessary to go back there, to walk with head erect among the trees of the bush, to look at the squirrel, to offer cigarettes to the chameleon. But now the life of the city was giving me back something I was afraid to lose down there; above all I feared to lose myself, not to resist. I had indeed decided that it had been a mistake, but a mistake which could not have been committed in any other way. Reality was this reality of city life, which calms and distracts: business, the bar, the white table-cloth, the supporting actress whose animation is meant for me alone. My day had taken on a slow rhythm in which my nerves had almost become calm. From the window of the room we occupied, the second lieutenant and I, one saw the spectacle of a civilian crowd—lazy, provincial, satisfied, but irreplaceable. If we looked beyond the gardens to the valley, where the sky stretched like an enormous back-cloth, our conversation suddenly died and we knew why. "The sea is in that direction," said the second lieutenant once, and I felt how his heart was constricted as mine was, too.

What need was there to say it? Perhaps my young friend did not know how to keep quiet, appreciated silence because the pauses were effective. But when would we see that dirty sea which was the same for all of us? Yes, it would be prudent to go back to the camp, to intrigue for furlough, alleging some intractable ailment. By staying there and losing time I could compromise everything, if everything were not already compromised. Perhaps down there in the mess my name was not mentioned with anger even, but with surprise and fear. Other officers were awaiting my return to ask for their own leave.

The second lieutenant had once more stretched himself out

on the bed and was reading that never-ending book of his. "I'm going," I said to him.

"Where?"

"To the camp. I'm going back." He began reading again and did not once raise his eyes, not even when I was really preparing my pack.

"Perhaps we'll see each other again," he said as soon as I was ready.

"Why not?" And he pretended to be looking at the pages, really angry. He felt that my flight made his resistance vain; he, too, would have to pack his kit and go. But just as in the preceding days I had comforted myself with the thought of going back with him, at least as far as the little town where we had met, so now I felt that I must go alone. Because I knew very well how things can end up—you decide to leave, in fact you do leave and at the first halt you turn back with a weight off your shoulders, determined to have a lark and to laugh off the consequences.

I was just going to leave the room when the second lieutenant called me. "You are leaving your watch," he said.

I went up to the locker and took it. While I was fastening it to my wrist—now I blamed myself for not buying another, but it was too late, the shops were shut that day—the second lieutenant added: "That strap is dirty. Change it, and *good night*."

"I'll change it," I said, and left without saying a word more, full of ill-will. Now I was glad of my decision to leave.

As I gradually left behind me the signs of civllisation, and the tar of the streets, and the bars disappeared, melancholy came over me again and foreboding about what was waiting for me in camp, where I would have to justify my very long absence.

The truck stopped at the command post, which I knew already, and the carabiniere told the driver to take somebody on board. He shouted towards the sentry-box, smiling to us as he did so; first the old native appeared, and then a child, the one I had seen so happy in the bush, so unwearying in his admiration of his young friend's dancing. When we moved off, I saw through the window of the cab that the old man had sat down and had his back to me while the child, standing up, was shouting with joy over the trip.

The old man had his back to me; I saw that it was curved and fleshless. He moved his stick between his long hands and stroked it with one of them absentmindedly, not listening to what the child yelled from time to time. He was looking fixedly ahead and his head moved irregularly with the bumps of the vehicle. After a few kilometres, when the evening was falling, I took advantage of the truck's stopping to get out. "I'm not going any farther," I told the soldier and stayed on that hill overlooking the table-land. In the distance I saw the mountains of my prison standing out; so the river lay in that direction.

When the truck had moved off, I remained alone; I did not know what to do, but did not regret my sudden decision. I thought of going back to A. That little town with its command post, with its girls and their gramophone, with its square crossed at this hour by the calm traffic of the women making for the well, might calm me. I must go back to the gramophone girls and never more set out on these hateful and ill-omened roads. The day after I would go back to Asmara. And to hell with the consequences.

Natives were passing, going towards the town, and they saluted me, stopping many yards away, waiting for me to notice them and allow them to pass. They went away gloomy and distrustful, perhaps surprised to see an officer alone in these parts. And why, as I climbed down from the truck, had I felt the need to give that coin to the child?

Half an hour later a truck passed and took me back to A. The evening had fallen and instead of going to the command post I began to wander through the quietest streets, as if seeking from the walls of these enclosed gardens the calm I had lost. In a little square I saw some soldiers standing cooking their meal on an improvised fire and went up to them. They invited me to supper. They, too, had to go towards the river, and I suppose they, too, had been held up by the oncoming evening, incapable of facing the solitude which would have awaited them in the low-lying country where it was always eerie, where what lay in wait was no longer men, but things, trees, shadows.

We ate in silence, since the thought of taking the road again the next day made them bitter. I was happy, all worry now being over and done with. It was inevitable that the talk should come round to the prospects of going home, and I got excited about it; the soldiers stood listening without enthusiasm to my optimistic arguments and did not contradict me. They did not wish to and could not contradict me.

"Lieutenant."

I rose to my feet and saw the major near the entrance to a hut where a light burned. Always elegant, his hands behind his back, his boots shining in the light of our fire. When I came up to him he invited me in and for an instant we stood in silence, he searching for the phrases for his stupid reprimand, I for the excuses. At last he made up his mind. He ought to report me, but he knew it would be no use. Yet he asked himself what pleasure I got from lowering myself like that. Unshaven I haunted the native houses, ate sitting on the ground like a gipsy. He asked me what my idea was in going native.

He had spoken in a very calm voice; it was all an excuse because he was bored. However, I pointed out to him that I no longer had a beard; I had sat down on the ground with the soldiers because they had invited me to supper and there was no refusing them; moreover I had eaten very well. As for the native huts, it was a misunderstanding.

He looked at me with surprise, and several times repeated the word "misunderstanding," with a query in his voice. "But if I saw you with my own eyes?" he concluded. I replied that we had gone there to hear a little music.

"What sort of music?" he asked, laughing at his own joke, and took a bottle of cognac from a shelf. So this was his hut. He lived among a pile of ration-boxes, stuff of all kinds. It seemed to set off his elegance, but my suspicion grew that there was a definite connection between the large ring he wore on his right hand, ornamented with a precious stone, and the reek of drugs rising from the boards of the floor—boards certainly used to bearing the weight of a flourishing business. We drank. The cognac was old and the heat of the night helped to befuddle us. We laughed, friends now, each respecting the worst qualities of the other.

The topic he had touched on interested him too much. He asked if I were married, and when I had answered him seemed satisfied: this was a point in his favour. On the table near his camp-bed there was the photograph of a very unpleasant woman. He saw that I was looking at it and said that it was his wife. In the tone of his voice I detected regret for a marriage made in haste for reasons he had perhaps forgotten or at least repudiated. Yet the woman in the picture was smiling. From that smile one could deduce without any effort the style of the furniture in their flat, the curtains, the mediocre orderliness that reigned there. And the boredom.

Then I sang the praises of the native girls; they were simple as doves, sweet, disinterested, part of nature. All you had to do was to pluck them.

"You are making a mistake," he said. He now addressed me in the formal third person.

"Not at all," I replied. I added that it wouldn't last much longer; in a few years they would acquire the sense of time, which they now lacked completely. "When they discover time," I said, "they will become like all the other girls in this world, but of an inferior type, much inferior. Now they amuse me," I added, "because they know how to waste time, like the trees and the animals."

So these were the considerations that led me to waste my time with them? And the major laughed. We drank again. I was quite dizzy. "And this," I said, "is the cognac from the first-aid boxes." He did not understand. I repeated the phrase and added: "In the medical orderly's box the brandy bottle is always empty." ("But perhaps," I thought, "the orderly would not have come.")

He poured out another drink for me and said curtly: "You're a youngster." And he got up. I thought I had offended him; but he laughed and left the hut for a moment, rolling on his feet. Then, impelled by truly childish curiosity, I opened his table drawer. I knew I would find there this orderly confusion, those boxes full of stumps of pencils, of penknives, of stamps and of pencils tied with string. And also odd bits of sealing-wax. I was satisfied. The major's elegance seemed to me like the facade of a sordid building which I could go round with my eyes shut. When he re-entered, I proposed to him to go and waken the two girls—I only wanted to see the one who had sat beside me again, look into her eyes and convince myself that my fantasies were not worth bothering about. The major agreed, pleased that it was I who proposed the party. He wanted to study the atmosphere, to check whether what I said was true. And I remembered the breast loose in her tunic but as one thinks of a clue that must be destroyed. My temples throbbed and I was already terrified at the thought of this vendetta which she had never contemplated. I thought that I would never go back to camp.

"Shall we take a bottle?" said the major.

The girls did not want to open and decided to only after long consultations; and one of them had remained in bed, lying half uncovered like a warm block of granite. Since there was very little light the major began to touch the girl, trying to make it look like a joke. "Get up, it's time to get up," he said. In actual fact he was putting his hand under her tunic, stopping as if spellbound and turning to me with exaggerated surprise, invited me to see that she was really a pretty girl, very well built, really very well built. "Feel here, lieutenant." Yes, he was just the type I had suspected that day when he had begun to walk up and down before the door. I now counted it a victory, although an easy one, to have succeeded in bringing him where I wanted.

The other girl pretended not to recognise me, or really did not do so; I no longer had a long beard and there was no reason for her to pretend. She stood up on the stool, wound the gramophone, slowly, full of faith in the miracle that would result; and when I took hold of her she smiled. Her feet touched the floor and I left her; in that body was the indolence I feared. I asked myself if it was for this I had let the truck go on over the hill, to find once again what I had already buried along with my other mistakes. "Are you going to begin again?" I thought. I was confused; then I sat on the hearth-stone and the major, perhaps embarrassed by my sudden serious behaviour, uncorked the bottle, laughing, asking for the complicity I could no longer give him. When he offered me the liquor and said: "Come on, let's drink," I refused. So that was the brandy from the first-aid boxes

He took a long drink to give himself a little courage, to give me some, otherwise he could not have stood it and we might as well have gone home to sleep. He could not have stood the shadows the lamp created in the corners of the room—shadows I had forgotten.

One had to drink. After a little I felt better, and could even smile at the worries that my mind amused itself by inventing. Everything was much simpler; I went on living and it was logical—in fact just—that I should go on desiring what I had desired before. If long solitude counselled me to put an excessive value on an indolent body and two eyes that still held the imagined light of past centuries, there was nothing wrong in that. "Let's take a lesson from her," I said laughing; and was going to move over when I was stopped by the noise of the other couple.

The major was trying to make the girl swallow a sip, but she defended herself courteously. And the major took the opportunity to throw himself on her, sure that I would no longer censure him. But the girl defended herself, although without conviction, and to me the scene seemed unbearable.

The other girl was in her bed, waiting.

Outside was the dark night of decadence, without thieves, without sleep-walkers. Many months before, passing through Port Said, I had seen from the steamer the last European night, the bars set up along the mole to give the tourists time to spend the foreign currency left in their pockets. And a voice like the one coming from the gramophone came from the mole. On board I could hear, at that distance, the sound of the champagne corks, the somewhat nervous merriment of the tourists who wanted to enjoy themselves but not to go the length of the excesses suggested by the night and the excitement of the return journey. And they were not very certain whether to give in to the Arab who was proposing a visit to such and such a house. Let's go. Of course, Africa is the sink of iniquities and one goes there to stir up one's conscience.

I went up to the major and said: "Stop it." He was not surprised and then I added: "Africa is the sink of iniquities, eh?" He burst out laughing and his hands went rapidly round the waist of the girl sitting beside him. I began to insult him, but he went on laughing and his sociable mirth, instead of calming, increased the uneasiness that tormented me. Was I this inflamed man? Did I keep letters, photographs, did I think myself better than all the others? There, the major's face presented itself like a long-awaited target. It was certainly someone's face, but at that moment were not the wrinkles that marked it words written by an old pencil demanding only the effort of translation? "If I killed this man," I thought, "I would also bury the worst part of myself." But since the major began to be inquisitive I said: "Go on, enjoy yourself, old fellow," and became sincerely moved when he embraced the girl again. "His hands merely wanted to do homage to the long boredom of exile," I concluded.

The other girl was on the bed; she was now looking at the walls of the room and I no longer saw her face. But I felt that she was absent, immersed in her dark patience, and her thoughts could not be very different from the thoughts which precede sleep.

Why was I in that house? What had I come to do there? When my tongue touched the still tender cavity in the gum I remembered everything. The day is over, tomorrow it begins again, and the only hope was perhaps that letter in the post orderly's tent. An unfolded letter, and within her fine round hand with a few words scrawled in haste the most timid signature that I know. I must reach the letter and that soon! And then. . . . Would I take the road to the river and the mountain again? "No," I said, "off to Asmara at dawn and to hell with the consequences."

The girl was waiting for me and I drank, until I saw the room spinning and the shadows with it. I drank with determination because I hate getting drunk and I did not expect any relief from the alcohol. I would certainly not have asked of it any other relief than I could not give myself by joining the girl in bed and convincing myself that one is as good as the other. "Nothing was left out; everything is in the grave," I said. For that reason one had to wind up the gramophone, to drink, to smack the girls' bottoms, to encourage the major; for one thing was definite—I would not go back across the river. Get put into hospital? We'll see.

The girls laughed to see us so merry, a sign that the party was a success. A pity they couldn't call the nine—or ten—neighbours with their children. Perhaps this was the moment to put on the military march? Of course, let's put it on in any case. When the major heard the martial notes he ran to take off the record and to lie down on the girl's bed. I could not bear his sudden free-and-easy manner. I went into the other room and stood looking at the woman, who was already in her bed and waiting for me without impatience. I sat down on the bed and looked at her, in fact I studied her. Her skin was not very pale and her smile was that of a good patient domestic animal. She remained motionless, not imagining that I saw her so clearly. "She was like this one," I said. "Like this animal—this mirage that solitude, heightened by boredom, offers you." Or was I perhaps trying to fool myself? Was I not looking for an excuse to comfort myself? I was happy to find it in the odour of the woman, a vegetable odour, like that of a patient tree, mixed with a perfume so sweet it turned one's stomach. I did not dare to touch her, and if the bed began to revolve, as I feared, I would have to leave. And instead I had to stay. I tried to look the woman in the eye; she had hazel-coloured pupils, like all the rest of the women in these parts. I burst out laughing. "Have you ever seen grey-green eyes; they don't exist here? Do you want to know who has grey-green eyes? Who has a mirror, please?" I went on laughing and the woman laughed too, patiently, without understanding.

"Major," I said. He answered with a grunt. "Major," I repeated, "have you ever been in battle?"

He answered: "Yes," with an effort, somewhat surprised. "Is it possible," I asked, "for a soldier to have his guts hanging out and get better?"

Although annoyed he said that everything was possible and would I leave him in peace. The girl lying beside me stretched out an arm and a cotton curtain divided the two rooms.

Did I have to insist? Would I not have learned it just as well by asking a doctor the next day, that doctor who reads his newspapers in the eucalyptus grove? "When you are wounded in the belly," I said, "it's another story."

"One of my men got away with it," answered the major, and I heard the girl laughing, perhaps because she was being tickled.

"Did they operate right away?" I asked and managed to sit on the bed. "Six or seven hours later." His voice expressed impatience with the dialogue I was forcing upon him.

"Suppose," I said—and the woman looked at me, patient, smiling, without wondering at the reason for my delay—"that I fired a shot at this girl's belly. . . ." I was already wondering what the major could know about it. Was it not useless to pose such childish questions at the side of that girl, who went on smiling?

"If you want to waste ammunition, go on," he answered. Then he added: "I'll tell you something that happened." And he told the story of a massacre at which he had been present. "They were brigands," he said, "and the colonel wanted to kill them all, the wounded, too. An eye for an eye, he said. And when he found one wounded he shot him. He shot him in the belly. And they lay there looking at him, covering their eyes with their hands, looking at him through their fingers. The doctor came along and said: 'But if you don't shoot them in the head you'll get nowhere with these people.' So the colonel opened fire at the head of the first wounded man he saw. The skull burst open and the colonel found himself all messed up. You should have seen him. He was in a towering rage. He heaped insults on the doctor. 'That's fine advice you give me,' he screamed. He had to go and change."

The petrol-lamp was annoying us all and I could not bear the cavernous light and the shadows it created in the corners of the room. The major rose and put it out. In the sudden darkness I heard him groping back to his bed, trying to catch the sound of my laughter; but it did not come. The woman beside me wanted to say something in my ear and laughed submissively.

"I understand," I said, "it's a question of light wounds." But the major did not want to continue the conversation and called out jokingly: "Good night." Then I had to lie down; my head was reeling; it was the fault of the liquor I had drunk. Now the night had penetrated into the house too, and the bed was floating up and down on the waters of a deep lake enclosed by mountains more unfriendly than those waiting across the river. And why did my gum still ache?

The woman lay beside me in silence. I had at least to ask her name; I felt her tranquil breathing and her soft body lying in a state of expectation, profound and sluggish; but I could not stand the smell of her—it was a thick smell, the smell of a Christian animal; there was the smell of sacristies and of stray dogs, and the smell, too, of tuberoses in a warm room.

"What's your name?" I said, but the girl did not understand. I was going to repeat my question when a soldier—who could it be but a drunken soldier?—beat on the door of the courtyard, and a rough voice called some words. I got up with difficulty. The girl, without moving, answered promptly, and the other intervened, too, calling out in her turn: she wanted to tell her companion not to let in the unwelcome guest, but she shouted as if the room was already invaded. The man outside yelled, then gave a bang on the door, and at last we heard him go off.

Then the girl caught me by an arm and pulled me to her, making me fall on to the bed. But suddenly I thrust her away and left her thus, surprised and already undressed, while I made for the door. I told the major I was going out for a minute and ran towards the square.

I stopped in front of the church; I thought I had heard laments. Going up to the huts at the side of the entrance I saw in the dark a tangled mass of rags and flesh—it was several natives; they were lamenting, but weakly, as if they too were sick of their

unanswered cries. Seeing me draw near, they fell silent, waiting.
They were beggars, I imagine. I threw them some coins and set
off again towards the command post. There I would wait for the
dawn and the first truck going towards the river.

4

I had not yet looked at the valley which fell away at that very
point. The table-land broke off, and soon the first decline would
begin. When the soldier climbed on to the running-board of the
truck, which had stopped at the checkpost, I recognised him—it
was a soldier from my company. Then I saw two more soldiers,
then three, then all my company. "And what are you doing here?"
I asked the soldier who had climbed on to the running-board and
was saluting and smiling. "What are you doing here?" I repeated.

He told me that the battalion had been moved here five days
ago. And he laughed happily.

My look must have betrayed my horror, but the soldier read in
it unexpected joy at news which he had been the first to give me,
and which meant another stage towards the coast, even if the
coast was still so far off. Then he laughed at my surprise, took the
pack from my hands and began to tell me the details.

We went along a narrow road, and shortly the first tents of the
camp appeared. And the soldier continued to talk of going home,
as everyone did, I imagine, now that there was nothing more to
do. He wanted to have my impressions, then he asked if I knew
about the workmen's camp.

"What workmen's camp?" I asked.

"The one at the bridge." The soldier was happy to tell me what
had happened. There had been an attack by brigands and they
had wounded eight workmen. And that perhaps was the reason
why the battalion had been moved. Meanwhile the *zouaves* had
already combed the area and now we had to stay and control the
whole line of the river. Certainly there were patrol duties every
day, but hadn't the battalion come nearer to the coast? And
wasn't it a nice place? A thousand times better than the last one

on the mountains, where the lice came rushing into the tents now the wet season was beginning. "Yes, of course," I said.

On the bank overlooking the road and the valley the soldiers sat and talked of their imminent return. The move had rekindled the hopes of even the most pessimistic, and now they were all encouraging each other with cries that leapt from tent to tent. Each soldier knew the secrets of at least one other, and this was a magnificent opportunity to refer to them, making the joy of others one's own, fancifully participating in future betrothals, in future weddings. They would all see each other again in Italy, and the friendship born under the roof of their tents would give a rosy tint to even the gloomiest memories and make everything, after a few years' interval, seem happy and pleasant, even the ten-day marches, even the thirst and the fatigue, even the heat and the fear.

Now I had to face the officers, my superiors and my friends. I decided that I would face them all together—it was a piece of elementary astuteness. In the major's or captain's tent the conversation would have been serious, in the mess tent other factors would come into play, the pleasure of finding oneself at table, the unexpected cries of the colleagues at my appearance. I had brought a packet of cigars and two bottles of liquor. And a lot of books. They would forgive me.

When I appeared on the threshold of the big tent everyone looked at me like policemen looking at an elusive criminal who has evaded capture for years and comes to give himself up after his case has been filed away. Perhaps they did not expect me any more. Or else the move had made my absence seem short. Or else they had already reported me for desertion. No, impossible. But I did not understand. Who did these people not answer my greeting and stay with their spoons in mid-air? Why were they all silent? An idea flashed across my mind: they have found her. I left a clue. Or I was seen. But by whom? I stayed on the threshold incapable of taking a step further.

"Welcome back," said the major curtly, too curtly; and then I realised that he did not know anything, that no one knew anything. It was the tone of voice of an angry superior officer; nothing more.

My joy burst forth. I was still running through a list of excuses when the laughter of my friends began. Lieutenant B. laughed too much and had a fit of choking—he was eating at the time-and this diversion turned to my advantage. Then the doctor unwittingly came to my aid by shouting out that some woman had kept me. Things having taken this turn, very soon no one spoke of my late return but only of the reasons for it. And everyone hazarded guesses. And everyone meditated a delayed return in future when it was his turn. I had made a glorious precedent for breaking the rule.

Yet the major did not look at it like that, but remained wrathful, incapable of restraining the others' mirth and incapable of taking part in it. At last he made up his mind: "I suppose," he said, "that your tooth doesn't hurt now." He spoke with irony, weighing the words, certain that he had scored a hit. I pulled out my pocketbook: "Here it is," I said calmly.

I had won. That burst of laughter told me so. But I had to sit down, eat, tell my story, provoke further laughter. It was inevitable. When later I entered my tent there were two letters on the bed. I sat down, at the end of my tether, and for a long time merely looked at them, incapable of opening them.

THE GOLD

1

A T REVEILLE THE captain ordered me to get ready for a tour of the valley; I would be out all day with my platoon. He spread out the map—not that incredible map, another one; and pointing out the spot I feared said that I would be well advised to go as far as that, besides, there was a fairly easy short cut; and in any case I should look and see if it was worth improving since the men had nothing to do and got into a bad state if they had leisure. In any case we would have to improve the short cut at many points; it was too rocky.

While the captain was speaking I looked for an excuse but found none. I had in some way or other to make up for my long absence and no excuse could have any effect. When the captain asked me if I had understood, I stood there without saying anything, embarrassed. "Take the map," he added.

The platoon was ready. They all knew the locality we had to inspect. This displeased me. It meant that the captain did not trust me and looked to the sergeant to have his orders carried out. It displeased me further because the idea which in the meantime had flashed across my mind became impracticable; the sergeant, too, had his little map and it was now impossible to take the company off its road towards another point on the river and let them have a bathe or start looking at the view—a programme which the soldiers would willingly have shared. There was nothing to be done about it. The sergeant would have let himself be killed rather than give up what he considered a military operation; he wanted to be promoted and was already proud that the captain had honoured him with his trust. I could not say to him "I am not coming"; he would have been delighted to command the platoon, he would have done miracles, but for that very reason the affair would have come out. I had to go. And to keep a good eye on the short cut to decide which bits it would be as well to improve.

"Will we find water?"

"Yes," I answered thoughtlessly, then added that I did not know, but that perhaps we would find it. And I smiled, thinking that we would find soap, too. Or perhaps the ravens. . . .

I had to go back again. The affair was profoundly repugnant to me, and so it is not always true that murderers are drawn to revisit the scene of their crime. Perhaps this repugnance of mine meant that it was going too far to talk of a crime? Good, there was some slight food for comfort. Going down towards the river while the soldiers sang, I felt that every trace of fear was vanishing and that instead a calm curiosity was taking its place; the curiosity of the diligent reader visiting the places described in his favourite novel. I could tell myself to be at ease, nothing would happen. And then what could happen to me? I certainly was not afraid of unfortunate meetings with disbanded warriors. I knew that they preferred to be inactive by day, and, if anything, tried to strike when there was something to carry away. But what could they have taken from a platoon, except letters and thoughts about going home? As for the woman, she was lying very quiet, unless some hyena had been strong and zealous enough to take away the stones one by one. And that might have happened, but the hole was deep and the stones big. No, the woman was still there, I was sure of it, and would have dried up under the stones I had arranged, and arranged with such care, as if afraid of hurting her.

In an hour's time we had reached the mule carcase. There was not much of it left, but the stench still spread through the fierce heat; and, more than the bush and the valley which lay before my eyes as on that other day, it was that stench that brought back the memory of what had happened.

I went on, ahead of the others, not to test my courage, but solely to prevent anything forgotten from turning up. Was I certain that I had forgotten nothing? But what about that envelope? That was an example of the sort of thing one should never allow to fall out of one's pockets. The presence of another envelope could not have been explained. But that, too, was the kind of idea that comes when you are taking a short cut and the soldiers are singing.

The sergeant came up to suggest that I stop them. He explained that we might easily fall into an ambush if we announced our arrival like that. "That's right," I said, "make them keep quiet." "Although," I thought, "the woman would not have minded." And the soldiers fell silent against their wills, because the soldier protests by singing and thus relieves himself of all his misfortunes, and singing he does not think about going home.

Now I was looking into the branches of a tree. "Halt," I said. There was something, a bundle; I could not see clearly. I went on with my revolver in my right hand, hearing, as I went, the confusion in which the soldiers got ready their weapons. What was the bundle? A man. But a man standing in a tree? A scout? And he doesn't move? Suddenly I saw that it was a hanged man. Hanged in his shirt, with his forehead bent towards the ground, as if meditating on his misfortune, his hands stretched along his sides, his limbs swollen. I would not have recognised him if, at the foot of the tree, there had not been, in pieces, that screeching violin. It was one of the young men, the fiddler to be exact.

The soldiers stood back and did not speak. No one spoke. There was a silence so unpleasant that a soldier fired into the branches of the tree. The ravens fled, a big bird fell, shaking itself, losing its feathers. Other similar birds, although too gorged, attempted to fly off and settled down, lazy and happy, among the branches of a nearby tree. I made a sign not to fire. The flight of these birds was too much, it was better not to provoke it.

"It is one of the brigands," explained the sergeant.

"A brigand who played the violin," I answered; but I did not want him to understand, it was not necessary.

The soldiers had already discovered another corpse at the foot of a nearby tree and were looking at it, keeping well away, unable to take their eyes off the immobile and decomposed body. It was the other adolescent, the one who had fallen behind in his dancing and leapt here and there, so happy to be alive, even in a piece of bush near the river, without cinema and without bars. When we went on a soldier began to sing too gay a song, and the others listened to him, but at the refrain no voice joined the first. We were near the dry water-course, we had to go on quickly.

There now, perhaps I had to mark down to my account the death of these two youths as well. I felt confusedly that the blame was still and always mine. Before asking the sergeant I thought that the disappearance of the woman had enraged the men of the village. The brigands who had attacked the hut were only men indignant at a crime. Had they discovered the woman's body? Of course not, and the old man? The old man who goes about looking for the woman in the houses that are open to all, and drinks the coffee I have refused and collects the butt-ends of my cigarettes? No, no one has looked for the woman except the old man. And who listens to an old man when he presents himself at the door of the houses that are open to all to ask for a girl? For a girl who has left the bush for a better life—a much better one.

When I asked the sergeant why they had hanged the two youths he answered that, in fact, part of the stolen property had been found in their hut.

"Perhaps the bandits left it in their flight," I said.

"Of course," said a soldier, the one who had fired a shot and who was now following our conversation. "If they had stolen it," he went on, "would they keep it at home?" And he looked at us waiting for a reply whereby to size us up. In his own village the soldier was a smuggler and was now taking advantage of the occasion to form an opinion of us. "What had they to do with it?" he added.

"You're forgetting the example it sets," said the sergeant. He repeated the phrase several times and meanwhile looked at me closely, expecting help, a final word, or perhaps only to remind me that such would have been my duty—and that he saw himself forced to take my place. He was a strange man, the sergeant; he had modelled himself on the disciplinary code, and when he spoke, now cited the letter and now in a few words expressed its spirit. He allowed himself few adjectives—those approved by the press and military custom. The ration was "excellent"; and if an aeroplane went over it was "one of our brave fighters." Encouraged by my silence he concluded: "The example means that these people will think twice before stealing."

"It's easy to see that you have never stolen," answered the smuggler with profound contempt, casting a glance of sympathy towards me. And our walk continued.

So, I thought, the woman was not the reason for the attack on the hut. It was not my revolver shot that set the avalanche in motion. The woman was something that concerned me alone. Me and the old man. But only for a little while longer. The old man would not press on with his search or would die. Is it possible to live long in bush like this? I would leave the country carrying with me a few photographs as my only memory. I would forget the woman, my error, everything. Oh, her ghost at the foot of the bed was most unlikely.

2

Having passed the water-course we took the path on which she had appeared to me that evening carrying her basket of offerings. Now that everything evoked her presence I was calm; it was almost as if I was about to see her again and nothing had yet happened. The path must lead to that thicket which she had pointed out to me as being her village.

I had put my revolver back in its holster; my right hand had become numb—all the fault of my scratch which had not yet healed. I was walking slowly and the soldiers followed singing. And they sang the song the gramophone had played, the one they had sung when they left and which, when they went back, no woman would sing. I was walking slowly because these were her haunts and they seemed familiar to me as they had been to her. Perhaps the sand of the path still kept the imprint of her feet.

Three hundred yards off a bush moved and a man emerged and fled. I was barely in time to stop the sergeant from firing, but could not stop him from shouting, and the man—but was it a man or was it the distance that deceived us?—hardly turned round and continued his disorderly flight. We saw him fall into a ditch, reappear shortly after, searching for a way of escape through the bushes, look at us, then continue his flight.

"Let him go," I said. But the sergeant threw me an ironical glance. He had to "capture him". I tried to make him understand that there was a great deal of logic in the man's escaping as soon as he saw us. He had found out how easy it is to hang from a tree if one has a dark skin and was trying to put the greatest possible distance between his neck and us, who were probably carrying cord. He was fleeing like a wild animal, without asking himself whether we were led, because of his flight, to consider him guilty. He was making for safety, he was trying to reach safety. It would have been too much to ask him to wait for us, smiling, showing us his certificate of surrender in the cleft of a curved stick.

They were still going about with their certificates of surrender. In the early days they had presented themselves at the various posts to recognise the new chiefs and to swear fealty or only obedience. They wanted to live in peace and had often asked for a tangible sign of their good will from the first soldier, because the first soldier one meets is always the most dangerous. And the soldiers had amused themselves by giving them certificates of their own, no less valid than those distributed at the command posts, indeed more picturesque. It was not uncommon to meet them with out-of-date tickets from some lottery, it was their most precious document, the sign that they were not to be disturbed. They had submitted, accepting the will of the Eternal. And others carried bits of paper with unrepeatable expressions on them, or else invitations to take a kick at the bearer; and so they went about full of new confidence, along the new roads, abandoning the short cuts.

We saw the man escape and then halt, uncertain what to do. He was looking towards us; he felt himself lost and amazed that we did not fire; he saw us on his trail, following him implacably.

"It is a child," said the smuggler.

"A child?"

He had stopped at the foot of a bare hill where the path came into the open. He would have offered us too good a target and had stopped. When he saw us coming up to him—yes, it was that very child—he began to run again. He began to climb catching hold of the bushes, no longer keeping to the path. His fear moved the soldiers to pity. "Let's stop," said one of them.

I had thought the same, but had not been capable of stopping. Now I had to catch up with the child. I shouted to the sergeant to stay there with the men and made a sign to the smuggler to follow me.

"Don't run away," I shouted to the child. But wasn't it stupid of me to shout? He could not understand me, that was certain. The smuggler who could have got ahead of me and caught up with the boy was instead following me lazily, not in the least convinced that it was necessary to catch him. Perhaps he was reliving some similar adventure where the bad part had fallen to him—that of fleeing and of feeling behind him the heavy breathing, the cries of the pursuers who are paid for their work and carry it out.

The child had stopped, leaning against a tree a few yards above our heads. He had given in. I saw his little body shaken with fear; he had seen that it was useless to go on. Because of the fatigue I had to face when pulling myself up, I could not smile at him until I was a few yards away. Only then did I see that he was wearing my shorts, the ones I had given to the woman.

Well, the matter was beginning to be complicated. These shorts were too clear a message for me to trouble to decipher it. For a second I saw the woman smiling again and looking at me with her halfshut eyes, and this time almost to warn me that things had not worked out as I had imagined. The child was wearing these shorts as his only garment; they reached from his chest to his feet and as soon as he saw me looking at them he took them off, leaving himself naked, and made to hand them to me. He was giving them back to me, he recognised that they were not his and he took the occasion of this meeting with a "signore" to give them back.

I gave him to understand by signs that he could put them on again, but he would not. He held out his hand, offering them to me, determined to recognise my right to them provided I spared him. When he understood that I had not wanted to take them he left them on the ground delicately and ran off again towards the brow of the hill.

"Come on," said the smuggler. And we followed the boy who was now more and more amazed at our pursuit. Had he not managed to placate us? The smuggler picked up the shorts and very soon we were on the edge of the clearing.

On the other side, two hundred yards away, were the huts all under the trees. There were few huts and they miserable ones; one could see, too, the remains of those which had burned. On the others fluttered white rags—the rags of surrender.

The child stood naked in the midst of the clearing and looked towards us. He called something when he saw us appear, and a man who was shovelling earth stopped work and turned round, then he went on working. It was the old man. It must be an important task if our presence did not prompt him to stop it and greet us. He was working beside a grave and said nothing when we looked into it. The old man was busy filling it in and said nothing. I lit a cigarette because the air was still full of the heavy and clinging odour of corpses insufficiently covered by the earth. But the old man was in no hurry and threw the earth calmly, without looking at us, trying to fill the gaps.

He was not afraid of us; he did not think it necessary to smile, to give the greeting, which I had so often seen. He threw the earth, using now his hands, now the spade. He would stay there until his work was finished without looking at me, or perhaps waiting for a kick from me to send him to join those corpses he was covering up, things which must be removed from the curiosity of wild animals and from the ravages of the weather.

I could not tear myself away. The smuggler had gone to one side, and sat on a stone, convinced that the dead must bury their dead. He did not understand why I stayed there offending the old man by my presence. He certainly thought me a fool or perhaps only an officer. When we got back to Italy we would be on opposite sides of the barricade, he being from the first compelled to earn his daily bread at the risk of his life.

He was a difficult character, that boy, one of the people for whom I have had most regard. Well, they were both there a few paces from one other, the persons I have most respected, the smuggler and the old man, and never addressed a word to each other. But their thoughts were the same, that I felt, and it was I who was the target of them, for I represented the law or something that resembled the law. "Good day," I said. What else could I say?

The old man turned round to look at me. His face expressed no feeling, neither surprise at my greeting, which was equivalent to defeat, nor the hatred which my person must inspire in him. He had squatted on his heels and his thin legs projected from the toga which he had gathered round his belt to work. "Good day, lieutenant," he answered. It was a harsh voice but it had correctly pronounced the words "good day", which the natives always mispronounce. And in the girl's house, too, he had pronounced his greeting properly.

He looked at me, but could not recognise me; we had scarcely met and I was protected by the shadow the lamp cast in the corners of the room. "A providential shadow," I thought. He was looking at me attentively, perhaps astonished that I had addressed him. And then I asked him, pointing to the grave, "Are some of these your people?"

This was not a defeat but surrender at discretion. The old man shook his head and went on throwing earth. He no longer looked at me and certainly wanted me to go away. But instead I had sat down on a big stone and was smoking. "Do you speak Italian?" I said.

He nodded. And then I added: "Tell me about it."

The old man rose to his feet and looked at me fixedly. For a moment I thought he wanted to cry out or throw the stone he held in his hands at me. But no, nothing happened. Perhaps he had read real sympathy in my eyes; I had felt like expressing it.

"You know about it, lieutenant," he answered. Then he shouted something to the child, who began to carry stones to him, one at a time.

The child had now recovered his courage; my brief dialogue with the old man had made him nothing short of audacious, and now he frisked about the clearing, expending all his energy on collecting stones so that I should admire him. He left his stone near the old man and ran to another one, full of zeal, picking the biggest ones, putting aside the little ones after rapid reflection.

The smuggler was not bored. He was rolling himself a cigarette, but he took no part in our conversation; he knew all about it, it was an old story now. He did not like the natives, but neither did he like those who killed them. He, who was forced to wander over the Alps unarmed—if they had taken him with arms on him that would have been the end—had learnt to hate whoever uses arms, aims them at the earliest possible opportunity and fires to give weight to his opinion. These natives were nearer to him than to me; therefore he did not feel himself bound to put on any act. The dead bury the dead; there's no use asking questions of the sexton. What's the point of these remarks from a passer-by? "How did it happen? Tell me, my good man. I'm sorry."

This is what the smuggler was thinking; you had only to see with what rage he licked his paper. But I was not playing the part out of curiosity and he could not know that.

I asked the old man why he spoke my language so well. Then he pulled out of his trousers an old pocket-book and looked in it for a card, which he handed to me. The old man had been an askari in his prime and later had come to live here. I wondered

how he could live on such a miserable hill, shut in by the valley
and with no trees that were not unpleasant.

He was called Johannes. I was amazed that he had not intervened to prevent the slaughter, but I knew that, at that time, he
was on the table-land. I still asked him why he had not intervened, why he had not shown this document which everyone
would have respected. "I was not in the village," he said, pointing to the child. I thought I heard in his words remorse that he
had been away on the very day that his presence would have
been helpful; instead, it was satisfaction at having saved the child
that made him lower his voice. What if they had snatched that
piece of paper from under his nose?

The Zouaves would have done it without thinking twice about
it. They had come on horseback to do this quick job; they were
passing that way and it doesn't take long to burn two or three
straw huts. And on the other hand the zouaves remembered
what the asaris had done in Libya, they, too, paid by the same
master; because this is one of the elementary secrets of a good
imperial policy.

And Johannes looked at me, but without curiosity, perhaps he
was not even looking at my person, but beyond it; he was looking at the edge of the table-land and the valley which opened out
under the sunshine of that sultry day. "And this old man," I
thought, "persists in living here where the hyenas will come, if
they have not come already, if the corpses in this grave have not
attracted them already."

"Darky," said the smuggler and the child scampered towards
him, trustingly. The smuggler handed him the shorts and made
him put them on. Thereafter he always spoke his own dialect and
the two understood each other perfectly. "Take it," he said, and
gave him half his bread which the child did not wish to take, but
then ate calmly. The smuggler thought hardly of me; I felt it. I
was confining myself to academic exercises in pity; I would
never learn. He, with a couple of shouts, had put himself on their
side; everything had been said between them, and not even the

confusion of tongues was able to divide them, because they understood each other as if bound by common roots to a dark destiny, full of unknown evil factors. "Here," he said to the old man and the old man caught the bread in flight and hid it in the folds of his toga. That was that. And I stood there and asked questions and would be looked upon by the old man as if I were the commander of the firing squad, who is not to blame, but all the same it is he who lowers his hand and then says: "Someone had to do it."

Johannes began to fill up the grave again; he wanted to finish his work before the sun was too high and the shadow of the trees had disappeared. I spoke to him no more and went up to the boy, who was eating. I did not know how to translate the question that I longed to ask. Was he perhaps the woman's son? I walked round him pretending to look at the landscape. I asked the smuggler for a match so as to have a chance of a better look at the child. I smiled at him, hoping that he would smile. I would have recognised that smile.

There, I was going into details; my curiosity was really worthy of a student of the place. Son, brother, nephew, what did it matter? Were not these very eyes with their green and grey, that gesture—full of modesty—as the bread was carried to the mouth enough?

A few minutes later I left the village much happier than when I had set out.

My guilt had almost vanished. "They would have killed her all the same," I thought. And how they would have killed her! I had anticipated her cruel destiny by a few days, sparing her a much more painful end. She had not seen her people being killed, nor the huts being set on fire, nor heard the cries of men who kill for the sake of killing. This I went on repeating to myself as I went down the hillside path. And I even got the length of being pleased that I had killed her.

But why was the old man following me now? Did he want to speak to me? I stopped and he rediscovered the salute he had known when he was in his twenties. "Lieutenant," he said, "do you want the child with you?" The smuggler and I looked at him in astonishment.

"He's a good boy," said Johannes, "he'll learn to look after you. There's no point in his staying here."

"Johannes," I said, "thank you, but I cannot take the boy. You know that I am not master of my actions. If you send the boy up to the camp we will give him bread every day, and other stuff, too, but I can't take him." And I smiled.

"You can take him," he replied, almost insolently, but avoiding looking at me.

"I can't," I replied. And since he was now looking at me I met his glance. He was looking at me fixedly, as the captain had done that same morning. He said nothing and went off.

When we reached the water-course we saw that the child was following us—I suppose the old man had ordered him to do so—and was following us calmly, hiding now and again when we stopped to look at him, but peeping at us through the branches of the trees. The soldiers were having fun out of it. The game had been reversed. He was following us and would come to the camp, and I would find him in front of my tent with those grey-green eyes, and the sentry would take a kick at him. I was about to lose my head. "What will we do with him?" I asked the smuggler. "He will be wanting more bread," I added, but I knew that it was not for the bread that he followed us.

"We'll see," said the smuggler. I went and took him and put him at the tail of the party. I did not know what to say and the sergeant dared not say anything.

3

The smuggler was not a prey to vanity, he did not know what to do with the "darky." He was a simple man, he had begun to earn his living as a child himself; he wanted to teach the child to earn his own living and taught him to do so in a few days. He would send him into the little towns of the old Colony to buy things and they re-sold them together, splitting the profits. In a week's time the child already knew all the words necessary for his trade. He ate his bread and slept among the sacks in a store, and no one said anything to him, things were so slack, and in a month or so, maybe more, maybe less, the day of our departure would come.

When he was not plying his trade the child would come and sit in front of my tent as I had foreseen. He was obeying the orders of Johannes. I was his "father." It was to me he turned when he had doubts about the advisability of any piece of business. He would sit a little to one side of the opening of the tent, and he looked at me until I deigned to look at him. Then he smiled and bent his head to make it quite clear that he was at my orders and this business with the smuggler was only a way of passing the time.

"Well, Elias, how are your profits?"

He replied with the exact figure, he held out the coins in the palm of his hand—just like the woman—so that I might dispose of them at my leisure. And he stayed there, sitting on his heels just as the old man sat on the hill guarding his dead. But I did not love the child and his presence annoyed me, above all because of those smiles, of his way of holding things out with his palm open, because of his way of gazing at me for a long time with extreme admiration without taking his eyes off me. I accepted him as a punishment, the mildest it was given to me to choose, but as a punishment.

"How many women were there in the village, Elias?"

The boy thought for a long time, then said that there were three.

"Were they very old?"

The boy was uncertain for a moment, then he indicated that two were very old but one not.

"And did the young one die, too?"

The boy shook his head. She was not dead. She had gone away in time, seven days before. "Gone away? Where, Elias?" The boy raised his head to say that he did not know where she could have got to. She had gone away, as women do go away to "marry" some officer or truck-driver. She had gone up on to the table-land towards the marvellous cities where people sleep in wonderful huts and there is everything that one can desire.

"She was your sister?"

The boy nodded several times. How had I guessed?

"All right, Elias, that's enough for today, the lesson is finished."

And Elias went off to his business manager to receive the orders for the day. He was happy, they had got together an old uniform for him and washed him often. But the next morning I found him in front of my tent like a hangover of my nightly remorse which time could not assuage, because the more I knew of the woman, the more hateful did my crime appear. I knew her name—Mariam—and from the stories of Elias I saw her laugh, sing, I saw her going towards the river or preparing the bread.

Elias had seen my interest in the life of the destroyed village and had thought that by my continual questions I merely wished to show him my sympathy. He thought himself bound to reciprocate in the only way he knew—by loyalty. One night I noticed that he was no longer sleeping in the company store but was lying near my tent. I heard his soft breathing through the canvas and I could not sleep. I thought that the next day I would have him chased away from the camp and sent back to the village, but was it possible? Had things not taken such a turn that I could no longer guide and control them? Was it not in itself a miracle that the old man did not also come and sleep outside the tent and the two adolescents, too, with the cord round their necks, and the whole village as well? And Mariam, too, while we are about it, why not? Just like that, all of them here round the tent.

I clutched my head in my hands so as not to cry out, so as not to leave the tent and to start kicking the intruder whom I had dragged there through weakness and stupidity. His place was in the village; what had I to do with his education, with his future? Some day or other he would go away, I said, as soon as he understood that he could himself do the same work as he was now doing with the smuggler. Let us wait a week or two and he will go away. I had seen children of four on the roads asking a lift from the trucks, offering to pay, so as to make journeys of five or six hundred kilometres in order to sell packets of cigarettes. I had seen a boy walk two hundred kilometres to sell a little can of oil and gain a few lire. They have commerce in their blood, these ones, and loyalty they understand as a way to attain one's confidence and then to abuse it. Don't worry, I said, he'll go away. And then it will be a sign that you have cancelled all your guilt.

I opened the tent and the child sprang to his feet, smiling.

4

One morning as I rose, I felt my hand numb; I took off the bandage, and around the scratch, which had by now almost closed, I saw that the skin was swollen and had become rough, taking on a pale violet colour. I touched my hand, felt the swelling and felt a hand that did not belong to me, that was no longer attached to my arm. The revulsion I felt was quickly overcome when, after having washed and moved about a little, I felt a dull and insistent pain rise in my fingers. After the agitation of the night the light of the sun calmed me and, having breakfasted, I was quite tranquil. I painted my hand with tincture of iodine, put on a light bandage and ran to inspect the men, who were setting off to the short cut to do road-mending.

This was an idea of the major's so as not to keep the men idle, but the short cut was now becoming useless. The passage of mules was irregular; for some time it had been possible for trucks to use the road. There should not have been much to do. But the soldiers, to cheat their boredom, took particular pains with the work; they wanted to make nothing short of a proper road, they put kerbs on it, arrows and signs, and one had to let them do it; in unnecessary work they found comfort for their forced labour.

It often fell to me to superintend their work. In actual fact I took the opportunity to chat with the soldiers. Or else I went off to the water-course and there looked at the village. The hanged men had been buried by the old man.

Sometimes, feeling as if I were challenging my fear, I halted beside the pools reading or pretending to read. I even pushed on as far as the boulder which had sheltered the woman and myself that night and I examined every stone, every tree, disappointed that the scene of my guilt should be on such a wretched scale. Four stones. Whereas in my memory everything had assumed vaster and more eternal proportions. Instead it was all there; our alcove, the boulder where the beast had crouched, the earth which had absorbed her blood, the shrubs prepared for burning, and up there the rim of the table-land not as distant as it had appeared to me that day now that I knew the road. Poking with a stick among the loose earth I found another cartridge case and kept it.

I could not yet make up my mind to see the woman's grave, but I imagined that everything would be in its place, even the bushes which I had put there to conceal it. Perhaps the rains would have deleted all trace, carrying more earth and gravel down on to the fissure, since the fissure ran down towards the ravine. The absence of any smell led me to believe—and in fact such was the case—that no beast had contaminated the place, and that in itself was a source of comfort. One day I went as far as the village. Three days before I had met Johannes on the short cut, and I wanted to see him again; I had with me a haversack with things that would be useful to him; and I flattered myself that he would be happy to have them. When I reached the clearing I called, but no one answered. Perhaps Johannes had gone off to find some food, had gone down to the tributary or else to some village on the table-land; I did not know how he lived. The village was deserted, and in the clearing the corpse-filled grave had been covered with large stones through which untidy and repugnant vegetation was already thrusting itself.

I called again and went up to the huts. I recognised Johannes', the only one which showed signs of a living being. There was a mat, a table, a few pots, some garments. The other huts were completely abandoned and Johannes had not even thought of taking possession of those things which might have been of use to him. He had left them in the disorder caused by the turmoil which had preceded the executions. It was not difficult to imagine what had happened. Swarms of ants had invaded the larders, and, having finished them off, were now devouring what remained—the few pieces of cloth, the wood, whatever had survived the massacre.

There were five huts, but I suppose some had been uninhabited even then; perhaps they belonged to people who had fled to the mountains some time before. I was looking, without wishing to admit it, for Mariam's hut, perhaps I would recognise it, but it was impossible; I did not dare to enter these ruins which repelled me with their heavy air of abandonment. I was on the threshold of a hut when Johannes appeared at my side.

"Johannes," I said with exaggerated cheerfulness, "where were you?"

"There," and he pointed towards the river. Then he stood there looking at me without saying more. I felt that with Johannes I would never have the better of it; it was wrong of me always to begin things, this must lead him to the worst possible deductions as to my capacity as an officer. I knew that the *askaris* do not like anyone who takes them unduly into his confidence, suspecting that it conceals injustice, which sooner or later they will feel to their cost. I knew of *askaris*, first punished and then let off, who claimed that they counted the punishment as a guarantee that future rewards would not be overlooked. I, on the other hand, did not know how to deal with these people. "Elias is getting on," I continued, "he earned at least a hundred lire this week."

The old man was indifferent.

"He's a good boy, he knows how to make people like him."

I had made another mistake. I was giving my words an exaggerated cordiality, not only so as to make him thank me, but worse, to make him see how friendly I was to him and how much he could depend on me. He took the haversack without looking at the contents. "Thank you," he said, and went and put it in his hut. Then he came back and made as if to accompany me although I had not shown the least intention of going away.

"If you come to the camp you will have as much bread as you want," I said. He thanked me again, but I understood that he would never come, that I would never see him in front of my tent saluting me, recognising me as the victor. Now the child annoyed me, and Johannes annoyed me; I felt him to be not hostile but inaccessible, determined to watch over his dead, determined not to pardon me; and there was something, some gleam in his opaque yellowish eyes that escaped me.

I began to talk about Elias once more. But I felt more and more disappointment, annoyance over a visit that was not even welcome. I had no illusions about Johannes' loquacity, but I had at least hoped for a sign of gratitude from him. After all I was not in any way bound to help him, and the motives that led me there had nothing at all to do with him, or rather he could not know them.

"You should go and live on the table-land," I said. If he went up on to the table-land he would easily find a better life. He was an old *askari*, he knew our language. He accompanied me as far as the water-course like a dignitary showing the road to his guest, impatient to see me go.

"Goodbye, Johannes," I said to myself as I left him, "this is the last time. I admire you, but the admiration costs me an effort, a great effort, and I hate walking consciences."

5

I had barely crossed the water-course and was walking on hurriedly when I heard someone calling to me. I did not dare to turn round. "You fool," I said to myself, "what are you frightened of?" And yet I did not dare to turn round and when I heard the voice again I barely glanced over my shoulder.

The smuggler was approaching. He came from the ravine and he was approaching with an air of conspiracy; he wanted to talk to me and it must be about very serious matters since he kept looking around to reassure himself that we were quite alone. I tried to smile and began to walk again; I wanted to get away, but the smuggler caught up with me and stopped. I then told him curtly to speak. He took from his pocket a clod of earth and handed it to me without saying anything, but looking into my face, perhaps enjoying my surprise in anticipation. I took the clod hesitatingly, I did not understand.

Look, he said. I looked at it and in the earth I saw some golden specks. They shone in the sun. I gave the clod back to the smuggler and, setting off again—more and more impatient to get away from a spot I had tempted too much—I said, trying to give my voice the calmest possible intonation: "Where did you find this stuff?"

The smuggler was not sure whether to show me the place but at last decided to. In his naive imagination he already saw himself rich, but he knew the formalities to be overcome before one was declared owner of such a fortune and he wanted me to give him advice. "I don't know anything about it," I answered, "but I don't believe this stuff is gold."

His disappointment was short-lived; he thought I was joking or even that I wanted to swindle him. He said that he would willingly grant me half the treasure if I guaranteed his possession of it. "This stuff wouldn't belong to you," I said. "We are in the army." And seized by an impulse that mastered my uneasiness, I wanted him to show me where he had found the clod.

Was this the tomb of Mariam, those miserable bushes? We passed close by, but I was not certain of recognising it. After a hundred yards or so, on the very edge of the ravine, the smuggler halted and picked up another clod. "It isn't gold," I said, "there has never been gold in this river and there's no use pretending to oneself. Many minerals look like gold, and this is not gold." And I thought: "The wind has removed the bushes; I should put new ones on it."

The smuggler did not seem convinced; I insisted. I was in a hurry to get away. As for really understanding what it was about, that was a matter of indifference to me. I wanted the smuggler to put his mind at rest; I attempted to persuade him. Without listening to me he began to fill his haversack with earth; and the same evening, coming back to the camp, I saw the whole company labouring under unwonted loads. He had not been able to keep his mouth shut.

In this way another worry was adding itself to the usual ones. I would have to see that the soldiers did not go tearing up the whole bush and find, instead of gold, what I had hidden there. Then I laughed at my fears. "Let them find her, no one will be able to accuse you."

I had reassured myself thus when the captain sent for me to ask me if I knew anything about this gold business. "I don't believe it's gold," I answered.

"But we must make sure. Tomorrow I will come with you." And that evening in the mess, the officers looked at me with new eyes. When the talk was of the gold, my silence increased their curiosity. "I maintain," said the doctor, "that the property belongs in part to the battalion," and this was the signal for a very lively argument. Each one defended his own thesis. The gold belonged to the state. It was, on the contrary, the property of the soldier who had found it. It belonged to all of us. It belonged to a mining company which we would found and which would allot us so much per head. "What do you think about it?" and they looked at me.

I answered that we should make sure first so as not to make fools of ourselves. "Have some of the stuff examined and then we'll see. But there's no point, *absolutely no point* in digging it up." Did my voice tremble as I said these words? Perhaps for that reason my reply was considered to be very clever. No one thought for an instant that I had put forward this doubt in order to calm my apprehensions and their imaginations. After the story of the dentist I had risen in my colleagues' estimation; they endowed me with gifts of wile and tact which I have never possessed and often the talk came round to my long absence, always arousing new peals of laughter. If someone went away everybody said he had toothache, and one talked of going to look for a dentist, not for a girl. And now I was bound to have a secret design; I was trying to distract other people's attention from this treasure which really belonged to everybody.

So that very evening attempts to wash the earth collected took the place of the usual game of cards. From my tent I heard the labours of the soldiers; this was a good opportunity to banish melancholy and instead mine increased.

During these days the pain in my hand had almost disappeared, but the circle of violet still remained and numbness that gave me food for thought. I went on attending to it myself; it would all clear up soon. I had even got thinner from constant lack of sleep; often I bled from the nose and this had to be attributed to the sun beating down on the short cut. So that evening my request for a month's leave to go back to Italy was received with loud laughter. Did I want to get ahead of them all in mining technique? But the captain did not laugh; he obviously thought a reply useless or else he merely wanted to show me that I had gone too far. Who had I not asked for my discharge while I was at it?

I was depressed. I would willingly have remained in my tent the next morning, but the thought of the tomb, which might be disturbed, forced me to reach the short cut and the ravine with its group of over-cheerful officers.

"This way," said the digging soldiers. I kept myself apart, and waited without joining in the chatter. "This is the worst test," I thought, "you must pass it." I had sat down near the woman's tomb, determined not to rise should anyone come to dig at that point. And I was watching, stunned by so much mirth, when I saw other officers arrive at the ravine, and the captain pointed me out to them, laughing. I was incapable of rising. The officers came up and introductions followed. They were from the post on the road and they congratulated me jokingly on my luck.

One of them had wine-coloured facings on the collar of his tunic. Perhaps the facings of the medical corps. But there was no use asking him.

They did not go away, instead they sat down near me and the officer with the wine-coloured facings—he might be a sapper officer or a *bersagliere*, but in the first case the facings would have had a black edging and in the second would have been flame-shaped—sat on the tomb. I could not prevent him. The soldiers went on digging more and more gaily. The captain wanted to discover the extent of the deposit.

"These facings," I asked, "are they medical corps ones?"

He said: "Yes." I asked nothing else, I did not ask how long he had been at the post or if he had recently come, after the attack, to look after the wounded. But he must have come recently; his tunic was new and on his helmet he wore sun-glasses. Beside he certainly could not keep the wounded at the post unless it was a case of light wounds. Perhaps he was an officer in transit who had stopped at the post before going on towards the mountains opposite; naturally he would be incapable of leaving the river to enter the melancholy region where there were neither roads nor trucks.

"You have just graduated, I suppose," I said. He had a youthful face; the troops would soon take advantage of his pliability by claiming they had all sorts of illnesses. He answered that he was a university lecturer. And a surgeon.

They did not go away; instead they lit their cigarettes and talked about going home. Even the officer in the new tunic talked about it, and I asked myself how he could allow himself to talk about going home—an officer with such a new tunic. And I asked myself, too, why he noticed nothing, that slight, almost imperceptible, penetrating odour. I smelt it, perhaps because I was tired, fasting, disgusted? Or was it merely the neighbourhood? No, it was an almost imperceptible odour but it brought to mind something definite. Perhaps the smell of the house of the two girls carried to its extreme limits, to corruption, and with it there was mixed the memory of the sun-baked carcasses. But I was the only one to smell it and I was not sorry. I had to pass the test.

The soldiers were following the lode which fortunately ran down into the ravine to climb from there towards the tableland. And no one came with his spade to say to me: "Excuse me, sir."

In the evening on the way to camp I fell to the ground. I was unable to rise again; my head was spinning, I felt nausea constrict my throat. "Go on," I said, "I am resting."

I heard the last voices of the soldiers going into the distance and looked across the valley at the disc of the sun drowning in its fiery sunset, awakening the first cries of the bush. I was broken in spirit. In all this sequence of incidents, in the child who slept outside my tent, in Johannes who showed me the door, and now in this ridiculous affair of the gold, and in the officer with the new tunic who arrived when it was all over, smiling, I felt the web of a treacherous design. But what was wanted of me? That I should begin to yell, like a penitent assassin: "Here she is. Dig"? I knew I would never give in to that temptation, that I would not even give in to the temptation to tell the story to a friend so as to ask him, as I told him the secret, for an implicit absolution. "After all," I said, "I have not repented. I could not have done otherwise."

The sun was setting; I must go back to the camp. The short halt had calmed me, in fact had removed every fear. I got the length of considering my guilt serenely and could think of no punishment for it. Even if they found the corpse, even if suspicion fell on me, until I admitted, cried out my guilt, nothing would happen. Once I had buried the corpse I had done my duty towards the others and now I must continue to do it in silence. The woman did not count, only my guilt towards the others. That, too, had disappeared from the moment when I did not reveal it. "Cheer up," I said, "you have a lot of accomplices, you could not even count them. And they only ask you to keep quiet. You did not have them that night, but now you do. With the woman buried the crime is not even yours any more, all sorts of other things come into it. A lot of accomplices and no trail; we are in enemy territory and worse things have happened. Your guilt will become guilt only on the day when you force H.Q. to put out a new general order."

Secretly consoled by what I was saying to myself, I set off again. Touching my brow I felt that it was burning; so it was only the fever that was making me excited. I would go away from there, never fear, and She would make me forget everything, even my deplorable weakness. She, my dearest accomplice who would never suspect anything.

But I had to get back to camp, go on with the stupid farce because everyone now knew that it wasn't gold and yet they went on talking about it, not entirely abandoning hope. "Here he is," said the major. They were all waiting for me, even the general, who had come, attracted by the rumour that was already running through the other units. "He's the discoverer."

There was no use trying to get out of it. The general was taking the business seriously and perhaps wanted to share in the triumph of the discovery. He advised us to make a statement to the governor of the colony, he would forward it that evening. I was writing it when a confused shouting called me back and I saw some soldiers trying hard to put out a fire which had broken out in a tent. The general had been burnt while watching an attempt to melt a certain quantity of the flakes. It was such a diversion that, three days later, when we learned that the gold was merely mica we quickly consoled ourselves by recalling the general's terror when the petrol stove burst. And in their stories, who had the joke fathered on him? I did. I had kept quiet for no other reason than to make them all fall into the trap, I had written the statement, I had advised the general to have the flakes melted.

"What amused me most of all," the captain would often say, "was the serious way you listened to the general."

My fame as a buffoon was thus assured to such a degree that I could not refute it. Even the major, who had some motive for spite against the general, found that my jest was in the best of taste. The fact that the government of the colony had been stirred up, made up for all our disappointment. The tents were emptied of the gathered earth, the haversacks were released. Some clods were preserved and served as candlesticks.

"I thought you were different," said the major one day, smiling, and that was meant as praise. We talked a long while for the first time in two years. Then I learned that he was really doing something about getting me my leave.

ALL MANNER OF SORES

1

I HAD NOT gone back to the short cut, indeed I did not wish
to do so; for me that chapter was now closed and, while
waiting for my leave, I intended to cure myself of the various
disturbances I wished to leave behind me, as I would leave the
memory of Mariam. Now perpetual somnolence had taken the
place of insomnia; and I was pleased about it, attributing it to the
calm which had entered my soul after so many agitations. If I had
not occasionally had severe headaches I would not have bothered in the least to go into the causes of that pleasant sleepiness.
I passed the days in my tent, reading, or else listening to the
noises of the camp which reached me, infrequent and smoth-
ered. And often I drowsed.

My hand was healing. The great swelling of the early days
having disappeared, there now remained on the back of the hand
a negligible lump. In the centre of this an excrescence had
formed no bigger than a pea, but it did not worry me, in fact on
touching it I scarcely felt it. I continued bandaging my hand so
as not to expose it to infection. Yet I was not satisfied. When I
consulted the doctor he reassured me, giving me an ointment
and attributing all my disturbances to the lack of fresh food from
which we had been suffering for some months. I sought the cure
for my tenacious ailment in rest.

Yes, my appetite had gone, and it was an effort to go to the
mess where—not without disgust—I saw the others throw themselves on the dishes with incredible appetite. My throat closed;
I had to invent a pretext for leaving.

But everything would pass off; my illness had temporary roots
and during the return voyage to Italy, on board the ship, the sea

air, the certainty of being for ever away from a country that oppressed me so much, all these would help me to pick up again. At this time the rains began; they would last for three months—that is to say until September. Every day, at set hours, we would have rain, and although it brought us some discomfort, yet—after so much sun—we saw with joy how the earth bathed in it. The soldiers lay in their kennels and sang, modulating the tone of their slow old songs to the melancholy induced by the rain. The camp drowsed under a slight mist; we thought of our cities. At night the drip of water on the canvas of the tent counselled rest and set the mind off on pleasant fantasies. I thought of her, of what my return meant to her, I re-read her letters innumerable times, always finding something new—added perhaps by my longing to see her again. Everything was ready to welcome me back there.

For some days Elias had been wandering in the cities of the old Colony and I no longer felt his presence near my tent. In fact I became more cheerful; on his return the rain would prevent him from remaining out in the open and he would go back to his store. But one evening—I had thrown myself on my camp-bed and was dreaming—I heard his insufferable breathing close by. At first I thought it was an hallucination, then I convinced myself that it was indeed Elias. He was beside my tent; he had covered himself as best he might with a sack and was resting. "Elias," I called.

"Sir!" The tent opened suddenly and the child appeared. I asked when he had got back.

"An hour ago, sir," and he showed in the palm of his hand the sum he had earned. He was waiting for me to say something to him; he stood still in that light rain ignoring the water that bathed his face. I did not tell him to come in and left him there. "Here he is," I said to myself, "here is the youngest of the conspirators and the most pitiless." All my old anxiety, which had been lulled to sleep during the days he had been absent, awoke of a sudden and I began to tremble with anger at the sight of this too obedient, too faithful child. He was more and more like the woman. I saw her face again.

Elias did not dare to move, waiting for a sign from me. "Come here," I said. When he was near me my hate exploded. "Get out!" I said, "if I see you again I'll have you arrested."

The boy was taken by surprise, then he smiled and made as if to touch my hand. Of course it was a joke—he wanted to say—I was joking. So he took my hand and laid it on his head in token of servitude, to say that I had complete power over him. This trusting gesture succeeded in precipitating my wrath. Blinded, I thrust Elias to the ground, out of the tent and ordered him off. The child had fallen and looked at me, still smiling, still believing that it was still a joke. Then I saw that his lips were trembling, the whole world was falling on top of him; he could not understand anything any more and burst out crying. But my yells made him stop. He got up and made off towards the road. I ran out of the tent and called him. "Come here at once," I said.

He came back as if nothing had happened, but he was trembling slightly because of the wetting, I suppose, and his lips could not find their smile again. I showed him the ration-box—I had to remove her portrait—and the child sat down penitently, trying to understand.

I wanted him to talk about the village, but he did not know what to tell me; perhaps he had forgotten. And he looked at me, unable to control the trembling of his knees. "What did you do all day?" I asked.

He lowered his eyes and answered with a gesture that meant nothing, or merely lack of interest in the things he had formerly done, which now appeared unimportant to him. "Didn't you play, didn't you go to bathe in the river?"

"Yes," and he smiled happily, but suddenly he became solemn again and lowered his head. "Alone?" I asked.

"No, with all the rest." Why did I want to make the memory more cruel, why did I want to know everything about her? Yet I felt that I hated her and told myself that the valley would keep its secret so well that I could now forget about it. It no longer belonged to me but to the earth, and to a country that I would leave for ever in a month or two. I could even persuade myself that I had done nothing that overstepped the laws of nature in these parts; perhaps in time I would even believe that I had not killed her; and already it was difficult for me to remember the scene, or else I saw it as if told by another. It was a very confused scene, and but for Elias I could not have remembered the colour of her eyes. Slowly I asked the boy whom he liked best in the village, but he did not answer; it was a new expression for him and I could not translate it. "Who did you like to be with best?"

Once more he spread out his arms to signify all of them. Or no one. When I asked if Mariam went to the river the child laughed shaking his head and answered: "She was frightened."

"What was she frightened of?"

"Harghez!" And he pronounced this word rapidly, with disgust and terror, but laughing. I asked him if he, too, was frightened. He nodded his head vigorously; he admitted he was.

"Do you want to sleep now?" Without waiting for his reply I took a piece of canvas and arranged it so as to shelter the spot where Elias had first curled himself up. I took another piece and threw it on to the wet ground and on it placed a blanket. "Sleep here," I said.

Elias slipped into his sack, saluted and curled up. In a few minutes his breathing was the only thing I heard, just as the condemned man, of all the noises of the prison, hears only the watch ticking in his confessor's pocket.

I was so irritated with myself—I had reforged the stupid chain—that I kicked in the bottom of the packing-case.

At reveille Elias had disappeared. He had left his piece of canvas and his blanket rolled up as the troops do and had gone off. I was surprised and even feared that his flight might conceal some plot on his part to make me sorry for him and bind him to me more closely. I asked for Elias; no one had seen him. The smuggler said: "These people have no affection."

These words relieved me and I thought no more of the boy.

2

When the order came to move camp to A. so great was the joy of the troops that even I regained hope.

Elias had not come back and would thus lose trace of us. Perhaps he might even catch up with us, the smuggler foresaw it, but not having to hear him near me was itself a comfort. During these days an unwonted gaiety possessed me and my colleagues in the mess began to laugh at me and my stories again. And the major told me again that he was seeing about my leave and that I should not worry. Six days later we were camped a couple of kilometres outside A. near another unit. There I met the second lieutenant.

Our meeting was not very cordial. I really could not pretend. Like all things and all persons which reminded me of Mariam, the second lieutenant, in my eyes, bore his share of guilt. And then I was depressed by my ailment which gave no sign of disappearing. On the contrary it had lately got worse. Round my belly and on my arms there had now appeared grey and pink spots; I often examined them, but was unable to make up my mind to consult the doctor for fear of a reply I did not even dare imagine. I saw myself in front of the doctor, half naked, and trembled at the fear which would follow the examination, at the serious look he would give me before saying the terrible word. "It's nothing," I thought, "it can't be anything serious. It is a disturbance caused by this frightful food. General Lettuce was quite right."

Therefore periods of optimism succeeded moments of profound discomfort; I told myself that the main thing was to get back to Italy as soon as possible, there I would be completely cured without beginning hasty treatment here. Suppose the M.O. made a mistake? I would finish up in a hospital acting as guinea pig for the study of tropical diseases. Instead it was a question of a few weeks now, and then the return. I had to treat myself, bear it. Besides the spots were not in the least sore. Nor did my hand hurt; even if the pea showed no signs of disappearing and, on the contrary, had become slightly—oh, very slightly—bigger.

"Where are you going?" It was the second lieutenant. Our greeting was becoming less and less cordial; we never referred to the time we had spent together which really should have stirred our memories. Something had risen between us; we had difficulty in recognising each other, but that day I could not ignore him. We had to go as far as A. together and it was better to speak—I could not have borne silence, in fact I preferred his stories. "Everything all right?" I said.

"Everything's all right," he answered. We walked along searching for phrases as if playing a tiresome game for a trifling stake.

And here was the square of A. the same as ever, magnificent, still watched over by the same major standing on the doorstep of his hut, not knowing what to do with himself, waiting for the night which now will take him to the house of the two girls. When he saw me a sly smile stretched his lips. "You ran away last time." He did not know what to do and wanted to follow us. Why had this person always to get in my way and why did his voice always strike me disagreeably? I could not escape him now, he was taking my arm. His face was cordial and I was more and more amazed at finding it repulsive, not untrustworthy, but darkened by hints I could never interpret; and so I avoided his glance, laden for me with absurd and perhaps insoluble mystery. He was a tall, fat man, glad to be alive, to uncork bottles and to open his box of cigarettes with a grand gesture, happy to speak and to listen to me, prepared to pardon my juvenile optimism. Suddenly he said he owed me a debt. "Thanks for having introduced me to Rahabat."

"And who is Rahabat?" I asked.

"Don't you remember?" The major sketched imaginary curves and thoughtfully added that she was an exceptional creature; she had no sense of time. He closed his eyes a little; this phrase— perhaps he had heard it once, but now it was his; and he began to describe to me the charms of Rahabat. I detested him. No I didn't; I envied his happiness, the security of his existence. He considered himself capable of defending his hut, his chests, his money, his business, for I was sure he was carrying on a business. I must imitate him if I did not want to succumb; I must think that the world and men were in a coalition against me and defeat them by cunning. He was convinced that I admired him—and it was true. I admired his defects, which might perhaps be necessary for me, or so I felt, if I was to live.

He was now talking with the voice of a military man who uses his rank to impose his opinions on every subject; and on every subject he had an opinion. He hated this land, he hated the inhabitants—except Rahabat—he hated everything. Or better still, he hated everything. Since his arguments annoyed me I began to contradict him.

He listened to me seriously—I hated this affected gravity of his—and finally he shook his head laughing. "Optimist," he said, "but look at these people. Do they look civilised to you?" I answered that they had qualities that are being lost in civilised countries and he said at once, smiling ironically, imitating me like a bad actor: "Can you tell me which ones?"

I said that these qualities seemed to me to be faith, perseverance and the other qualities of simple creatures. And then sobriety, courage. They had remained Christians.

"I'm a Christian, too," observed the major in amazement.

"And," I went on, "they lack those ambitions which, in our case, make the life of the average man shabby and unhappy. They do not fight for a fictitious existence. They do not fight for their cash-boxes."

"They haven't got a sou," added the second lieutenant, winking, "and are unfamiliar with the sorrows of saving."

"Quite right. And probably," I concluded, "if we had not come they would never have suspected that they can lead a less hard life provided they lose their good qualities and acquire our defects."

"So you like these people?" asked the major. I thought of Mariam and did not answer, it seemed to me superfluous. I pretended to be bored.

"They have a prudent reverence for the theory of least resistance," said the second lieutenant. "They remind me of the people where I come from. But here there is the advantage that they sing less."

The major laughed and with unexpected indulgence fired the shot he had kept in reserve: *"C'est la faute à Jean Jacques,"* he said, and his accent made me really angry. Then he added: "A country that had no roads."

"And not even motor accidents," added the second lieutenant quickly. At that point I felt that the words were acquiring the gravity of phrases already heard, or ones we will hear in connection with some event still indistinct in the memory. "Why," I thought, "do these words disturb you?" But the second lieutenant added: "Besides it has its short cuts." Then he lit another cigar. I felt I hated him, too—him and his cigars that required such attentive care; and his answers, too.

As we spoke we had arrived in front of the church and the major was pointing out the two porched huts near the entrance saying that that was the hospital and ironically asking us to admire it. I looked at the two huts and asked if the sick lived there. "Of course," answered the major who was becoming magnanimous, "they live there ignorant of the sorrows of saving."

I was beginning to feel unwell, perhaps it was the sadness of the evening and I asked: "Do they live on charity?" but I knew the answer. And I looked at the huts, I looked at the men huddled like animals, sunk in their desperate indolence.

"Of course," said the major again. The second lieutenant added: "Poverty knows no limits evidently. Here is a nation of beggars that gives alms to its poor." And he laughed. I wanted to go away, but was irresistibly led to go closer to the huts; but I did not want to leave the two officers who, for the moment, gave an assurance of fraternal protection. Seeing that they were going on I joined them, but I did not hear their conversation, which reached me confusedly. A treacherous kind of curiosity attracted me to the gate, and the square seemed to me to be much bigger. What were the two officers saying, why were they laughing, who were they laughing at? I, too, wanted to share their mirth, to feel myself alive with them, to affirm my existence. "They are leaving me behind," I thought. What were they saying?

Suddenly they saluted one another. The major went off and I

saw him get into a truck which at that moment had halted in front of his hut. I had to hold myself back from going with him, from going with this man with his cordial face, even if it were overcast by hints that escaped me, hints that I did not wish to explore. He turned, made a sign to us with his hand while he climbed into the truck; and I did not answer it. "Come on," I said to the second lieutenant, "let's visit the church."

We had to pass in front of the huts and my glance lingered on the miserable creatures lying there. A tremendous resignation had settled on their faces. Young and old, mixed, incapable of be-wailing their lot—only the night, as they well knew, was able to release their tears—incapable of finding rest. They moved in that brief span like larvae ousted from an old tomb; jostling, letting fall on to the pavement their filthy bowls and looking anxiously at the passers-by. But no one halted, and on the square the passage of the women going towards the well went calmly on. There, in the inn, the woman in pink was serving her silent clients.

The second lieutenant went on several paces ahead of me; we arrived at the door of the church after crossing a courtyard ornamented with tall eucalyptus trees. Strange how the evening had suddenly fallen. We did not enter the church, attracted by the peace of that courtyard where, as if sunk in meditation, some women wandered. Perhaps experience lies in the ability to un-derstand the power of certain words that life reveals to us slowly and sometimes not in vain. Faced by that calm vision I knew the words that made these shadows gather round the church as if in a limbo already touched by grace. Between the dark shadows of the trees, the light shadows of the faithful. And above, heaven. A heavy and gleaming heaven of deep violet, closer than one thinks, since there heaven becomes something you believe in, and these shadows certainly had it in their hearts, as I, too, already felt it. I thought of Mariam and wanted to go. I would go back to camp.

"What pretty girls," said the second lieutenant and he pointed to two girls standing leaning against a tree. They were talking quietly and we stopped to look at them. "Look at the dresses. They are white. What elegance."

I could not see clearly because the evening was closing in unexpectedly. "Let's go closer," I said, seized by an anxiety that I could not conceal. I crossed the courtyard and stopped a few paces from the two girls. Seeing themselves observed they turned away. They reminded me of Mariam; I did not know why, but I thought that it was certain to be some trap laid by my already overtaxed imagination. "You will see Mariam everywhere and that will be the time to put an end to it," I said. But they did remind me of Mariam. There was in their faces the same grave beauty, but veiled by centuries of obscurity, the same deep waters in which I had immersed myself for an instant and which I did not wish to see again. They were looking at me silently without smiling, and I saw that the second lieutenant was halting to look at the facade of the church as if suddenly attracted by its architecture. "It is a very simple kind of architecture," I thought. When I greeted them the two girls answered with a nod of the head and smiled. Then I called the second lieutenant. "Ask these girls if they have a house," I said.

"Of course they have." Then he added: "And it will be eternal, the best kind of all." Then he translated my question to the two girls and they made a sign of assent and smiled again, looking at us. "Poor limbo," I thought. Once again I recalled Mariam; in these girls there was the melancholy I had discovered in her eyes and her sleep.

"Now what do you want me to ask? That they should invite us?" I smiled. "It's a good idea," I said, and thought that everything is much simpler than one thinks.

The second lieutenant spoke for a long time with the girls and they shook their heads smilingly, but their smile was so different from what I expected that it filled me with sudden alarm. Why do they smile instead of hurrying to show us the way? Why are they shaking their heads?

"Nothing doing," said the second lieutenant. At that same moment, as if to soften their refusal, the two girls held out their hands to us.

They were hands already devoured by horrible sores. These

were the cause of their refusal. Thus they stood, serious, like children holding out their hands so that you can see that they are clean.

The second lieutenant looked at their hands—and I, too, looked at them—and turned to me with a smile doubtless intended to conceal his perturbation. "Leprosy," he said in a low voice. The two girls let their hands fall and followed us with their eyes until we had once more passed through the gate.

3

Why did my fingers now go to the back of my hand? "It isn't possible," I said to myself, but yet I noticed that I was walking along without seeing anything. And I felt my throat dry and a sweat run down my back. "It isn't possible." But meantime these hands were always before my eyes.

"Stop," I said. We sat on the steps of the telephone hut. Two happy soldiers were teaching a child to ride a bicycle, more to amuse themselves than to teach the child anything. I saw the bicycle cross the street, come towards me, turn away, go back; I heard the words of the soldiers, the cries of the child.

And then I chased that terrible thought away, attributing it to the anxieties of the previous days and to the sight of the square, which was already closing like a flower and engulfing us in its consuming sadness; for there the day was really dying and the word tomorrow was the most useless of hypotheses. No lamps were being lit, the number of people walking about did not increase, no illuminated advertisements called the crowds to the cafés, on to the street, to the theatres. I thought of the light of our streets, of the rain that multiplies it, of the fountains, of the newspaper-vendors calling the last edition, of the cars that graze you and of the smile one suddenly meets in the mirror of a shop window. "Don't get stupid ideas into your head," I concluded, "your hand will heal and it has nothing in common with these other hands."

"Do you want to smoke?" said the second lieutenant and offered me a cigarette, and while I lit it he steadied my arm delicately. Unable to bear that silence I said: "Poor girls," and the second lieutenant agreed. Then he said: "If we come back in forty years time we will still find them near that tree. We will find them old, terrifying, in pieces, but we will find them."

I asked him if the courtyard were a leper colony. But the second lieutenant was long in replying, as if the conversation was becoming extremely painful to him. He avoided looking at me or perhaps could not, because we were seated on the same step and he would have had to turn his head. "There is no leper colony. They stay there. They have at least the comfort of religion. Think of it, the church a couple of steps away."

"Still it is a comfort," I said. We fell silent and I was amazed that life in the square went on. The hostess was even laughing. "I would shoot myself," said the second lieutenant in a low voice.

"So would I." But the second lieutenant shook his head and before speaking lit a cigar, wasting a lot of matches. "We are used to hope."

"But in these cases hope is useless," I said. Now I felt myself calm, I had put all my suffering to flight and touched my hand, glad that it did not hurt. I had to go back to camp, perhaps the post truck had arrived.

"Quite useless. Some of them get cured and in ten years time it starts all over again," said the second lieutenant.

"In that case one would have to find the strength to shoot oneself," I concluded. The second lieutenant nodded his head, then said he could hardly wait for the day to get back to Italy. "That major, who is stuffed full of commonplaces, is right. This country is too sad. If the hyena is native to a country there must be something rotten about it."

"Yes, there must be something rotten," I repeated. And this something I already guarded in my inmost thoughts, no one would ever have understood, not even she.

"I can hardly wait for the day to leave," continued the second lieutenant, "the day when I will do what I used to once. Even the foolish things, especially the foolish things. And not to have to put up with the criticism of this land, the trees, the men, all of them grown old in their somnolence."

"You're right," I said. I had to go back to the camp now, perhaps the post had arrived during the afternoon, it was sure to have arrived. And the square still lay before us, that gloomy and marvellous square, it, too, fallen into decrepitude in the somnolence of the centuries. What were they saying to each other now, the two girls in the courtyard of the church? Would I ever forget their looks as we went away with the caution of those who do not wish to become involved? And would I forget their hands? They had showed them as if they were not their hands, but wished only to accuse someone. (No, they stood in the courtyard of the church because they hoped, they would always hope.) Yet there they were, four gnawed hands with a finger or two turned back into the palm and those dark excrescences of baleful red. But yes, do look, they were our hands and they will get worse and worse, they simply will fall off, and then someone will have to put the food in our mouths and will do it unwillingly, with his throat closed with disgust, in order to be worthy of that solemn and shining heaven which is above us. And other people will stop, attracted by our beauty, and will suddenly turn their backs, smiling at the unexpected, pleasurable, egoistic terror of the sight, relieved to be able to cross the gateway. Even if on their necks they feel our eyes.

"Why," I asked, "do these women live like that, free?" The second lieutenant turned towards me. "Everyone knows they are lepers," he said, "I knew, too."

"But you can't see it at all. And someone might go up to them," I observed. And of course someone might have gone up to them, if for no other reason than to render homage to the lesson of those eyes of theirs, which absorbed the colour of the evening. But the second lieutenant was lighting his cigar again. And he was not looking at me. Then he said: "No, it does not happen." And since I was silent he repeated: "No, that doesn't happen, it can't happen. They are untouchable."

"Untouchable?" And I had the strength to laugh.

"Yes, *untouchable*. They have a sign everyone recognises and then no one goes too near. Except hope." Then he added: "In fact no one is allowed to go near them."

The evening was giving way to the night, and, as punctual as the bat, melancholy returned, this time without escape. I was afraid to ask, I thought I had already guessed. I made an effort, and giving to my query the simplest intonation I could, I asked what that sign was. The second lieutenant rose to go: "It is the same sign as the priests'," he said. "A kind of white turban. It has a special name, but I don't remember it." And he added: "I'm going back to camp. What about you?"

"Me too," I answered.

After going a few steps I stopped and said to the second lieutenant that I had forgotten to buy something. "If you like," he answered, "I'll wait."

It wasn't necessary, I might take some time. Then he went off and I saw him move away with his slightly dragging pace of a person grown accustomed to walking along hot streets. He went off without haste and I refused to speculate on his thoughts. I wanted to call him back, the solitude weighed on me now, but if I had called him back he would have gathered something from my eyes and perhaps he already knew something. I saw he was getting farther away and felt I was losing the only person capable of comforting me; I knew now that his silences sprang from a calm which I had lost, they were the silences of a sensitive heart. And his cynical boredom was simply fear of giving way.

I climbed up to the well and stood there watching the women filling their water cans, but evening dispersed even the last stragglers and very soon I found myself alone. I did not know what I would do; it was almost unwittingly that I found myself once more in front of the church and then in the courtyard. I looked for the two girls and saw that they had sat down at the foot of the tree and were eating in silence. They sat there like two macabre picnickers forgotten by the rest of the party, with the night weighing on their shoulders, resigned to the darkness, speaking in a low voice. Their turbans made a single splash of grey.

They recognised me and immediately fell silent. Only one of them, the one whom I had looked at most, made a friendly sign to me, staring into the dark, and smiled slightly; then both began to eat again unhurriedly. I felt their annoyance at my presence. I was a few steps away from them. "Good evening," I said. They answered me together, in a low voice, and laughed.

What else could I say? I knelt down; I would remain there. The women were now laughing quietly, just like two girls who become vivacious when they see they are being watched. Something had not yet died in them and would for long survive the disintegration of the body. The one I was looking at most closely even arranged her dress with sudden coquetry, and once more for a second I saw that hand.

Meanwhile the custodian of the church was shutting the door and would shortly close the gate to the courtyard. When he made towards the gate with the great key in his hands, terrified at the thought that I might remain shut up in there and that the old custodian might prevent me from leaving, I rose suddenly and reached the gate. The old man cried something and his harsh and guttural voice prevented my turning round. I made my way back to the camp.

The soldiers were singing. The night was too beautiful for them to keep quiet. There was talk at this time of a new move and, now that the fear of a long stay in these parts had gone, they passed the hours of rest anticipating the joys of homecoming. These their imagination conjured up in such a lively form that from time to time there came from the tents shouts and bursts of laughter such as I had not heard for months.

I shut myself up in my tent and took the gauze bandage from my hand. Perhaps it had got worse. The hand was swollen and, touching it, I could just feel a distant pain like a voice coming from a deep dungeon. "I have made the bandage too tight," I thought, "and the hand has got worse, I cannot accept any other hypothesis. My nerves are worn and I am taking too gloomy a view of things."

Then I remembered the spots on the belly and on the arms. I

stripped, looked at them for a long time and felt my throat constrict, but was incapable of sobbing. I stood on the camp-bed, half-naked; the pain had been succeeded by a calm still more devoid of hope. I was alone, I would remain alone for many years, until the end.

My tormented thoughts returned to Mariam. I remembered her perfect body, so spotless, animated by that thick blood. "And yet the two girls are beautiful, too. Is it possible?" I said. I tried to remember and uneasiness came over me more and more. I remembered the resistance Mariam had offered, a courteous resistance in which she herself had not believed, her sudden resignation, the fury of her body which already knew itself to be alone and had asked of me what it could no longer have. Then there were those hands gripping me, surely trying to tell me the horror of her solitude, the temptation to drag me into it as well. And then her refusal to accompany me to the bridge, her wish that I should sleep in the bush far from anyone who could have warned me. And finally, the white handkerchief.

And I had arranged it on her face so that she might not see that I meant to kill her. I had twisted her unclean dress round my wounded hand so that the report of the revolver might be silenced. I had had pangs of remorse. "Ah, Mariam, you have won," I said, "I relieved you of a load and you have placed it on my shoulders. It is such a good joke that there is no point in getting angry. Let's accept it in its entirety."

Then suddenly I leapt to my feet; I looked in bewilderment at the objects in my tent, her smiling photograph; I listened to the laughter of the soldiers, despair overcame me and I had to smother my cries in the pillow so that no one might hear. I bit the pillow and remained face downwards on the camp-bed.

I took the revolver and put a round in the breech. "I will shoot myself," I had told the second lieutenant. It was the only advice he could give me, indeed he had already done so, and now I appreciated the unnatural cruelty of his words, that forced conversation and the advice not to trust in hope. I understood. Had I not trembled at the sight of those hands?

I was passing the revolver from one hand to the other, all that was necessary was to press the trigger a little, aim well; but my fingers refused and the barrel remained turned towards my breast, ready but also indifferent. Then I took from the chest a bottle of petrol and a rag and removed the magazine, leaving the round in the breech. My carelessness would be obvious. Everything was ready. But wasn't there a lot to do? Write for the last time at least, a letter like all the others? I would speak to her of my returning soon, or of the move believed now to be imminent, I would talk about the parcels I had received, ask for more books. That I could do. I wrote a letter, stopping often because my breathing became laboured. The storm would not break, I could not cry.

When I had written it, read it through and put it in the envelope, I thought that it was a letter which my hands had touched. No, I could not send it to her. And the others, all the others? It was not a valid reason for continuing to send her them. I tore up the letter and took up the revolver again, but I was trifling with myself; I felt that I would not have the strength to pull the trigger. And then at the very limits of despair there came what I had feared: hope.

There were too many things I had not taken into account. The woman did have a white turban, but she was washing herself, she had put it on so as not to wet her hair. I had seen no sores on her body. Her ambiguous resistance? She wanted to be overcome, that was all, to feel herself less guilty. I remembered her laugh when the night had freed her from all remorse.

Besides I must first consult a doctor, find out. And I could not give up my leave, the only means of escape that remained. In Italy I would be able to look after myself better, and the day when I had no more hope left—I would read it in her eyes—I would kill myself. Really kill myself. But now I could not run the risk of being kept in that gloomy hut where nothing is ever done and the bells sound into the empty air and the laughter of the orderlies runs through the corridors and dies away on the threshold of the rooms. Was I to stay here and wait for the fingers to curl up one by one, then for the hand to shrivel up and then for the belly to split and the throat to burst open? I must keep calm and go back to her, try to go back. There was even the possibility that it was nothing serious and I had to keep it in mind, that solitary, distant, gleaming possibility. I had scarcely come to the end of this reasoning when despair seized me anew, and once more I had to stifle my cries in the pillow.

4

I lay thus face downwards, deep in that bewildered agony, now watching the flame of the candle, now the stains on the canvas of the tent, when I began to notice a slight smell.

It was not a stench, but an almost imperceptible smell that reminded me of something, of the room of the two girls, and particularly of the girl I had had beside me. But this was a smell that was all the more unbearable because it seemed to me non-existent, a message that only I could apprehend. It was a message of victory, a triumphant smell; this at last was the cry of triumph that rises from the abyss. I sniffed at the blanket, the pillow, still numbed with pain, but I could not determine the origin of the smell, nor all the elements that composed it. But there was the odour of tuberoses in a warm room. This odour I smelt distinctly, although only at intervals. Then, something that recalled the hide of stray dogs, of stray puppies, and also incense; but a sweet-smelling incense, ancient, clinging, mixed with vanilla, to be overcome only by the fresh smell of wet and upturned earth. It had rained and it was logical that the ground should be wet, but why upturned? I lit a cigarette and although the smoke hung about the tent I was soon overwhelmed by the increasingly heavy and festive smell. There was added to it now the scent of lilies, the odour which is set free from the vase when one changes the lilies' water; not so distinct, much more subtle, an odour that no longer recalls the purity of the lilies but rather the corpse of the patron saint of lilies. And was there not also perhaps the smell of the ravine, the tepid and unbearable smell of dry bushes on the tomb? "They were dry bushes," I said; "they could not have any smell." And why, to make the potion more evil, this suspicion of cocoa?

Perhaps the sore? I sniffed at it and to the smell there was added tincture of iodine, but it was not the sore. No. Upturned earth, above all, and with it decaying flowers left there by pious friends, slightly damp with mist. "Ah," I said, "this is too much, Mariam."

I uncorked a bottle of eau-de-Cologne and sprinkled it on the bed and repeated to myself: "Mariam, this is too much. It is the odour of your victory; but aren't you satisfied yet?"

It was impossible to resist. Now even the eau-de-Cologne compounded itself with that putrescent mixture and even the tobacco, even the petrol—everything. "I haven't had my supper," I said, "and my stomach is letting me down." I still sniffed around, and since my jacket now seemed to be impregnated with the odour and was perhaps the source of it, I determined to burn it.

The fresh night air revived me and the fire distracted me. When I returned to the tent I saw a bundle, the usual bundle; Elias sleeping curled up in his sacks. And he had turned up the earth round the tent so as not to get wet. "Your stupid fantasies," I said. I woke the child and made him come into the tent.

He saluted as usual, smiling, and now I saw satisfaction in his smile—satisfaction at a completely successful joke. That was what his smile said. I took a deep breath so as to allay the anger rising to my eyes. "Sit down," I said. Elias sat down as calmly as usual without taking his eyes from my face, ready for the slightest sign. I asked him where he had been all the time. "With Johannes," he answered.

"What is the old grave-digger doing? Is he getting my grave ready?" I had spoken simply yet Elias did not understand. He went on smiling, putting his head a little on one side. "I'm asking you what Johannes is doing," I repeated.

"Nothing," he answered. My question was really superfluous. What else could the old man do if not watch over his dead and await death? But Johannes mattered little, I had called Elias because another ray of hope was trying to join the others. Perhaps he knew. "Listen," I said, "tell me about Mariam."

He shrugged his shoulders but did not reply. "You say that Mariam was young. Why did she live in the village instead of living here, in Asmara or in Gondar?"

"I don't know." Then he added: "But now she doesn't live in the village."

"Perhaps she lived in the village because she was ill." The child looked at me for a long time, frowning. Then he smiled. "I don't know," he said. This answer, too, sounded to me as if it had been prepared beforehand, a long time before. "Did you never hear that she was ill?" I insisted.

"I don't know." There wasn't much to be got out of him; they had sent him only so that one of the conspirators might be present at the triumph. I seemed to see Johannes and Mariam laughing at his answers. "You don't know anything," I said. He smiled, shrugging his shoulders, as usual. And as usual, after a little, I heard his gentle breathing, as slow as the breathing of Mariam. "You will have to get used to it," I said. I stretched myself on the camp-bed in a state of calm that was more and more void of hope.

At reveille I noticed that the night had calmed me. My bewilderment gave place to nonchalant serenity. I was more calm, I felt fit for anything; was this, then, the resignation of the condemned man? Now I had to know. I had to know and go back to Italy. I put away from me with all my might the idea of staying there, nothing could hold me back, not even the certainty of a speedy cure—an absurd hypothesis since I had scarcely begun. Then no one must learn anything from my behaviour; so that day I shaved with care and put on a new uniform, the only one I had left.

I called my batman. "From now on," I said, "I want to look after the tent myself. Understand?" He did not understand. He smiled with an air of conspiracy, perhaps he thought I wanted to bring in some woman or other at night and keep her hidden.

I must find out. I passed in front of the M.O.'s tent, tempted to go in, but I refrained. It might work out badly. I had renewed the gauze dressing on my hand, and had added a bandage the same colour as my shirt so that it would be less conspicuous. I walked with quick steps.

At that hour the square was invaded by merchants. I wandered for long between the stalls, looking at the goods with the absent and amused eye of the visitor who buys nothing. But I had another aim in view; I must find out. So I was looking for a sore like my own. Among the innumerable sores of those Abyssinians I would find one like mine, of that I was certain. If I found that sore on someone in the market my heart would burst with joy, I would run to the doctor. So I was looking for sores, but it was not easy to find any. I found that it really was not easy to find any. And yet every so often natives appeared in front of the M.O.'s tent to be treated, and the orderly treated them, shouting in dialect, annoyed at having to work for these interlopers and content to do it, repaid by their deep obeisances, by their smiles of brotherly humility.

They were quite different kinds of sores. I had to admit that they were quite different kinds of sores. Bigger than mine, yes, almost all bigger, but normal looking, like sores that want a little time to heal. The kind of sore that will heal if only they clean it every day. There was a child with a sore on his shin. That's right, he's going about barefoot, the dust will end by making it worse, unless it's necessary to cure it. No sores on the hands.

The merchant looked at me timidly; perhaps I was going to impound some unlawful merchandise, bought from the supply service, or allowed to slip into his hands by the major?

"You, show your hands." He showed me his hands and he, too, looked at them for a long time, as if he was seeing them for the first time and was discovering in them something new and unthought of. They were dirty hands but healthy ones. They were gnarled hands, dirtier than his feet, which sometimes inadvertently ended up in a puddle of water, but healthy ones. Yet this merchant had a sore on the tip of his finger.

My hopes were vanishing; I would never get to know. But I did not leave the square. I still searched among the stalls, I went up to the little groups, I forced myself towards the hospital. No, these sick people were "different." Sick, too, but people went up to them. A young woman had brought food for an old man and sat waiting on the edge of the hut. She rocked her foot to and fro and smiled to me. She had a sore on her foot. But it was a healthy sore, a different kind. Seeing I was looking at it, she looked at it too, as one does at an ornament.

Why did I not go back to the two women, why did I not ask them to show me their hands again? I would certainly have saved myself all this trouble, but perhaps at that hour the women were not there. They could not stay there the whole blessed day waiting for me! They certainly were not there. In any case let us leave the women in peace. Why offend them with my unhealthy curiosity? I remembered the agony of the days at school when they gave out the results of the exams. I preferred not to go, I preferred to wait for my companions to pass by and tell me the results by their behaviour. I wanted to guess from their faces. But the women weren't there in the courtyard at that hour, they must go there only in the evening. For prayers, I imagine.

I went round the square again and climbed up to the well. There, too, there were many sores, but always on the feet. Gaping terribly or already closed by a tenacious scab, but sores caused by the sun, by the heat, by bad food, by walking with bare feet. No one had sores on the hands.

At the inn, when I entered, the fat Ethiopian in pink looked at me with severe eyes. What was I doing there? Did I really want to drink bitter beer in these cups? I, a signore? "Good evening, lieutenant," said the Ethiopian in pink.

"Good day," I replied. She had a broad, open, generous face, and her hands, too, were light coloured, well made. She invited me to sit down, I smiled and made a sign that I had to go. Instead I stood still in the middle of the room looking at the few drinkers. They rose to their feet and saluted with their hands. Not one sore.

Near the telephone hut there were sellers of perfume, of fake carpets and of umbrellas, of Arab prints illustrating the doughty deeds of the Crusaders and of the Mussulmans. The Crusaders were ugly and dirty; the Mussulmans vigorous and well-dressed. The merchant had no sores, I had a sore. And that almost imperceptible odour was undoubtedly the exhalation from the perfumes, from these rotten, sweetish perfumes the merchant had laid out in the sun.

5

The square became deserted and then came to life again. I took the road away from the camp and then the path which led to the eucalyptus grove. The doctor was sitting in his deck-chair, and a little way off, the soldier was preparing to leave.

When I drew near, the doctor turned round but returned my salute with a tired air. He did not show the least pleasure at seeing me, nor did I expect any other welcome; I knew him by reputation—he was one of these slothful characters who love solitude and know how to preserve it. He had set himself down there, far from everyone, because Africa had awakened in him one fear only—the fear of being disturbed. He defied any danger in order to nurse his delicious boredom, he read newspapers a month old, perhaps he did not even look forward to the day of his repatriation; everything must be a matter of indifference to him. My visit, however, worried him. I would not stay long, long enough to find out, to ask him for a book. But a pretext had to be found. When he handed me the tube of aspirins he said I should have asked my unit medical orderly for them. I replied that my unit was not in the area, and since he remained silent, looking at his newspaper and already regretting having given me a topic of conversation, I added: "My unit is the other side of Gondar. A week's walk." And I followed it up with a laugh.

He was not in the least interested, he wanted to be left in peace. And I had to go on talking. "Can I sit down?" I asked. He did not answer, but pointed to a stool which I had to clear of the litter that covered it. There was the same disorder as the first time, except for the motor-cycle which was now mended—only the wheels were missing. "Allow me to introduce myself," and I gave him a name picked at random; but he did not even hear it and I thought that he was the very man I was looking for.

But I still had to find an excuse.

Before going off, the soldier came slouching up to ask if the doctor needed anything. The doctor made a sign in the negative, and yet began a long and detailed speech which the soldier must by now have known by heart—errands to do, certain letters to post, this to be asked for at H.Q. and that from the hospital. He kept starting over again, explaining calmly, getting mixed up, contradicting himself, and the soldier stood two paces away nodding his head—he would not do a thing. Finally the doctor saluted him curtly and began once more to read the newspaper.

Would I manage to break the silence? "It's a nice place here?" I said. He replied that it was a nice place, repeating my words, too bored to look for new ones; and if I did not find a topic the conversation would dry up. I must find a topic. "You could paint here," I said. He did not answer. "You could write, too. It's the ideal place." He looked at his page without even raising his eyes towards me and when I said: "I shouldn't imagine you like shooting," replied with a curt "No," intended to conclude the dialogue.

But I could not go away. "You are in charge of the hospital?" I asked. Getting no reply, he refused me one, he wanted to ignore me and stared at the road almost as if meditating flight—I added, could I have a look at his papers, it was months since I had seen one. By reading I could at least justify my stay. I turned the pages of the first paper that came to hand, it was a comic paper. Then I said that it seemed to me to be in the worst taste to insult the enemy like that.

A moment later I saw that the doctor was observing me through his coloured glasses. He kept his lips tightly closed and held his breath while his eyes, which had suddenly become lively, examined me from head to foot. The little head on his great mastodon's body seemed to light up. Perhaps he wanted to chase me away. I was about to rise to my feet when the doctor suddenly let out all the air and said slowly and placidly: "Yes, in the worst taste."

He had replied, but now he was on the point of immersing himself in his paper like a hippopotamus diving back into his muddy water after the visitor's offering. With the utmost rapidity I exclaimed that, after all, they had defended their own country. He nodded. Behind his glasses I saw his eyes already half-shut with annoyance at the effort; a slight grimace expanded his mouth, he puffed once more and said: "Question of taste."

"Just so," I said vivaciously.

And hearing him sigh I added that I would be delighted to hear him discuss the subject. He passed a hand over his brow and spoke, dragging out the words, thinking them out, at times exclaiming them. I even forgot the reason for my visit and when he asked me what I did "at home" I discovered in his voice a comforting note of courtesy. I answered that I did nothing. But suddenly I remembered that I must return the ball and added that once I got back to Italy I intended to begin writing. I would write about the places here and my experiences. "In fact I am writing now," I said, "I *am* writing.

He was no longer listening to me. His attention had wandered and his head seemed to have got smaller or perhaps only sunk down on his neck. In a louder voice, already losing patience, I repeated: "In fact I am writing a long story." I sketched the plot: an engineer comes to these parts and falls ill. They had described the country to him as a mine of riches and he finds only death there.

He said politely that it was a good subject. Encouraged I went on: "I thought you might be able to advise me on the illness to give the engineer. A tropical illness." Here I fell silent, I had to take a long breath, then I said: "Perhaps leprosy?"

The doctor twisted his mouth: "Yes," he said. He did not seem convinced. I felt my heart throb and hoped the doctor could not hear the thuds which I distinctly heard. I asked him then whether he had a book he could lend me on the subject.

"I believe I have something." But he did not move. He stayed there looking at me and again he looked hard at the street meditating a possible flight. Perhaps he had never risen from that deck-chair. He listened to me with one ear and lay back on the canvas, relaxing. I thought the chair would give way. "I'm pretending," I said, "that my engineer catches the infection through sleeping in a native's bed. Can that happen?"

He referred to inheritance of the disease and contagion. Everyone allowed that there was contagion. Smiling—an infantile smile that accentuated his corpulence—he added: "You become a leper as you become a tyrant: by heredity or contagion."

I managed to laugh. "And would it be sufficient for my engineer to sleep for one night in a native's hut?" I said it in such a calm voice that I was amazed. Interested at last, he answered that he could tell me only by examining the native first. With a quiver in his voice he added: "Or your engineer."

He was looking at me now with different eyes, there was something in his glance that worried me. Irony perhaps. Why had his voice that gurgling note in it? Did he really believe in the story of the engineer? Never mind, he had sunk so easily back into his deck-chair. He asked nothing from Africa except to be left in peace. At last he said that if I wanted the book he would go and get it. He went heavily into the hut and came out shortly afterwards holding a thin book in his hands, but instead of giving it to me, he sat down and began to turn the pages, and a long silence followed. I now cursed myself for my carelessness. Slowly I unfastened my divisional badge from my tunic. He did not notice anything, he was reading, he had even forgotten about me. "Your engineer," he said suddenly, "has slept in the house of a native infected with leprosy?"

I started. "Yes," I answered, as readily as a witness.

"Has he slept in the sick man's bed?" (Why did he speak as if the case had really happened? We were talking about a fiction, a story.) I answered with a nod. "It seems naive to me," he continued, "to make an engineer sleep in an Abyssinian's bed."

I was cursing myself more and more for having chosen this

excuse. I kept silent, waiting for him to make up his mind to give me the book. But he kept on: "Have you ever seen an Abyssinian bed?"

When I replied patiently that I had seen some, he asked me if I thought there was an engineer anywhere in the world who would think of sleeping in one.

Perhaps he only wanted to make a criticism on the grounds of verisimilitude. "It's a literary hypothesis," I said. He agreed, but since we were dealing with hypotheses one might as well make the engineer sleep in the house of a native *woman*. I pointed out to him that it might seem a worn-out excuse. He smiled and said that it was *at least* the most plausible. "Yes, the most plausible," he repeated.

I then stressed the theme of an engineer who goes into a promised land and finds only death there. It doesn't matter how. It was a secondary question. I kept on speaking, trying to calm my fears; now I would have liked to go away, but flight on my part would have awakened or confirmed his suspicions. And meantime the doctor was smoothing his moustaches, calmly; then in an unexpectedly serious voice said that "the engineer"— and here it seemed to me that he was stressing the words to show that he was playing my game but would beat me at it— would die much later. He began to turn the pages of the book, but did not find the paragraph he wanted to quote or perhaps pretended not to find it. Only after an interminable silence—he kept on licking his fingers to turn the pages and always began from the beginning—he succeeded. "It says here that persons seriously ill can remain alive for twenty, thirty, sixty years, until a recurrent or chance illness puts an end to their sufferings." He smoothed his moustaches again. "So," he concluded, "your engineer will live a long time in his promised land. Not having been able to refuse native hospitality for one night he will accept it in spite of himself for ever." Then he continued, smiling. "Unless your engineer decides to follow an old native ritual."

A stupid hope assailed me and I asked too quickly: "What ritual?"

"Here you are then," he replied, "your engineer should bathe every year in the blood of a new-born child. A perfect allegory and one that would give a positive solution to your story."

I had risen to my feet and was looking at the road, incapable of controlling the trembling of my legs. When he finished speaking—I don't remember what he said—the doctor picked a tobacco pouch from the ground and began to roll a cigarette. He held the paper up to the light, unfolded it, chose another, thrust it deep down into the pouch and drew it out full of blond tobacco. He could not make up his mind to go on, as if he had been struck by an unexpected thought. And I did not know what to say, although I felt that my silence was the most explicit of confessions. I stood motionless, fascinated by the way his excessively fat hands strove to press the paper together. Threads of tobacco fell on his shirt. By now the torture was unbearable. His fingers strove, but there was either too much or too little tobacco and finally the paper tore. I offered my box of cigarettes. He refused—he smoked only sweet tobacco. Then I said that I would not follow the odyssey of my hero until his death. "It's sufficient if I know that he is condemned to death." Then, more calmly, as if the matter was not one I had at heart, I added: "I could choose another disease. But what one?" And without leaving him time to reply: "Well," I said, "what is important to me is to know how the engineer knows that he has leprosy."

Here I saw that I had made a mistake. Seriously, with a voice that had suddenly become fraternal, he said: "I suppose he would go and see a doctor."

"But first of all he would have symptoms," I answered. "And that is where your book will be useful to me. I will take a look at it and come and give it back to you tomorrow."

"It doesn't matter, I'll make you a present of it," he said hastily. With a rude gesture he threw me the book. Only for an instant his sleepy cat's eyes looked at me, fleetingly, as if they were afraid to linger long on my person. I recognised my own glance when I looked at the two girls.

I thanked him. The doctor was getting up now and was making for the hut. He walked quickly in and I heard him humming to himself. He put on his boots, took his belt with his revolver and in a loud voice asked if I was going into town. He would come with me.

Something gripped my throat. He was going to denounce me. Or perhaps not. But if he decided to move, it was a sign that he wanted to denounce me. When he stopped a minute to look for something on the table I was taken by the impulse to flee, but my legs did not obey me. I must flee; he certainly would not run after me; perhaps he would fire. He wasn't the kind to aim well. My head whirled and I was incapable of moving a pace. The little book was already damp with sweat, the sweat of my hands. When he reappeared we set out and as we went along the path he began to speak again. He liked my theme, but he advised me not to make a case history of it. And I could not but admire his patronising air. "The engineer," he said, "will discover that he has leprosy, that's sufficient. He will have sores, pustules, boils, analgesic nodules." Since I remained silent he added: "Nodules that do not hurt when touched. But keep things vague. A good writer never goes into details."

I replied that such was my intention. My throat was dry and I could scarcely see the path. In my pocket my hand felt like lead. "Therefore," he went on, "leave his bodily ailment"—and once more he stressed the words—"to the intelligence of the reader. Remember that leprosy sometimes takes ten or twenty years to declare itself."

I felt my legs giving way, but the doctor, with studied slowness, went on to say that there were numerous cases of rapid contagion. "Three months, a month, a week even. In young patients, of course. In these cases the infection is transmitted through a cut or wound."

Someone was laughing behind me, a long way off. I turned, it was a soldier coming along the path throwing stones at some animal among the grass. I stopped. I wanted the soldier to go on and leave us alone. "It's terrifying," I said.

"Yes, it is terrifying," repeated the doctor smiling. "I'm not a dermatologist, but all the same it's terrifying."

He was now looking at me fixedly. He was, in fact, looking at my hand, which up to then I had kept in my pocket. Why did I instinctively put it back in my pocket? I said nothing. Indeed an instant later I could have sworn that he had not seen the bandage, had only been curious to watch a scorpion crossing the path. He was calm. "There's something wrong with this country," I said. I was thinking of the second lieutenant who also "knew."

"It's an infectious Empire," I added and managed to smile. I had to speak to him, to thrust my confidence upon him. He made a sorrowful gesture and said that imperialism, like leprosy, is cured by death. He wanted to play my game, but in his eyes I suddenly saw pity for my already stricken state. My strength was leaving me, I had committed the error of not going back to camp and I had not eaten since morning. When I leaned against the doctor he moved away as if I had wanted to strike him, then blushed and looked black. I admired him. His corpulence, crowned by an infantile and blondish head, even made me think that everything would turn out to be a joke. We had already conceded each other mutual friendship and we knew that the deal was shortly to come to fruition. We both hesitated before committing the irreparable act that would separate us for ever.

Now to the reproaches I heaped on myself for lack of caution was added the reproach of having recognised a friend and of having to lose him at the very moment of discovery. He, too, was thinking the same, I suppose, but he could not neglect his duty. Each of us had his duty to discharge towards the other. "Come on," I thought, "why don't you call to this passing soldier and get him to help you to carry me to hospital? You must make up your mind."

The soldier went past whistling.

I began to talk again—I still wanted to show him that I was not agitated, but he now avoided my glance and seemed sunk in a painful thought. At that moment I felt that he loved me like a brother. Everything had now been said; we could only repeat ourselves, and we did not dare to go on because we felt ourselves incapable of a sacrifice. While speaking I had unfastened the buckle of my holster. I saluted him. "Thank you very much, doctor." I should have liked to kiss him; it was up to him now to decide whether I was the only condemned man.

"So you're not coming into town?" he asked.

"I prefer to take a turn round the camp," and I stared at him. I was offering him the last piece of extenuating evidence—my calmness. I besought him not to believe in my leprosy, seeing me so calm, and to put away any suspicion he had. The doctor thought a minute and then said what I was afraid of: "After all I won't go to town either. It's late already. Why don't you come with me instead and have supper?"

It was not an order but an invitation. An invitation to accept my illness and to give up a hopeless struggle. I could not accept it because I refused to believe in my ailment before I had left the country. I was not ill and no one had the right to see if I was. The doctor repeated the invitation in a lower voice, he wanted to appear indifferent. He was trying to put some gaiety into his voice and this clumsy touch of comedy made me indignant. Why could he not make up his mind to draw his revolver and point it at my ribs? Why did he not confront me with an accomplished fact? There you were, his insolent laziness was giving way, and now he was behaving like a brother, but unfortunately like a younger brother. The feeling that I was stronger and more decided than he was taking away all my courage. He was inviting me to supper, knowing that afterwards he would have to destroy the cutlery, the glass, the plates, to keep me and meanwhile call someone from the command post and the hospital. The last supper, in fact, of our short-lived friendship. Who was he moving impatiently round me but always avoiding looking at me? He knew he had a bad part to play and he was begging my pardon, never imagining that I was already prepared to do worse without feeling myself under any obligation. "All right," I thought. "I'll be the stronger one." But at that very moment the doctor had set off towards the hut. He was going in front, trusting to me. He was so calm that I followed him.

Nothing mattered to me any more, they could take me if they wanted. Always at sunset this lack of self-confidence came over me, this presentiment of death and the certainty that it was useless to fight. I followed him in silence like a prisoner. He went into the hut to take off his jacket, wrote something on a sheet of paper, laid down his belt. Then I saw that he was taking the revolver out of its holster. Then I fled.

I ran a good length of the path without turning round and squatted behind a tree. The blood was pounding in my temples and I thought that if he denounced me it would be the end for me. Once I was caught, no leave and no going home. But I must go home. Go back to her. At any cost.

Now I must be calm. In fact I was calm. There was no one else besides the doctor in the hut. The soldier was in town and would never take the note to the command post. He must not take it. And above all it was necessary to avoid leaving clues, or to destroy them. I remembered the bottle of petrol and the rag. That's right: while he was cleaning the revolver.

The doctor was looking for me. Perhaps he thought I was nearby and seemed to be impatient. When he called I answered and seemed to reassure him. "Did I leave your book there?" I called.

"No," he replied, "it must have fallen, but I will look for it later." And I turned back. I was calm, so calm that I felt surprised and even flattered. I drew the revolver thinking that I had to come within two yards and aim at the head and that I must not make a mistake. One shot, that was all; you don't kill yourself by mistake with two shots. The doctor had sat down and already appeared absorbed in the grey of the dusk. "Perhaps he would do the same in my place. At least I should like to think so."

I was now near the hut and the doctor had not heard me. And I had come up so quietly, just like a ripe assassin who does not give more than his professional attention to his movements. I was near him, but he could not see me; I was hidden by a tree.

"Lieutenant," said the doctor. He had raised his head and was looking at me with unmoving eyes. Then, quickly, I fired.

I saw him start, he had moved an instant before. He had moved, he who sat whole days in his deck-chair without moving an eyelid! Quickly I pulled the trigger again, but now the revolver did not fire. It had jammed; perhaps not; at any rate it didn't fire. I pulled the trigger again; it did not fire.

The doctor was on his feet, he was running towards the hut with that unexpected agility with which only the lazy are endowed. I fled towards the road; threw myself into a ditch then set off running again and crossing the fields reached the perimeter road so as not to be forced to enter the town. I stopped when I was a long way away; I heard no suspicious noise—perhaps the doctor had given up following me or had never thought of it. Probably he had telephoned from the hut.

I was in a fix all the same. They would catch me. Only then did I remember that the revolver had not fired. With trembling hands I examined it. The magazine was missing. How? I didn't remember. Suddenly I burst out laughing, but it was a dry, rapid laughter, which shook me and forced me to lie down on the grass. I had left it on the packing-case, the magazine, beside her photograph and the bottle of petrol during my ridiculous attempt at suicide. Soon I noticed that I was sobbing, they were long lamentations that I could not hold in, and I was amazed at them. "My suicide has been a complete success," I repeated.

I began to run towards the camp again. I had to organise an alibi at least, or flee. I had to think it over, but soon I quickly had to admit that there were no plans which did not envisage flight, in fact desertion. What answer would I make to the court of inquiry? I could deny that I had fired, maintain that the shot went off through carelessness—and it was naive to hope to convince anyone—I could still deny my illness, and it was downright silly to hope to do that. So make an end of it or desert.

I had a few hours yet, the carabinieri would not come right away to our camp, they would search among the officers in transit at the command post, they would stop trucks. There were other units near ours. If I had another night my flight could succeed. I would leave the camp after supper, for then it would not occur to anyone to look for me, and my absence could be explained away until the morning. But where would I go? "And yet," I said, "I must flee."

These words struck me as if they had been spoken by someone else, and once more I had to sit down, in a state of collapse. There you had it; Mariam's plan began to appear in all its treachery. She wanted to "isolate" me more than I was already. "There will be a general order from H.Q.," I thought. Isolate me and take me away from her. Overcome with hate I shook my fist at the valley, which I could feel far off, under the lean mountains standing out against the violet sky, and cursed Mariam.

So it was flight. Avoiding the road I reached the camp, prepared my pack, added a blanket, and when, to avert all suspicions, I went to supper, the captain announced that I had got my leave. My friends congratulated me, but with reluctance.

THE BOLT

1

THE NEXT DAY I was in Massaua. The steamer would leave late at night; I was attracted to the principal quay and saw its name in white letters, freshly painted. "Perhaps I will succeed," I thought. I had to get on board, but first and foremost not let myself be caught. I repeated this phrase to myself several times.

Was it impossible to understand anything in that heat without repeating it several times to oneself? Blank apathy was coming over me and I stood there more than an hour considering my sorry state. My leave was a trap. They would catch me on board or when disembarking at Naples. But I must go on board all the same and hide, paying for the connivance of someone on board. I had to reach Naples; get back to her.

Not let oneself get caught. I remembered my departure from camp at night, my halt in front of the doctor's hut. There was the doctor; in his eucalyptus grove, asleep in his camp-bed, his papers scattered on the ground and his coffee machine on the table. Perhaps he had his revolver under his pillow and perhaps he was lying awake thinking about me. Of course he was thinking about me. With pity, but with anger, too, at my attempt to kill him. And he would never know that I had been a few paces away from him, more than an hour, tempted to kill him properly. But what would I have gained? Having reported me, he had lost all importance, had saved himself; if I killed him it would be a stupid act of vengeance, meaning further suspicions and fewer accomplices. Yet I had hesitated before going away, thinking: "Suppose his sloth had been such as to advise him to put off his report until tomorrow?" No, I mustn't delude myself to that extent over a doctor's laziness. "So," I said, "let him sleep in peace, this doctor friend of mine who moves his head so ludicrously."

At dawn I stopped a truck after walking all night across the fields. And in a few hours' time I had felt the hot and salty breath of the sea. "Is it the sea?"

"Yes, it is the sea," the driver had answered. All my irrational hopes had awakened and I arrived in Massaua singing to myself. Now the city was evaporating and the steamer was lying ready with its name newly painted; but it showed no sign of life. On the contrary it had about it an abandoned air such as makes one foresee a delay in sailing or, quite simply, no departure at all. On the other hand I knew it would leave late at night.

I climbed the gangway and found myself on the promenade deck. There was a nice smell of warm paint and nothing more, no more of that imperceptible odour which from time to time things on land gave off around me. Warm paint, the nice, good paint of ships that lie in the sun, an odour which made me bewilderingly confident. I went into the saloon and here the air was warmer, more intimate. I looked at a divan and it seemed to me the newest thing in the world. There were also a lot of easy-chairs and, on a table, a tray with three crystal glasses. I took one of them, it was a tall glass and when I touched it with my nail it gave out a sound I had not heard for a long time, a festive sound, full of promise. "I will succeed," I said.

As if summoned by the sound a half-naked man entered and asked me what I wanted. He was obviously some one who had to do with the engines, he still had traces of oil on his temple and a tired somnolent air. Perhaps he was the only person awake on the ship, the others must be lying in a state of collapse in their bunks. I told him that I was there to embark, I was going on leave. He replied that it wasn't time to embark and that I must leave the ship: no one could come on board before the time appointed.

"I am an officer," I said. I had made a mistake. Precisely because I was an officer he wanted to humiliate me. "My leave pass is in order," I added.

He looked at the paper without curiosity, then said: "And the stamps? At least go and get it stamped. And don't come on board before the time appointed."

"What time?" I said. And was unable to bring out the speech I had been preparing ever since I ran away.

"I don't know." He stood on the gangway and I descended. Get the paper stamped? I stopped on the quay in the sun before making up my mind to go to the military post on the very same quay. Curiosity, stronger than any fear, compelled me towards the office.

The post was open, a soldier in brief shorts had posted himself out with his legs wide apart under the fan and was looking at the ship, he was staring at it without seeing it with that lost look the heat induces—the heat and the drowsiness caused by the glare. A carabiniere was also sitting in the door in the shade, looking at the ship. He raised his eyes to the funnel, then counted the portholes, the life-boats, looked at the funnel again and the wireless aerials, and the limp and dirty flag. Another carabiniere in shorts was there in the background, leaning in an archway and fanning himself with a paper fan. He looked at the steamer, the anchor chains, the dirty water drifting around the hull, and spelt out the name written in letters of white.

At this hour there was no one else on the quay. Loading was finished, the native porters were in their dens, and so there was only myself on the quay, myself and the soldier with his legs wide apart and the two carabinieri. All of us looked at the empty ship with the same nostalgia. The stoker came down and went to talk to the carabiniere; I did not hear what he was saying to him; then he went off towards a bar with his unsteady and broken gait.

Perhaps this was a good minute to go into the office, have a stamp put on my pass; they would not even look at it. I went closer, trying not to distract the carabinieri from the sight of the ship, but when I was a few yards from the door I saw that the carabiniere on the quay was tearing himself away from his meditation and making for the office; perhaps he only wanted to chat to the other carabiniere and the soldier. I stopped and pretended to be interested in the ship. These carabinieri were there waiting for me—what else were they doing? There had never been so many carabinieri in offices of that kind. They were waiting for me, they knew that I would come there in the long run, impelled by those stamps that meant embarkation and, in a week's time, Italy.

Now another carabiniere was coming down the gangway of the steamer and joined the two standing talking. I took my pack and went off pretending to be looking for something I had lost. There, you see, the ship was ready, really far too big a trap for such a small mouse. Of course another carabiniere was waiting for me in the officers' mess, reading the paper, looking at the clock, amazed at my lateness. And the soldier who stood with his legs astraddle under the fan knew my name, and if I had gone into his office would have given a sign to the carabiniere, an arranged signal, so as to prevent me from doing anything stupid, drawing my revolver. And that ambulance already waiting behind the Customs, with its driver sleeping as if they had killed him, was for me. The orderly knew my name. They all knew it, my name.

I could not risk it. It's easy to identify a lieutenant. No use cutting one's moustache off. There's still the bandaged hand, the colour of the eyes, and other details the doctor must have noted, just because he is lazy. I must not go on board with my papers in order but climb up by stealth, hide myself and mix with the troops she would carry. It was a risky undertaking, but it had to be tried. While I was going back towards the ship, two sailors were pulling in the gangway for no other reason than to prevent impatient officers from coming on board before the time appointed.

I went to the bar and sat down. At the end of an hour I was finished, defeated, and would have gone back to the post to give myself up if the stoker, in passing, had not smiled to me—and surely for no other reason than to excuse himself for his rudeness of a little before. He went off pale and broken by the heat. Perhaps he was looking for a house to spend the afternoon in, before going back into that oven; but when I joined him he looked at me with unexpected mistrust. We went into a house; the stoker was certainly in a hurry to be left alone with the woman—I could see her coming and going half-naked through the half-open door, she was beginning to wash herself, overcome by the heat too, absolutely deaf to our conversation—and with difficulty brought himself to listen to me. He stood there thoughtfully for a long time, he was mistrustful, and finally he said: "Impossible."

The woman was washing and was looking at me over the screen. I smiled at her—her opaque face was enlivened by a red ribbon in her hair, and it was a calm face, one that had survived the disaster which had overtaken the body. So I smiled at her and continued my conversation with the stoker who was listening to me. But I saw his inexpressive eyes give way under the pressure of his boredom. "Impossible," he repeated with a yawn. He didn't want to hear any stories, he would have to pay too many accomplices.

The woman came and lay down on the bed half-naked. She was a native; she lay down and listened serenely to our discourse; no one told her to go away and I thought she did not understand. It was so hot that she undressed and lay there naked, impassive, her glance vague and fixed on the ceiling. When I had finished talking the woman said without moving: "Why not, what does it cost you?"

The stoker did not even answer but lay down on the bed and I was afraid he would fall asleep. Then I pulled out my money and I saw that he was tempted, but he didn't want to make up his mind. "I must talk to my friends first," he said at last, but appeared to regret having promised even so vaguely. When I left him a few notes, he became more expansive; he promised he would try. In fact he said that I must be on the end of the mole at eleven o'clock. His face was calm and serene, and now he was talking as if he were used to this kind of job. While I was drying my sweat I saw—or was I mistaken?—that the woman was smiling at the ceiling, lost in thought. I saluted her and, suddenly modest, she covered her belly with her dress.

I collected provisions for a week and at eleven was on the mole.

I saw a unit going on board, the men were climbing up cheerfully. There were other people walking on the mole—it was the only point where a light breeze blew. Two workmen had brought their camp-beds and were talking quietly.

When the stoker came at midnight and said "Impossible," I looked at him so despairingly that he began to make excuses. He would go back and speak to his friends. I listened to him and remembered the soldier I had left alone with his overturned truck at the first hill going down to the river; the stoker was talking the way I had talked, knowing that I would not come back. Then I gave him a letter to her which he would post in Italy, a letter written with infinite care—I had scarcely touched it. I told her not to worry, that whatever happened to me it would never prevent me from coming back to her. The stoker took the letter promising that he would try to win over his friends—in short he left me with some slight hope. At one o'clock the steamer silently detached itself from the quay, passed in front of me, and once more I read the name in white letters, newly painted. It was huge now, the steamer—and so silent that it seemed empty; the soldiers on board waved to the sparse crowd on the quay without shouting. They were muffled adieux, veiled by the dark, by the heat and by the envy of those left behind. Through the portholes I saw people busy, happy, preparing for the first Red Sea night. A young man stuck out his head and said quietly: "So long, Africa."

As soon as it had reached the open sea, the steamer gave a salute with three long hoots of her siren. The two workmen had fallen asleep and awoke with homesick curses, turning every now and again to watch the dark blot of the steamer disappear.

And now I still had to read the little book. I opened it with repugnance and the first illustration was my hand. "I knew it," I said. Determined not to let myself be upset I put the book back in my pocket. And I went back to the woman.

2

I found her lying on her rickety bed where sandals and boots had left traces of a uniform grey. She was reading a paper-backed novelette which she threw to the ground when she saw me come in, but did not seem surprised and perhaps had long known that I would do so. I told her my misfortunes, and the words came from me more and more brokenly and impetuously. Finally I threw my pack into a corner of the room and asked her if I could stay. I waited for her answer and meantime looked round the room; to me it seemed infinitely sordid; the men had left traces everywhere. Photographs were stuck in the mirror and on the coat-hanger I saw a tunic of brown canvas, perhaps left there by some drunk. And I sniffed. But there was only a nice smell of eau-de-Cologne. An excellent smell. "Funny," I thought.

I could have slept in the open air, on the mole, and instead I had come to that house. Why? To ask her for protection or to test it? I didn't know yet. "Well," I said, "can I stay?"

She was a long time in making up her mind, perhaps she was expecting customers; or else she found my action disturbing. At last she said I could, I could go in there, into the shower. There was a broken camp-bed. "That will be fine," I said.

I arranged my blanket on the bed and lay down. "Something must happen," I said. But very soon fatigue and the heat prevented me from thinking, in fact the depression caused by my failure to embark was giving me a pain in the chest—the ache of suffering too long borne. But I could not weep, I knew that that would be the end, that I would become soft with self-pity and the next morning would run to the hospital begging to be taken in. I told myself that if I wept I had given in; and instead I must consider my situation very coolly and try every possible means of returning to Italy. I was pulling myself together thus when the street door opened and I heard a voice call to the woman. "Mimi," the voice repeated and shortly after the woman got out of bed with a sigh, let in the visitor and spoke to him. Perhaps she was telling him that there was somebody there. "So soon?" I thought. And I managed to smile.

The man replied that it didn't matter, but from the way he moved about the room, hesitating, I gathered that he could not make up his mind to stay; and meantime the woman had got back into bed, had lit the lamp and was turning the pages of her magazine again.

"Don't stand about," she said. The man sat down on the bed, then muttered that if that was how things were he was going. The woman answered him with a bored "Good night" and went on turning over the pages; thus we passed some minutes in a silence full of mutual suspicion until I heard the noise of a slap on someone's hand. "Make up your mind," said the woman quietly and the other replied that he was going away. He must have felt hurt in his pride, or else he was pretending; or again perhaps the two of them were winking at each other and barely suppressing their laughter. When I pretended to snore the visitor, more annoyed and disappointed than ever, rose to his feet and repeated that he was really going. It was then that the woman asked him when he was going back to Genoa.

I smiled again. How closely events were working out as I had foreseen. Come on, bring out your well-worn phrases, trying not to laugh. "In ten or twelve days, as soon as we have finished loading," said the man. His was a calm voice, with a lilt in its Genoese accent. I raised myself up, leaning my elbows on the bed, and listened; the woman was speaking in a low voice and after a long silence the man said he would need to think it over. "Of course," I thought. Meanwhile the woman had made him sit down near her and was asking him: "How much do you want?"

"He'll ask exactly what I have in my pocket, or a little less, so as not to give himself away," I thought. I held my breath. The sailor asked who it was that was to go on board; but since the woman kept silent, considering a reply unnecessary—how badly they played their parts—he said: "Sixty thousand."

I stretched myself out on the bed; that answer had suddenly comforted me and I laughed at the futile fantasies I persisted in nursing. I did not possess more than twenty thousand lire and if the man asked for sixty he was really a sailor. He had not refused and that was a good sign—it showed he was a man used to that kind of risky business. But the fact that he had not asked for nineteen thousand lire—that was an excellent sign. Of course it would be absurd to persuade the sailor to accept an advance until the rest was paid over on disembarking, but his blunt reply was a guarantee of his seriousness. He had named the figure like a poker-player raising the stakes.

When the woman came to my bedside and gave me a sign to go in, whispering: "He is the captain of a tramp steamer," I caressed her thighs with gratitude. I slipped on my shirt and trousers quickly, but first of all I took off my badges of rank.

The woman introduced us with a gesture, and my adversary touched his cap. I decided that I could trust him, he was just the type to live by taking risks; a broad face marked with deep wrinkles, a huge, avid mouth, two eyes which gave sudden piercing glances but preferred to avoid mine. While he spoke he was uniformly hard and surly. On his head was a white peaked cap, one of those caps the oyster vendors in Naples also wear; it made him look like a boy. That cap filled me with tender faith. The captain was standing against the head of the bed, with one hand he was touching the woman's knees, but gently, as a gambler touches the cloth, waiting for his opponent to make up his mind. He had no idea what new hopes, what new confidence his cap was giving me. When I had finished speaking he said that he would not know what to do with the money when he disembarked. And he concluded: "If I take it here, I can buy stuff."

I answered that I accepted. I would give him the money when I got on board. We fixed the day, the hour, the place; at that point I felt that I must not let the question of money worry me; I would sail. I had ten days' time.

I went back to the camp-bed happily. The woman had not spoken again, now she was accompanying the man to the door. I heard the sailor's steps in the street, then I heard him knock at the door of a nearby house and my mind was set even more at rest. There was no trap; everything was clear. When the woman came back into the shower she sat down on the end of the bed with her back leaning against the window and for a moment we were silent. I felt relieved at the thought that I had trusted her. I had hit the nail on the head when I came back to her house.

The woman remained silent. When she was not moving about the room and not speaking, her face was still the naive and impenetrable face of a woman from the interior. The cosmetics simply laid a puerile veil over her face, and I remembered young girls making up for the first time, anxious to affirm their puberty and to challenge the first comments. But her body was already worn out, in perfect harmony with her wide bed which occupied all the room and was impossible to ignore. You had to sit down on it or else keep standing in contact with the walls, and they, too, bore traces of unmentionable traffic.

She was an advanced native, she read novelettes—reading matter which must be a source of pride to her; and so she kept the magazine on her bedside table and turned the pages, perhaps even imagining romantic situations. This was a good situation; she was protecting a man. And she did not even suspect what absurd motive had made me enter her house. What absurd but implacable motive had forced me to go to her, who talked like her blonde heroines and had acquired a sense of time and the romantic. The motive I did not even know fully myself, indeed it had been more an impulse than a motive, and now I asked myself if the heat had not played a bad trick on me. She was silent, honoured to be able to offer me her hospitality. "Yes," I thought, "that smile at the ceiling was suggested to her only by the stoker's boredom, not by the unforeseeable outcome of my adventure."

She was a good woman, a little worn by the heat. Nothing more. Now she was sure to be wondering what I could have done to get into this cul-de-sac. She knew nothing. When she asked me if I had the money already, I said yes and thanked her. Had I not tempted logic sufficiently by trusting her without going on to test the accuracy of my fantasy? So now a new peril was looming up and I had to banish it. The next day she would make the proposal once more to other sailors, prompted by the thriftiness innate in these women, until a carabiniere came dressed up like a sailor to offer possible terms for taking me on board. And the woman would swallow the bait.

In the little room there was a fresh odour of eau-de-Cologne; there was no doubt that it was the odour of the woman. She had to wash herself, not to pass the time but to combat the heat.

There now, with the greatest light-heartedness, with my usual extreme light-heartedness I had given myself away, imagining that I was foiling all sorts of plots and upsetting all kinds of plans and thus gaining time. I had set myself a new, invisible trap with my own hands. Perhaps I would be well advised to talk to the woman right away. But if I did speak to her now that she had expressed her sympathy for me, would she find in my worries a certain misgiving or a rebuke for her unsolicited solidarity? Finally I said that I'd given up the idea of going away, I could get away without paying anything if I waited a few weeks. Since she did not answer I added that I was not a thief or a murderer. Not even a deserter. "I am an engineer," I said, "and I'm tired. I've broken my contract and am going back. That's why they won't pay my passage."

"Why are you tired?" she asked. It was the question I least expected. "Aren't you tired? Do you like staying here?" The woman shrugged her shoulders—of course she must like it. She had attained the enviable position of a house with a shower, she had customers, she could read, she read novelettes in which blonde girls marry an engineer. And she had never got to know engineers, except in their drawers.

She shrugged. She was hot and had the ennui of Massaua in her bones. "What sort of an engineer are you?" So she could even distinguish between two different kinds of engineer. "Mining engineer," I answered, and could not help smiling. But of course, what a stupid idea. I would go away; the woman had smiled at the ceiling only because the stoker had woken up at the sight of the money. Hadn't I smiled, too?

The woman rose and invited me to come into her bed where it would be nicer. I was just going to rise when I remembered and said that it was too hot and I was tired. Then she went into her own room; perhaps my refusal had offended her—it really wasn't worth while worrying about an engineer even if he was really an officer who had to hide. A little later she came back carrying a bottle of orangeade and sat on the edge of the bed while I drank. Poor Mariam. She had learned to read, she went to the cinema, she didn't wash herself in the pools of dry water-courses, she did not refuse silver coins, she had forgotten the village by now. She could stay naked not because of her extreme innocence but because she was past all shame. And if she covered her belly with her dress, suddenly, it was certainly not from fear of my revolver but from belated coyness. Her dress came from Naples, her magazine was printed in Milan. But I didn't want her to touch me.

Her steady and serene gaze did not annoy me, and yet I could not recall who else had looked at me like that. Certainly not Mariam. Who then? She sat still and untroubled, her face made no attempt to express anything, but her eyes, which I only now saw distinctly, were no more her own. And the imperceptible odour—perhaps I had brought my hand near my mouth when drinking and the tincture of iodine was mingling with the sweat, or perhaps someone had thrown flowers into the courtyard—that sweetish stench was already filling the room. I was amazed that she did not notice it, yet she did not take her eyes off me but sat still and silent. "Johannes," I thought, and from that moment knew why I had come to this house. The conspiracy was continuing and I would not foil it. I hurled the bottle out of the window and she started aside. She thought I wanted to hit her. "Sorry," I said. Then I added: "Has someone thrown flowers into the courtyard?"

She leaned out of the window and said: "No." Now the almost perceptible odour was stagnating round the bed; the stray dogs were well washed and the flowers had not yet withered, but there was a hint that they would wither unexpectedly. "Perhaps

I shall go mad," I said softly. But the woman did not hear, she had gone back into her room and was opening a drawer. She came back quickly with a biscuit tin. In it were all her valuables—her medical inspection book, some silver jewels, necklaces, bracelets, photographs. She showed me her post-office account; she had eight thousand lire in it. "That's not enough," I said, (there was no use pretending now) "and even if it was enough I wouldn't know what to do with it. Tomorrow I am going back to the workmen's hut."

"What are you putting on this act for?" was what her eyes said. But I had to insist, make her understand that there was nothing else for it, or that I couldn't do it any other way. I added that I would come back in a few days. She remained silent. Then she took off her dress, went behind the screen and turned on the spray. Although I could not see her I felt that she stood tired and motionless under the water. "All we need is a raven," I thought, "and it would be complete," but I could not manage a smile. When she came out from behind the screen she stayed near the window drying herself in the warm air of the night, and powdered herself with a big powder puff. "Don't you want to wash?" she asked. I said: "No," and clenched my jaws so as not to yell at her to go away to her grey bed and get out of my sight. I trembled at the thought that she might sit down beside me and notice the odour which was becoming more and more rotten, inevitably. I thanked her for everything, even for the things of which she could have no idea, but next day I would leave for the table-land. "I'm going back to the workmen's hut," I concluded bluntly, "and I won't leave again, I'll start work again." I wanted to ask: "Are you happy now?"

The woman came and sat on the edge of the bed again and touched my brow. "I'm not ill," I said and pushed her aside. Why did she put her hand to her nose? I started up and went to the window, but there were no flowers in the courtyard and no refuse either; in fact it was a clean courtyard. Perhaps the flowers were in the next door houses, and the refuse, too. No wonder, we were near the port; the stagnant water was certain to give off the stench that now filled the room and laid itself over every-thing like a veil. "Of course, the stagnant water," I thought. "All you need is a dead mouse in this weather." I was at the window when the woman came close to me and made to put her hand out to my neck. "Come," she said. I stopped her. "Don't touch me."

She flinched as if I had slapped her; she turned pale, she thought that it had not been worth while keeping me and offer-ing me her savings, which were indeed hard earned. Could I not forgive her for being a woman different from those who peopled her reading? That was what her eyes said, and I could not bear their glance. "Why?" she asked. When she understood that I did not wish to discuss it, she burst out laughing and once more stretched out her arms towards my neck. I stopped her. I thought that this time I was playing Mariam's part. What if I gave in? Was it not all foreseen down to the smallest detail? If I infected her because it was useless to refuse what was offered me before it was too late? Or perhaps the conspiracy expected at least one good action from me? Very well, I put the woman from me and she returned to her room, to that bed streaked with grey and as unsteady as a raft. She turned over the pages of her magazine quickly still muttering, not reading. Then she put out the lamp.

I could not hear her breathing, she was not sleeping. Her eyes, open in the dark, made me uneasy. "What's your name?" I asked. She answered that she was called Mimi.

"O.K., but they call you Mariam, don't they?"

"Yes, Mariam." ("Well," I said, "what's funny about that? They're all called Mariam in these parts.") "Good night, Mariam." And I had to restrain my laughter. She said nothing, she moved and was perhaps smiling at the ceiling as she had smiled when I was trying to convince the stoker.

I lay a long time looking through the rectangle of the window at the pale night sky; few stars succeeded in overcoming the tedium of that oppressive veil. When I heard the siren of another ship saluting the city I gave up hope of sleep and was once more overcome by sorrow. I would never go back to Italy, I said.

There was no use trying, I would pass from one hope to another because I had not the courage to face the only decent solution. I must die, the flowers were rotting and waiting and I was procrastinating.

3

After a long hour I decided to go out, I would make for the first hills; there, perhaps, the wind from the sea would temper the unsupportable stifling atmosphere of the houses. The streets were hot, pale, and as dirty as rags. On the quay the empty berth had been taken by another ship and the native porters were unloading cases. They were singing in order to put some energy into their work and moved about in groups of ten where two persons would have been enough; but that is how they work, without conviction, like drunks.

I took the road to the station, then I struck towards the first hills and when I saw the whole city I stopped, because the sun must be going to rise and the heat would be unbearable. I sat on a hill near an abandoned hut among big bushes, eaten by the dust. I opened the little book again; it was exactly my hand and these spots were my spots. I began to read.

"... In the story of St. Elisabeth of Hungary by Montalambert details are given of the ceremony of *separatio leprosorum*. The rites of the dead were celebrated in his presence; then the utensils which he must use in his solitude having been blessed, and when those present had given alms to the sick man, the priest, preceded by the cross and accompanied by all the faithful, led him to the solitary hut which had been set apart for his dwelling. On the roof of the hut the priest placed earth from a graveyard saying:

'Si mortuus mundo vivens iterum Deo.'

Then he addressed to him words of consolation pointing out the joys of Paradise. Then he planted a wooden cross in front of the door and they all departed...."

"That's enough," I thought, and put the book back in my

pocket. The port was full of ships at anchor, and among them was the ship that would take me to Genoa if I found sixty thousand lire to give to the captain. One thing was certain, it wasn't a question of a mere stoker, but of a captain who trafficked and needed money. A captain who had gone wrong. Which was his ship? Perhaps that red and grey one near the mole? It must be that one, a down-at-heel ship, with a captain who has found work only because there is a big demand and has put to sea again, determined to get rich this time.

I took the revolver from the holster and examined it, thinking meanwhile that the captain would make me his guest at table and that when I got to Genoa I would disembark at my leisure and we would salute one another, friends for life. But there was no use now looking for the thirty-two thousand lire, even supposing Mariam wanted to make her fine gesture, concealing God knows what new piece of treachery.

The sea was there in the background; a grey that was hardly darker than the sky, steaming and hot, a sea accustomed to miracles; but it would not open this time for me, for an untouchable. I put back the safety catch and at that moment the silence was broken by a trumpet sounding reveille. And where was the barracks? Right under the hill where the slope ran into the plain.

They were long huts, painted grey, and up to now I had not noticed them. That wide-open space was the sports ground, it could not be mistaken with its wall all round it and the sloping bank closing one of the short sides. I saw that at the sound of the trumpet men began to hurry out of the huts, naked to the waist, and went to wash, but no shouts reached me. After a little they all disappeared and another scene followed.

First there came a detail of armed men—perhaps twenty of them—commanded by an officer, then the guard with the orderly officer. They must be going to hoist the colours. Funny, the orderly officer was wearing his blue sash, and since leaving Italy I had not seen them any more. Then gradually all the companies—eight in all—came from the huts and formed a square in the centre of the camp. The soldiers wore long trousers and tunics. Perhaps they were celebrating the raising of the regiment or some other military anniversary, unless it was Sunday. No it was not Sunday, it was not a question of Mass. Only curt commands could be heard, then the trumpeter sounded "Attention" and a soldier ran up the flag on its staff. The flag remained inert, wrapped round the staff, while the troops presented arms.

Other commands reached me. The formations formed up beside the bank moved so as to leave it clear. At the "Stand at ease," the troops remained still and silent while the officers gathered outside the square and talked, but always keeping an eye on their men, every now and again shouting an order that was immediately carried out with a rapidity that astonished me. "It must be a newly arrived unit," I thought, "if things still go as smoothly as this."

Time passed and nothing happened. I was tempted to go away, but fatigue led me to stay and I rejected the idea of going back to the woman's house, full as it would be of the warm smell of night—hers and mine. The revolver in my hands embarrassed me.

The men still stood motionless; no one asked to go away as always happens when a unit stand at ease for a long time. No soldier had sat down or taken off his helmet. They were all silent, only the group of officers talked, but quietly, without moving. Another long time passed. Between the barracks some soldiers in their underpants peeped out, but withdrew suddenly, considering it wiser not to let themselves be seen. They were the cooks, the malingerers, the sick. No one moved. Soon the sun would rise, a ship was leaving port—not the red and grey one—and the siren gave three long whistles. The soldiers did not move; one or two turned their heads very slightly towards the port. And now when a dog emerged from a hut to come bounding with joy towards the troops on parade a soldier ran towards it and threw stones at it until the dog decided to turn back, stopping every now and then to see if he were really the object of this unaccustomed welcome. Someone hit it on the back and then it fled and was seen no more. "The colonel hates dogs," I thought.

An instant later an officer entered the camp, running from the main hut, and immediately I heard other words of command, more decided this time, the definite words of command of great occasions. It was perhaps some general who wanted to review one of his regiments, but it was funny at that time of day. Then I decided that it was not funny, the heat would shortly make any manoeuvres tiring.

A little procession was now leaving the main hut. There were various officers and the regimental chaplain in cope and stole. Perhaps he had to bless the new regimental colours in that box near the flag-staff. The little procession advanced as far as the flag-staff and took up position in front of the detail. An exceedingly fat officer placed himself in the middle of the square with his back to the bank, took a document from a brief-case and began to read. I could hear nothing. The soldiers stood motionless at perfect attention. Between the barracks, the men in pants had formed groups and did not move.

The officer finished reading and turned towards the detail. "Stand easy" was ordered, but the soldiers made no perceptible movement, and no sound broke the silence. And it was then that I noticed that among the little group of officers there was also a soldier.

Funny that I had not seen him before. He stood with his head bare, his hands behind his back, beside the priest and two other soldiers. A pang went through me because now I knew. I wanted to get up, but I stayed nailed to the spot, incapable of going away, hoping only that I would have the strength not to look, but I knew it was impossible.

The three soldiers and the priest moved towards the bank. The priest was speaking into the soldier's ear, he was walking blindly, for the priest had now and again to support and guide him.

While the four walked towards the bank the detail moved silently and an officer gave a sign. The men prepared their weapons. I heard no noise, perhaps they were already loaded. Between the huts some of the soldiers were going away.

Now the officers were all in their places. The priest was still speaking and the soldier nodded. A cold sweat bathed my breast and back and ran along my legs. I threw myself on the ground near a bush; I did not want to see or hear anything. I began to tremble and tried to hide behind a bush. I wanted to hide. That was my execution; that's what it would be like, and I had got up in time, had taken this road, had chosen the best seat.

The soldier was still nodding and the chaplain embraced him. Then he kissed him, made him kiss the cross and withdrew, looking at him, while the two soldiers also withdrew. The bare-headed soldier looked at the chaplain, then he raised his head a little towards the hill. But he could not see me, I was hidden in the bush and he could not possibly imagine that there was any-one up there at this hour. He looked at the hill and he looked at my bush too, and for an instant I saw his pale face. The men levelled their rifles rapidly. The soldier was looking at the hill, suddenly he fell forward as if struck down by a blow from a fist, and I heard the volley.

I gave a scream, but no one could hear it. I sat there behind the bush while some officers went up to the soldier and the priest waved the cross.

Now two soldiers were carrying the box from the flag-staff to the bank, two others put the soldier's body into it, shut it and stood back without speaking. From the huts there advanced, swaying from the roughness of the field, a little van.

The soldier's last look had been at the hill, but he could not possibly have seen me: I was three hundred yards away and hidden by a bush. No one had seen me, not even the soldiers who were now going back to the huts, still keeping order; not even the officers who without looking at each other were going into the main hut to take a cognac or a coffee; not even the chaplain who was waiting beside the van, waiting to climb in.

I lay down and looked at the sky trying to calm myself. It was not my execution; I was neither a deserter nor a traitor, I was merely ill. They don't shoot sick men. I had a leave pass in my pocket. As for the doctor I would have denied it fiercely. And then? What does "then" matter? I must go away, go back to her, and stay near her. And then, perhaps even hospital, but first I must go back. "I am sick," I repeated; "they can't shoot me, they can't kill me, I must live." Then I said: "What about the suicide act then, why do you keep on thinking about suicide? I want to fall to pieces," I answered, "but to live to the last moment. I cannot leave the sky, even if it is a leaden sky like this; I cannot leave anything, not even this bush, not even the dullest days and the darkest nights, or the persons I hate—nothing."

I stayed there half an hour until the ground became roasting. Various trumpet calls had informed me that the life of the barracks was resuming its usual course. Now the dog was running freely in the open space and it was only among the huts that a soldier or two lingered to look at the bank. Then I went down towards the plain again, and I was happy because I had decided to live.

4

That day went by. When the night came I did not go back to the woman. Going farther in the city I had noticed some huts set aside for units about to embark and at this time empty. I moved into the showers and stayed there to escape from the infernal heat of the streets. I spent many hours stretched out on the concrete, seeking in the showers relief from the itching spots on my belly and arms. They had got worse.

Sometimes I smiled at the thought of the carabinieri who were perhaps looking for me and did not know that I was a couple of steps away. But these were short snatches of optimism; suddenly a longing to leave rose up and I had to calm myself with a thousand arguments. I had time—a great many days—to find the money and I turned over in my head the idea of going back to Mariam next day. I would accept her savings. Once and for all I must rid my head of the stupid ideas oppressing me. And the rest? I would find it. I couldn't get her to send it to me. One had to fill up forms, go to a bank; or give oneself up.

Thus I waited for the dawn, and with the dawn the first sleep for many nights. I emerged from it refreshed, and kept telling myself that in three weeks I would be in Italy. Ten days to find the money. Almost too many. I would do something, and although I could not say precisely what, I still felt that I would not fail to procure the thirty-two thousand lire I needed. On going back to Mariam's I did not expect to find whom I did find. But hadn't I shown him the road? There I found the major from A., the corpulent and self-sure major from A.

The door was half-open and I went in. Mariam must be in the shower, I heard the water falling in the little room and a noise of feet splashing. "Mariam," I said. Over the top of the screen I saw appear not her calm and childish face but the face of the major from A.

"And what are you doing in these parts?" he asked immediately, laughing. I had not been able to withdraw and he had seen me. But why was he laughing? So he knew nothing about the affair with the doctor, or else the doctor had not said anything about it. I tried to laugh too, said I was on leave and showed him my pass. He burst into a loud laugh and added that he knew all that, he had seen me going about enjoying myself for months now. Then he asked if I was going to Italy and I said: "Yes." He came out from behind the screen, half-naked; he had a towel round his belly and with another towel was scrubbing his chest and back. He was pale in colour, had a feminine breast and slender legs and his face expressed more strongly than ever a mystery I did not wish to solve. His belly, no longer held in, protruded solemnly. He sat on Mariam's bed and began to rub himself again. He was almost pleased that I had surprised him in this house, almost one of the family. We were all members of the family. But he was pleased.

I asked him if he had been long away from A. and he replied that he had been away two or three days. So he could know nothing, and the short-lived hope which had comforted me disappeared. One task remained—to see to it that he never did know anything, and not to compromise my embarkation. An easy task—he did not know my name; we had introduced ourselves hastily and he could not possibly remember it. Now I had told him another name. He must like me. I was, in his eyes, one of those officers who are the legend of every regiment—incapable of doing anything, who fall asleep when there is a general inspection or blow up the magazine out of absentmindedness. And he was too pleased with himself not to like me. "Do you know Mariam, too?" he asked.

"Not as well as you do," I answered laughing. At that moment the woman came in, she had been out shopping. Seeing us engaged in conversation she set about tidying the room. "This is your transit hotel," I said to the major, pointing to the sordid room where traces of the men were everywhere and made our presence too suspicious. He laughed frankly, shaking his head. He was passing through—a brief look in and a shower. He felt himself to be very young, to be loved and humoured because of the new, unexpected youth I had revealed to him. He said that Mimi was a good girl, she never complained, and he caressed her back, letting his hand rest on it. The woman did not even turn round, and in the silence that followed I felt that she was hostile to me. After a while the major and I went out to go and eat. His presence was an alibi such as I could never have hoped for.

He was very pleased, the major. I had unexpectedly discovered a new, Bohemian side to his existence, and that was what he must be feeling happy about. Having laid aside the gravity of his rank, which had caused him to advise me to shave the first time we met, he now seemed to ask me for the complicity natural to my years. Of course he could treat me like a boy, with the fatherly condescension of fortunate and experienced men towards young men; but now he had lost all his envy. I thought of that drawer of his, not now perhaps in such miserly good order. He slapped me on the back with a cordial gesture, forgiving me for not being like himself, for not having his good fortune, which he now appreciated at its true value. He said: my truck. So he had a truck, not an army truck, but a real private truck. And he was doing business. He was not alone. So he treated me like a boy who has a lot to learn from life, a boy who looks at the bright side of things and loves the natives because in them he finds the virtues other people are fortunately losing. I had a lot to learn from him, of this we were both convinced.

Yes, he must like me. "You," he said, "are one of those officers who, when they are orderly officer, allow the barracks to empty, even the sick go out and no one comes back that evening." And he laughed. I laughed too, modestly. I noticed that from time to time his cocksure elegance relaxed into familiarity and lost all its vulgarity. But at these moments he grew old, and hence his unceasing smile, the wily glint of his eyes. He was fighting his own decadence.

He looked at the port with other eyes than mine. I saw it as starting point of my flight; he, as a bigger and better hut. The packing-cases came from that quay and went into his blue truck. There was not much exertion needed, only the exertion of taking a packing-case and putting it on a truck. He was not even furtive. And it was I who had revealed to him the existence of all the Rahabats who have no precise idea of time. I smiled, thinking of the wife in the portable frame. When he went back home the major would go on making use of his second youth, with the help of the winnings he was accumulating in the meantime. The wife would remain in the portable frame. It was her place now, and she did not seem displeased to stay there. She was smiling.

And I was thirty-two thousand lire short. In fact, at that moment, forty thousand.

It was after lunch that I had the idea of asking him for it. We had gone to the bar and were absorbing the indolence of the afternoon, drinking orangeades. I thought he could not say no. In fact he must not. It was only later that I understood the reason for this absurd claim of mine. I felt myself to be his natural creditor. What could it cost him to give me the money? Knowledge of the source of his gains authorised me to consider myself his accomplice. Besides I would make him look upon it as a debt of honour. In Italy I would deposit the sum in his name in a bank he would name to me. I would be eloquent, enthusiastic, I would admire him to the utmost of my powers. It was really a naive hope—nourished by the heat of an implacable day and by the way his face suddenly succumbed to the fatigue of the game he had imposed on himself. "Major," I said, "I must ask you for a loan."

"Willingly," he answered, "how much do you need?" I was going to name the figure; he had already put his hand in his pocket and taken out some hundred lire notes. He was spreading them out, offering them to me, almost as if to hear their beloved rustle till the end. I saw that my request had surprised him, perhaps made him angry or made him downright suspicious. Then I laughed and said that I didn't need anything, I had been impelled only by curiosity to see if I had a friend in him.

Reassured by this, the major insisted that I take the money, he wanted to put it into my pocket and I had to repeat that I had been joking. "What do you think I would need?" I said, "I'm going on leave." To reassure him still more I showed him my money. Only then did the major put his own back in his pocket, happy to have proved his good will. He became magnanimous, and while I looked at him, concealing my suffering—I saw now that I would never find the money—he went on with his speeches. I did not listen. The ships anchored in the port were baking in the sun. I looked at them with the deepest envy, I envied the sailors collapsed in their bunks who would sail away without appreciating their good fortune, cursing it instead. "Must I stay down here and rot?" I thought. And how long would I avoid capture? Now the major was my natural enemy. His cock-sureness offended me.

I saw him again walking up and down in front of the house of the two girls, with his old straight back that disguised so ill the lust that had accumulated in the mediocre orderliness of his domestic life. I saw his drawer again and his gesture when he ran his hands under the tunic of the sleeping girl.

He was speaking. He was really sincere when, slapping me on the shoulder, he said: "Apply to me for anything." While he was repeating this offer he opened his eyes generously and all his rosy face, full of little wrinkles and with veined apples on the cheeks, lit up. I thought that we were two animals of a very different species and, almost involuntarily (what voice suggested the words to me?), I said: "I want you to take me up on to the table-land, here I'll die of heat and I'm bored. The next steamer leaves in a week."

He exclaimed that it was an excellent idea, happy that he could count on my company. He informed me that he would leave next day for D.

D. was a place on the other side of the river. Although I felt an instinctive repugnance to the idea of going through these places again I said I would be happy to see them for the last time. The major smiled. I was incorrigible. Then he announced the time when we would leave and the day we would come back to Massaua; he, too, wanted to be back before the ship left. "We'll take turns at the wheel," he added.

"Yes," I replied. While he was talking I was looking at him really on the verge of tears, overcome by the clarity of the image that had formed in my head and was now projecting itself far away, beyond the major's back, with rapidity and precision. I saw something fall into a ravine and the image was projected again almost as if I were incapable of controlling it. I was standing there like a fool when the major, disconcerted by my silence, asked: "Perhaps D. is too far?"

"No," I said, "it's high enough up." But he could not understand. And I smiled. I thought of the second lieutenant who had a taste for paradoxes. Knowing my story, he would say that from now on good deeds were forbidden me if I wanted to go to paradise. The road to my paradise—the one she lived in (which I now glimpsed from afar, beyond the river, among the lean mountains jutting into the violet sky)—was a special road, but I had to follow it.

5

Having reached D. we were to leave for Massaua next day. On the journey the major had finished off his business and collected his money which he now kept in a leather purse. He kept it constantly at his side.

We were to leave at dawn and I had not a minute to lose. Before supper, as the major had dozed off, I went up to the truck. I already knew what I had to do and unscrewed a bolt on the track rods. There was one for each wheel; I unscrewed the one for the left wheel, leaving it at the last turn so that it would be easier for me to finish the job when I got out of the truck. I only unscrewed it; I would take it off at the opportune moment. I then went back to the tent and, pretending to search among my things, I took the major's belt—he did not notice, thinking it was my own. I took out the revolver, unloaded it and returned it to its place. Now I had to keep calm and wait for the dawn. At dawn we would leave for the river, as I had left four months before to have my tooth taken out.

During the trip the major had been gay, our friendship had grown closer. The major had not even concealed the nature of his feelings towards his wife. He detested her and was very pleased to be far away from her. The new fortune he had accumulated undoubtedly made the woman in the picture frame seem an obstacle to his future. I followed him along the well-worn path of comments on women and meantime I was thinking of her, of what I was doing to be able to see her again. I loved her so much that I felt, like an adolescent, sudden pangs at the heart whenever I had doubts about my scheme and therefore about my return. During the long hours in the truck, when the major was silent, I once again lived through the moments of our happy life up to the hour of my departure, when I had seen her flee from the quayside unable to bear the comedy of farewells—flee sobbing and turning to wave but without seeing me, with those smiles of hers all drowned in tears.

More clearly than ever I saw her making that gesture; I lost sight of her in the crowd, she reappeared near the band, pressing a hand to her breast to restrain her grief, thinking I did not see her. Then she waved once more, hastily, and finally disappeared, jostled by the porters and the customs officials; near the gate she stopped incapable of going further, incapable of finding the way out and of looking at the steamer. She stood there until the ship cast off amidst the din of goodbyes. And my cry did not reach her, drowned by the clangour of the brass.

I must see her again, what I was doing seemed an obvious step to me—one to which the major had he known of it could have taken no exception. The major and the doctor, two stones to be removed from my path and cast on the tomb of Mariam, on that unsated tomb. And in homage to her. Nothing else. Because I loved her and wanted to see her again.

I was getting fond of the major who, apart from his elderly vanity, was a good chap and had begun to wish me well, considering me maladjusted to life. I considered him as one already done for, and from time to time stared at my victim, who persisted in laughing, talking, in busying himself with the follies of everyday life. Only once did I ask myself if what I was doing was right. "Once one begins," I replied, "one goes on, and perhaps it isn't a question of adding new chapters but of perfecting the first." There was not much choice; perhaps the shot which had cut short the sufferings of Mariam had also killed the major. Fate willed it that I should seem likeable to all my victims; they found me a nice, good-natured boy; indeed, that was the essential condition. I recalled the doctor (now I was almost pleased that I had missed him)—that lazy doctor with his taste for aphorisms, for coffee and slippers, whose friendship I had felt suddenly, just as one suddenly feels the spring on a dull winter's day as one walks under the trees in a garden. Had not he, the misanthrope, been willing to talk to me for an hour before he noticed that I was merely ill? Why had he not drawn his revolver at the right moment?

Now there is the major who thinks I am a young chap who can still be saved, one worthy of confidence, one whose every word breathes admiration of his good fortune.

Nor could I draw back—everything was going on outside of me with apparently unsolicited approval. In fact they were crimes that had been committed a long time ago; I was only going over them again. A work of restoration. Now I thought that from our first meeting on the square at A. I had understood. From then on, something—perhaps his way of walking, the way he put his belt right, the surly air under which he hid his extreme and elderly lechery—had caused me to foresee that I would play a part in the major's history.

Coming down to the river I had noted that other units had camped on the south bank near the first hill. So I told the major that I would get off to say how do you do to my cousin—he was an officer, too—whom I had not seen for a long time. I would leave the next day with some truck or other. There were still four days to go till the steamer sailed—and six till the tramp left.

"If you like," he said, "I can wait an hour for you." I answered that I would prefer to stay longer. He made no further objections, he only seemed less cordial than usual. Since we arrived at D. he had changed—perhaps his business was to blame.

I had seen to everything except the money. I decided that I must take the money from him without threatening him with the revolver; he would give a yell and then I would be forced to fire, to attract someone's attention. I had to rob him—the word no longer frightened me, but the difficulty was to get near the purse without awakening suspicions. He always kept it on him and I certainly would not be able to reach the truck in the ravine and search among the wreckage or among the embers of the fire. I had to take the money before leaving, but how? I told myself that I would think up something on the spur of the moment, then I scolded myself for this rashness of mine and tortured myself to think what manoeuvre would work best. Thus I lay awake all the night; the purse was on the table, but I could not have taken it without touching the major's camp-bed.

At dawn when we were ready to leave, I had not yet made any decision and was already on the point of giving up the idea, tightening the bolt, going back to Massaua, waiting for a passage that cost less and asking Mariam for hospitality. But the occasion offered itself when I least expected it. The major, having laid the purse at his side on the seat of the truck, climbed out for a moment to make sure that the tyres were all right, and at that instant—I thought my heart stood still—I opened the purse, took out a wad of notes—they were five-hundred-lire notes—hid the wad in my pack and lit a cigarette: just in time, for the major, satisfied with his inspection, climbed in again and took his place at the wheel.

Now the plan had to succeed. The nut would hold until I took it off, then there would be the bolt left, barely held by the grease, and the sudden movements which the curves of the descent demanded would cause it to jump out. And then the major could not in that narrow road—made for going straight on and made, anyhow, without kerbs—have avoided the catastrophe waiting for him. He would fall over with his blue truck among these cardboard trees. No passing driver would ask himself if it was worth while going to have a look, the truck was empty, there was not even the chance of salvaging the load. He would fall like a toy which, in its course, goes over the edge of the table. Even if someone did go down—but this was expecting too much of the curiosity of those who crossed the valley—he would find a purse full of money and a missing bolt. And a major with no bullet wounds. The matter would end up with an entry in records, with a telegram to the wife.

I had been long in dressing so as to give the other trucks time to go on ahead of us. There was no fear that any vehicle might follow us—it was at D. that the road ended—and not even that any vehicle might meet us; the traffic was so regulated that the trucks never met, for the very simple reason that the carriage-way did not allow two vehicles to pass. We left, and I had the strength to talk up to the very moment for getting out; this was the greatest strain, since the major did not seem to me to be in his usual good humour, and my jokes scarcely made him smile. When I told him to stop he braked suddenly and seemed pleased at the way the brakes worked. Did he perhaps suspect something? I got out quickly and let my match-box fall to the ground near the wheel. While picking it up with a sigh of annoyance I took off the nut and put it in my pocket. "Goodbye, major," I said.

He barely answered. Yes, he suspected something. When I had taken the pack he closed the door; it was the sign that my plan was succeeding. That sharp sound gave me courage, but only for a little; it was like the noise of a coffin shutting and I was on the point of jumping on to the running-board and confessing everything. I saw her weeping face again and restrained myself. It had been done before. "Goodbye, major," I said. Then I added: "And thanks for everything," but without a shade of irony; I really wanted to thank him. And that pink face of his, serious now, suddenly seemed to me to have become old and dead. But he was so calm that I immediately dismissed the vision his face suggested to me.

I began to move off, my legs moved with a jauntiness that was not new to me, the same elated jauntiness as when I had found myself safe and sound on the edge of the road looking triumphantly at the landscape of the valley and the truck upset in its cloud of red dust. I had hardly gone any distance when the major called me back. He was pale. "Come here," he said. I was tempted to flee. He would have run after me, I thought, and instead everything must go off calmly. He had climbed out, too, he had the purse in his hands and was waiting for me, suppressing his wrath; his face had gone white. "There's some money missing here," he said. "Do you know anything about it?"

I shrugged my shoulders in amazement, but was incapable of saying anything—his pallor was taking all my courage from me—and once more I saw the vision I had had before, annoying and distant. There, had I not anticipated this scene? Why did the condemned man not resign himself?

"Out with the money," he said curtly. Then I saw that if I gave in it would be the end and I became contemptuous, saying that I knew nothing about his money. Then, since he made to take my pack from me, I added: "But of course I've taken it and I'm going to keep it."

It was a well-aimed blow, for he remained stunned, incapable of answering, suffocated by anger and surprise. Then I said it over again. I needed the money, I would let him have it back in Italy. Now I needed it. If he kept on about it I would fire. If he reported me, I would report him. "And spare yourself the trouble of drawing your revolver," I added "because it is unloaded."

Perhaps only death—his imminent death—would bring such a pallor to his cheeks. "You are a scoundrel," he muttered, and I saw that he had given up trying to open the holster. I answered that I didn't mind; he must let me have the money, otherwise I would talk. Perhaps they would choose the occasion to make an example of someone. I felt that my words gave him food for thought. Instead he sat down on the running-board and smiled. For the first time he smiled. He looked at me and smiled as if savouring his victory. "All right," he said, "go on. But you won't leave on any steamer."

"There are a lot of steamers," I replied, because I found his irony was disturbing.

"None for you," he repeated, still smiling and stressing his words. "Not even the smallest and most broken-down tramp." And he looked at me calmly, waiting for me to open the pack and hand him the money.

His words told me that he knew, and only from incredulity had not referred to it before. But now he had proof. So it had been Mariam. Now I grasped the meaning of his muttered words. The accounts were being rendered and all the Mariams were acting as one. But I had the nut in my pocket.

The major was waiting. "Well," I said, "do you want to report me?" He nodded seriously, still gazing at me. Then he added: "I thought it was merely ill-will. I have been a fool, but it doesn't matter. I know your name, better than you think."

And since I stood there unable to make up my mind, his face lit up with craftiness, the craftiness I already so much detested and which he—like a bad actor—was unable to hide; and he said: "Why do you leave so many letters lying about?"

"All right then, I'll denounce you, too"; but I said it in a low voice pretending to be worried, so as not to let him see that my game was going too well. "But you won't report me," I added. "You will take other packing-cases and make good the loss in a single journey," and I said it almost like an entreaty.

"No," he said stubbornly, "I'll report you." But I touched the nut through the cloth. "Think twice about it before doing it," I said. I had to keep a hold of myself or else I would have laughed. He shook his head and shrugged. "Why should I?" When I said that reporting me would not do him any good, he got to his feet and said: "We'll see." Then he came rapidly towards me; I thought he was going to strike me—besides he had his revolver in his hand—but he restrained himself: "Rascal!" he cried. I did not answer, I thought it was a good thing if he relieved his feelings.

He climbed quickly into the truck, shut the door and said: "I'd be interested to know where you'll go to." Then without waiting for a reply he burst out laughing and added: "Have a good holiday."

Then I laughed, too, and when the truck drove away automatically gave the military salute. And I went on laughing, seized by and relieved by my mirth. And of the major there remained with me his smiling image, and that final good wish so often added as a climax to waiting for the train, to the reiterated farewells, the good advice. So he went off, and already he was having his revenge.

I saw the truck accelerating and could not take my eyes off it; I thought: he will fall off at the first bend, at the same one where I capsized four months ago. It was a coincidence that I was waiting for. So I saw the truck going into the distance jolting up and down because it was empty, just like mine, and I waited for it to face the first curve down at the foot of the hill. It was going fast, the truck; the major trusted to the brakes and the brakes did in fact function. But the wheel would not function and the report would remain with his thoughts, in his last thoughts, to be eaten by worms in a few days' time. "Goodbye, major," I said. I was sad.

The truck was nearing the bend; it slowed down, took the corner and I saw it disappear behind the bank of the road, slowly.

"Then it will be the next one," I thought. Incapable of turning back, determined to be a spectator of the crash, I ran to the corner. The truck was still running along the road, the distance made it seem smaller—almost like the toy I had imagined. It was bouncing because of the potholes, but it was running along, leaving behind it a cloud of red dust. I saw it disappear behind another curve in its dust.

I began to have doubts and took the nut from my pocket to make sure that I had removed it, and in the meantime I asked myself how the bolt could still be holding. Then I said it was sure to happen—that road had a hundred bends before you reached the river and they were much more dangerous than the first. The bolt would jump out. The truck must not reach the river. If it got there the major could warn the road blocks and the command posts by telephone. And he would do it. Then, as my last way of escape, the bush would be left to me, but for how many days? For how many days can an officer wander about the bush with a last-century map? Or through the low-lying country, or among the hills asking hospitality from the brigands, the ostriches, the "possible shepherds," the hyenas? If the truck did not crash I could simply make my way to the nearest H.Q. and give myself up. I would at least save my life, and I had to save it. But it would crash.

Racked by these thoughts, I remained on the verge of the road waiting for the truck to reappear in the bottom of the valley. From that height the road looked like a pink ribbon on the back of a sleeping animal. I waited for an hour and my hopes were born afresh. It had crashed. Another ten minutes and I would go away, in fact I would go down the road as far as the river looking in the ravines, and from there reach the other edge of the table-land by following the short cut. Another ten minutes and I was safe, I said. If the truck does not pass I am safe and I can embark. Now the truck will not pass any more. I checked the time on my watch.

I saw an old native coming from the hill above, he was going to the river and stopped a few paces away waiting for me to notice him. He had his certificate of submission stuck in the cleft of a cane. I smiled to him and he went on, black and trusting, saluting. He didn't smell at all. "Good," I thought. I let my attention wander for a moment to follow the old man and when I started to watch the valley again I saw the truck as small as a blue mouse running slowly along the red-pink ribbon. It was running along it slowly, like a performing mouse, swaying in the dust. It was moving forward at a pace that seemed to me the cruellest of mockeries, and its delay told me that the major had discovered the damage and had done something about it. "Damn the bolt," I shouted.

So it was moving along slowly—to avoid further surprises of course—then it disappeared among the foliage of the bush, and with it there disappeared the certainty of reaching her.

Now what use would the money be to me? I counted it—there were fifty thousand lire.

THE BEST HUT

1

W HEN I awoke the sun was already up. Twenty yards away ran the yellowish waters of the river, still in full flood. They reminded me of the waters of that other river, which are always just as yellow, and it was like meeting a friend on the pavements of an unknown city. But a friend who looks at you absent-mindedly, does not recognise you—or pretends not to do so—and continues on his way, carried along by the implacable crowd.

I was stiff from the long walk of the day before, and, when I remembered what I was doing there, black apathy came over me again. There, that was the first obstacle to overcome to reach Massaua. I had spent the night doing nothing except look at the river, listening to its deep murmur, the only quiet voice among the hysterical cries of the bush. Now I had to swim it and the thought did not frighten me as much as the possibility that a crocodile might make the attempt end in failure. I was still more frightened by the conviction that there was no longer any use in fighting against fate; for it had already struck me a mortal blow, and was now amusing itself by putting academic difficulties in my way. But perhaps there were no crocodiles in that part of the river, since the banks sloped steeply and the crocodiles love the hidden beaches and the sun that bakes them.

I heard myself saying this to myself aloud and took fright; it was the sign that I would give up the struggle if I did not do something. I had to act, let myself be taken when I was finished, half-dead, but first have a shot at it. I began to call myself names; and this time the sound of my voice comforted me; I took advantage of an access of energy to choose a point where I could reach the water. When I had found it I thought it was better to have breakfast first. I had boxes of cheese and biscuits with me—I had taken them for the unsuccessful embarkation—so for some days I would not suffer from hunger. As for my thirst, the water of the river in my dixie did not seem to be muddy. I made the coffee, put some into my water-bottle and stripped. I searched round the foot of an old rotten trunk and shortly had a little raft of that accursed cardboard to lay my pack on. I tied the raft to my left wrist with a string, pushed it into the water and followed it, trying not to touch the bottom with my feet so as to avoid the slimy contact of the mud; it was a question of letting the current have its way and of intervening when it became rapid towards the middle of the river.

It became more and more difficult to keep afloat—it had not occurred to me that fresh water doesn't hold one up much; and perhaps I had been unwise to tie the raft to my wrist, but I had to get across somehow. And I would get across on only one condition—that I let the river have its way. The longer I was in the water the more the odds improved in favour of the crocodile, but if I exerted myself too much trying to get out of the water I diminished the odds of getting out at all. The bridge was barely two kilometres away, and I saw the banks going past at a speed that worried me. And the opposite shore was still a long way off. Suddenly I was carried to within a few yards of it but was seized again by the current and carried back to the centre of the river.

I was considering abandoning the raft when, moving my feet, I struck something soft and resistant, perhaps even alive. As I cried out I began to swallow water. Then I frantically decided to save myself and struck out with hands and feet, thus succeeding only in swallowing more water and increasing my panic.

The thought that I might lose my life in the river filled me with profound regret—regret that proved stronger than shame at my fear. When I was exhausted, I let myself go and the water took me under for a second. Then, still more determined to save myself, without shouting out, I was able to grasp hold of the raft and thrust my feet towards the bottom. I touched it.

The water came up to my neck. A moment later I was on the bank and lay there naked, vomiting my breakfast and laughing. I stayed on the sand until the ants began to annoy me. Downstream I could see the bridge—a convoy was crossing—and when I tried to pick out the point where I had entered the water I saw that I had travelled almost half a kilometre. As I looked the surface of the water rippled and the water boiled sluggishly. I at once began to put on my clothes.

My clothes were now dry, even the bank-notes were dry, I had lost nothing. I had not even lost the will to live, to save myself, although my bathe had brought me back to reality—I had had to bandage my hand again. But that I had not lost my clothes was an excellent sign, because naked I would not have been able to get farther than the first post. I even recovered some of my spirits by thinking what sort of a state they would have seen me arrive in to give myself up.

Thus, laughing, I faced the first rise without further fatigue. I had to reach the short cut, follow it to near the edge of the table-land and thence cut across country, avoiding the road. Once on the table-land I would follow the old Abyssinian mule-track to A.—a journey of eighty kilometres which I had to do in two days, avoiding the posts, the camps and the villages. I had not yet began to ask myself how I was going to do it, I knew only that I had to do it. The bathe in the river had given me back the necessary optimism, and I was now anxious to get out of the valley which I knew so well.

The river was behind me and the knowledge that I had overcome the first grave obstacle made me certain that I would overcome the others too, right up to Massaua. I was in no hurry, but I knew that if I stopped I would have had difficulty in going on and so I repeated to myself that all the obstacles were imaginary, as imaginary as the crocodile I had felt under my foot—the crocodile that was only a tussock of weeds, or the carcass of an animal caught in the weeds.

I reached the path leading to the short cut at the very spot where we had found the two hanged youths; I recognised the grave Johannes had made for them. I bore towards the short cut, and soon reached it. Here the path became easy and the arrows the soldiers had put there as a joke showed me which way to go, this time without any possibility of error, and the phases of this too-protracted comedy ran through my mind. And my thoughts went back once more to Mariam, to the death each had given the other according to a secret plan—I to remain alone, she to drag me into her solitude. "A pity," I said, "that I didn't have the doctor's opinion on this literary hypothesis." And I laughed because now I could laugh at everything.

"My dear doctor, the engineer and the native woman kill each other, each of them with the means at his or her disposal. The engineer kills like a practical man who *has no time* to verify a phenomenon already sufficiently tested by experience, and without debating the consequences of his act. The native woman kills as her country kills, *with all the time in the world*, of which it has such a mistaken conception."

While I was imagining the doctor's weary reply a rifle shot broke the silence. I plunged into the bush, squatted among some stones, and waited. But I heard no other sound and was about to make up my mind to go on when voices came from the path and two soldiers appeared on it, they, too, making for the table-land. They were walking calmly forward, tired already, speaking a dialect I did not know. One of the soldiers had a rifle in his hands and was looking for a target worth a shot, a bird, a squirrel; the other, more tired, walked on ahead of him, wiping his sweat and urging him to be quick. When they were nearer I saw that they were carabinieri and that they had fired to cheat the silence surrounding their tour of inspection. Or perhaps it was me they were looking for.

I lay low and with one hand drew my revolver; I tried to put forward the safety catch, but my fingers were bathed in sweat and trembling.

"Come on, get a move on," said the one in front. The other still lingered, then he took aim and fired towards a bush, but without hitting anything, for I heard him mutter. Then he hurried off.

I would wait twenty minutes before setting out again, and I looked at my watch. I had to give them this start; at certain points the short cut came into the open for long stretches, and they might see me. After twenty minutes I started off again, keeping off the path and climbing up on to it only when the ground became too rough. I crossed the road at the same point where four months before I had waited for the truck, and a low hum of motors told me that a column of trucks was climbing the hill. The trucks passed, raising clouds of dust. Fortunately I did not let myself be too much distracted and thus had time to see the two carabinieri coming running back along the path determined to jump on to the running-board of a truck and thus get back sooner. They passed in front of me, a few yards away, without seeing me, and jumped on to the first truck, laughing.

Then I left the short cut and struck towards the table-land; provided nothing unexpected happened I would reach it. I arrived there a few hours later, but I could go no farther, the path led straight to the old camp and there was no way of skirting it without attracting the attention of some sentry.

I had intended not to allow myself to be seen. If a sentry communicated his suspicions to an officer, it would mean the loss of my initial advantage. Of course I had to reject the idea that all the carabinieri in the zone were on my tracks, but by crossing the river I had gained an advantage that I must not lose through imprudence of that kind. Perhaps they were looking for me and would still look for me towards the mountains or on the low country, down-river from the bridge. Reluctantly I turned back and took the short cut again, making towards the river. I had some lunch and thought how lightheartedly I would have run into the arms of my pursuers. And yet I had decided that I would keep away from camps and villages. It is not possible, I thought, to reach A. in less than four days. And Massaua? A month. Two even, if necessary.

Besides, if I reached Massaua quickly it meant giving myself up to the major. In a month or two the major would have forgotten my very existence, while at the moment his desire for revenge was certain to be making Massaua into one huge trap. I remembered his words: "I'd be interested to know where you'll go to," and I regained confidence. Did he really think I would not dare to cross the river? Did he think I would remain in the mountains? Well, I had tricked him, I was eating with relish on *this side* of the river, making for his trap which in two months' time would be sprung.

And what about Her? It was the thought of her that impelled me towards Massaua, and therefore I decided that henceforth I would distrust any decisions taken with her in mind. The final goal was not really Massaua, but Italy, in fact her house. Until I had reached that house and knocked at that door I must look at my task coldly and not give way to any irrelevant sentimental suggestion. I was carrying out a task. I simply must not yield to the lure of Massaua, to the lure of the sea with its promise of certain liberation. Because now when I recalled them, those days in Massaua appeared to have passed in a dream, and I felt a nostalgia for them. The lazy life in the bar and in the hut with the spray; the nice, unfaithful face of Mariam, only made up for fun, and the sight of the ships—among which, if I had patience, I would find mine—were already images from a lost world I would need time to reconquer. "It will be a fine thing," I said, "if you haven't even learned how time works in this country. You will have your whole life to die of leprosy, and now the ground is scorching your feet and you want to finish up in a hospital with a couple of court-martials that will postpone your return for at least three years."

When I passed by the tomb of Mariam I was calm, and did not even stop; I was going straight towards the tributary in order to follow it up-stream and come out just beside A. I had taken this decision after looking at the map. The tributary rose south of A.; and if a path ran along one of its banks I would save myself a lot of walking and all sorts of encounters, because that area was entirely devoid of camps and carabinieri. I plunged into the bush with its scattered termite heaps and reached the tributary; it lay down there, still calm and inviolate as on the first day of creation.

The gorge which led to A. ran between two high walls, about a kilometre apart at first, and narrowing later, while the river became rough, with short falls. Had I followed it I would have seen it become a torrent and then a mere rivulet. However the sun was already past its zenith and I was unwilling to face the idea of allowing myself to be overtaken by nightfall in these parts. I calculated that by walking at a good pace I could cover twenty kilometres before evening. And that map, that optimistic map, showed at least fifty.

I decided that if I found a cave I would spend the night there, otherwise I would have to turn back. But back where?

I sat down and lit a cigarette to gain time. I no longer managed to deceive myself, and thought that if I turned back from fear of losing my way that was all right, that was a valid excuse. But other fears—the shadows of the night, the animals,—were foolish fears. I could not allow myself such luxuries. If anything, the beast ought to fear me, for I had nothing to lose this time. And then what beasts? When I set out again I was convinced that I would not admit to myself that I was afraid, but in a few minutes I decided that I could not fool myself to that extent and press on with such a perilous undertaking. My nerves were taut and leapt at every little rustle; I found that I was walking along revolver in hand pretending that I only wanted to make certain that it was loaded.

Half an hour later I met a mule. It was a white mule and was lying stretched out with its belly in the air, but I could smell no stench. I drew near and the mule turned its head and looked at me, then rose lazily to its four feet and went off. It was a white mule, not a yellowish one, a supply mule; it still had the chain round its neck and dragged it along the path.

Perhaps there was some camp in the neighbourhood? But then they would have tied the mule to the picket line or to a tree. No, it had no saddle and walked with difficulty, free at last, although near its death. Perhaps they had left it on some other path and the soldier had not been able to shoot it through the ear nor to cut off the hoof with its number on it so as to put in a return for its death. He had left it dying and the mule was now standing in my path and looking at me, fearing that I wanted to disturb the peace it had won at the price of toil and sickness.

"Come on," I said to it, "we'll go along together." I was happy to have found a companion, a companion from Italy, like me, and who, like myself, perhaps wanted to return there. It followed me tamely, but when I tried to make it carry the pack it went off at a trot and then stopped to look at me, uncertain whether to go on or no.

I caught up with it and tied the pack on to its back with the cord. Then it turned round and set off for the river again at a lively pace, trotting along; I followed behind barely able to hold it back. It was carrying off all my things and all the money, determined not to listen to my calls. With an effort I caught up with it and seized it by the tail; it pulled me along in spite of everything and I had to let go in order not to fall. Then it stopped to gnaw the bark of a tree, but as soon as I attempted to approach it fled, still trailing its chain on the path. It went against the grain to kill it and I had to follow it as far as the bush, cursing. At last it allowed itself to be caught by the chain and I was able to recover my things, but by now my energy had been used up, and, tired, I lay down to rest; the mule grazed and watched over me, tired, too.

I would not go up the tributary again that day. The sun was already sinking, and the melancholy of the evening was forecast, the light draining from the mountains. "I will never get out of this valley," I thought. "No one wants me to get out of this valley." My thoughts went to her, full of longing, and in order to assuage my sorrow I re-read her last letter, then the others, but by now the water of the river had washed away the ink and in many places I could no longer decipher the words. I thought that one day my tears would complete the process, because these pages were all that remained to me of her.

I took the road towards the torrent again and the mule followed me, keeping at a distance. The sun was setting when I arrived in front of Johannes' hut.

"Good evening, Johannes," I said.

"Good evening, lieutenant," he answered.

"I am very tired," I said, "and I will stop here a while."

The old man did not reply and went on mixing flour on the stone. He was mixing it without haste adding water from an old tin; and when he had made a repugnant soft dough he threw in an oval stone he had been heating in the fire and wrapped it up. He put the dough near the fire and waited.

I sat in a corner of the clearing and looked at Johannes who was watching his bread. When the bread was cooked Johannes took it from the fire, opened it like a fruit and let it cool, then slowly began to eat some, stopping every so often to look towards the table-land, or towards the river, without ever directing a glance at me.

2

At dawn I wakened suddenly, as the birds perhaps do, from a dreamless sleep. It was the first night after so many months that I had not dreamt, and all the fatigue of the previous days seemed to have vanished; but I still had a confused memory that became clear when I saw the huts still plunged in shadow. And the mule wandering uncertainly about the clearing, now nosing at the grass and now at the grave mound. It was still trailing its chain with a noise like a bundle of keys carried along a corridor. I did not know yet whether it was the corridor of a convent or of a prison. "Damn the mule," I thought.

My only anxiety was to leave the village and set out again, but torpor paralysed me. I was lying on my blanket in the same position as when I had gone to bed, my head on my pack, my hand on my belt, near the remains of the fire on which I had heated the coffee the evening before. I felt ready, but when I tried to rise I could scarcely move; my limbs refused.

And yet I had to go, to climb up the side of the tributary to get back to A. before sunset. When the mule came up and stood looking at me I was on my feet in a bound. I prepared my things and shouldered the pack; I would leave the beast to its obvious fate, determined to rely on myself alone. It would have been of some use to me if it had not been so bad in harness and if its mishaps had not made it more stubborn. It had already made me lose a day, and if it were to fall where the path was bad, I would risk losing my pack. And I would also have to see to its fodder; and it was difficult enough for me to provide my own.

Seeing that Johannes was awake I went over to his hut to greet him. When I moved my legs they felt like lead, but the march would limber them up and I could not allow myself a longer rest without arousing the suspicions of that insolent old man. He must already suspect something because my bearing was already that of a fugitive and no longer that of an officer.

"Goodbye, Johannes," I said. I saw that Johannes was rising from his couch; then the red earth of the clearing came up to meet me, the sky disappeared and a second later my face was in the dust. I shut my eyes and remained thus a long time. When I came to myself the sun had already risen and flies were drinking at my eyes. I was unable to chase them away; I thought intensely of chasing them away, but my hand refused to carry out the brief movement. A few paces away there was Johannes, squatting on his heels, impassive, sipping something from the tin that served him as a glass. He was sipping and looking about him; he had not noticed that I had opened my eyes.

Then we remained in silence for some minutes, I incapable of speech, he looking at me without curiosity, his hands leaning on his long stick, smoothing the cane with the forefinger of his right hand with an unvarying movement. Seeing that I was opening my eyes, he rose and made a sign to me to wait and went off towards the path. He walked with a stoop, with sunk shoulders. He was going away and I was incapable of movement; he had already disappeared beyond the edge of the clearing when I succeeded in giving a cry. The cry emerged unexpectedly, strangled, but Johannes could not have heard it; only the mule had heard it and turned its head towards me, dragging its chain along the gloomy corridor. I tried to move and it was only then that I saw Johannes' head reappearing over the edge of the clearing, then slowly his whole body. He was coming back.

Seeing that I was in a state of collapse he asked if I wanted anything. I had already forgotten the harsh, guttural sound of his voice and to hear it again did not comfort me. I made him a sign to stay. A little later I asked: "Where were you going?"

"Up there," and he pointed to the table-land. He was going to ask for help, he did not want to have trouble. I made a sign that he must not go away and then he obeyed. He put his stick in his hut, took off his toga and once more asked me if I wanted anything. I wanted nothing. I only wanted him not to go away, and when he went off again with an empty petrol tin he had to tell me several times over that he was going to get water from the river and would come back at once.

"Johannes," I said when I saw him reappear, "I must stay here."

"Until tomorrow, lieutenant?" he asked.

"Yes, until tomorrow." "Tomorrow I will be better," I thought, "and will leave this place; I will not sleep another night beside these corpses and will not see the bark of these trees nor the sky shut in by the lips of the valley."

Drops of water streamed from the tin on to Johannes' feet. He said nothing and I did not dare to look at him, I looked at his dusty feet and the water that washed them. At last he said: "You have the right to stay," and he said it shortly but he did not mean to be discourteous. He recognised my right. "Thank you," I said.

Johannes went off; a little later he came back and, sitting on his heels once more, asked me almost with solicitude: "Are you hungry, lieutenant?"

I was hungry, or at least extremely languid, but I answered no. The biscuits and the cheese, even if reduced to a pulp by their bath in the river, were still preferable to his badly kneaded bread cooked among the earth of that clearing. I would eat later so as not to offend by too open a refusal. However he prepared a very strong coffee and when I had drunk it I felt better. "It's only a passing indisposition," I said, "and I had better set off on my way." Instead I fell asleep. But such was my fear that the old man would take advantage of my sleep, and go away, that I called him several times, waking with a start; and he always came to reassure me.

"You mustn't go away," I said to him.

"But you are ill," he answered. And added: "If I don't go it will be my fault." Then I took his hand, I was overcome, and almost wailing I repeated: "You mustn't go away." He looked at me without understanding, or pretending not to understand why I confessed, not daring even to draw back his hand, which was dry and rough like a piece of iron eaten by rust, and I added: "No one must know I am here."

He went off towards his hut scarcely turning to look at me, still more severe, because he had understood and must not pretend any more, and I had dealt his convictions a mortal blow. But he was satisfied. This was how he would continue to look at me in the days that followed.

After the third day I felt well, but had no desire to set out again. The road to Massaua seemed interminable, and the more I studied the stages of the journey the more I became convinced that I could not face even a couple of them in this condition without immediately feeling the effects. I must first get back my strength, and this, after all, was the best place, even if everything concurred to make it gloomy. Perhaps with time I would even get used to Johannes.

That day the old man was working on some poles for a new bed and asked me—an unusual attention—how I was; and in a voice I had not heard before. It was a more friendly voice; I might even have caught a note of sympathy in it if his eyes had shared the weak smile that accompanied his words. No, the eyes of Johannes still remained too open and immobile when they looked at me. He always seemed to be surprised to see me. All through that day I could not get out of my mind that the old man was planning something against me. I remembered the words of the smuggler: "They're not a people that get fond of you," and I translated them: "They are a treacherous race." But I could not expect Johannes to shower me with attentions; and I had made up my mind not to spoil my days of rest by a thousand and one suspicions. I had put myself in the old man's hands, and if he betrayed me it was a sign that I was asking too much of things. Yet there was some comfort in the thought that by delivering myself into the hands of my executioner I was foiling the plot. It was a dangerous move, but it might succeed. Compared to the risks I would have to face if I left the village at once, the risk of denunciation was preferable. The hill commanded the path and if a patrol came I would have time to hide. There were trees everywhere and there was the path leading to the tributary. Then if Johannes invented an excuse for going away I would go away, too, mounting the tributary, and covering my tracks. In fact I told Johannes that I would have to make for the plains on the borders of the Sudan and he appeared to believe me. He knew the road to the plain and I kept him talking while I made notes. I interrogated him about the tribes of the plain and he was full of information, so that at the end of our long talk he had no doubt that I really wanted to make for these parts. I also asked him if he had recently been on the table-land.

"No," he answered. Now he no longer called me lieutenant and for the first time I did not have the heart to point it out to him. "And your pension? Don't you want to draw it?"

"I go every three months," he replied.

"And that is when you buy the salt, the flour and . . ." What else could he buy?

"Yes," he answered without taking his eyes off his work. He was working slowly, pointing the poles with his knife, but breaking off frequently to look at the clearing and almost forgetting my presence and his work. They were sure to be poles for a new couch; then, counting them, I noticed that there were too many of them, perhaps he wanted a very comfortable bed or to replace some pole in the hut.

Sometimes he remained with the knife in his raised hand, but his eyes no longer saw farther than beyond his fire, or the first tree or the mound in the middle of the clearing. When he began to hack with his knife again—and his slowness irritated me because he often did not even succeed in scratching the wood of the pole—he seemed to be doing it only in order to chase away some unpleasant thought that immediately laid hold of him again. Sometimes he came to tell me more about places in the plain, pleased if he saw me take my note-book and jot them down. Johannes, too, I suppose, did not know the meaning of time, and in these parts the seasons barely alter the hue of the atmosphere; and so he lived through a single season without ever asking himself whether one day it would come to an end.

On the fourth day I wanted to shave, and I had already lathered my cheeks—and Johannes was watching me because the operation must seem to him to be a clear sign of my departure—when I decided that I would disguise myself by letting my beard grow. I would need to have a different face, and in a week I could have one. "An officer with his chin adorned by however light a growth," I thought, "passes for a man on good terms with society." The carabinieri would hesitate before asking for my papers, saying: "It can't be him." Because a beard calls for that daily care and the lack of imagination which a fugitive does not possess and cannot afford. A chestnut beard, two light eyes, that was more than enough to puzzle an ordinary police agent. "Here's for the beard then," I concluded, and when I removed the soap from my cheeks Johannes shook his head and sighed.

3

My strength was returning, but slowly, owing to lack of food. When Johannes saw that I had finished my provisions and was searching my pack and muttering, he came and offered me part of his bread and I accepted. But it was so tasteless that I could scarcely swallow it; and then I remembered that in my pack I had a packet of salt; I ran to fetch it and offered it to Johannes in exchange. He accepted it without thanking me, as an act of homage due to him, then suddenly put his tongue into the packet and appeared satisfied; but he did not favour me with a glance. He put the packet in his hut and I sat looking at him, already repenting my childish and impulsive gesture, which had not even been appreciated. I asked myself how I would get more salt. Johannes, like all his kin, was bound to consider it the most precious of minerals, preferable to money and—now that the war was over—to cartridges. I had given him a treasure without obtaining a glance in return. The only card I could have used against him I had thrown away; and now Johannes would go on giving me a portion of his bread every day, and I would not even be able to ask him for the use of "my salt" just because I had made him a present of it.

Towards evening, after a longer absence than usual, Johannes came back to the village and, passing in front of me, stooped slightly to give me something—two eggs, which I sucked at once. They were very fresh indeed. I asked him if he could give me them every day, I was willing to pay him any amount. He replied that he would try, and in fact the next day he had two more eggs, but not even one on the succeeding days; and when I pointed out to Johannes that I would really pay any sum if only I had some more he shrugged, and cut me short with an ugly muttering. I clenched my jaws so as not to give way to the temptation to strike him and went off in a state of dejection, cursing the apathy that tied my hands and put me more and more in the power of the old man and his insolence. Now I could no longer regain my ground, and I consoled myself by saying that my departure would put an end to all the humiliations. Sometimes I was seized by anger to such an extent that I would lay hold of a stick and come up to the old man beating my boots, ready to strike him full in the face if he gave the least sign of trouble. But then he pretended not to see me. And I wandered round him, impatiently, provoking him with sharp blows against the leather of my boots; until at last I threw the stick away or brought it across the back of the mule, talking at the top of my voice and showing that I was prepared to go to any lengths.

On the morning of the seventh day I found Johannes busy preparing something in his pot, and the rank smell of the chopped mess constricted my throat; but when Johannes invited me with a sign I could not refuse. I had to abate my hunger somehow. I have never wondered what animal furnished the flesh, the worst I have ever eaten, extremely tough and yet sometimes unexpectedly yielding, so much so that it melted in the mouth like fat and was just as difficult to swallow. Johannes had added to the concoction a very hot spice, obtained by grinding down certain damnable red peppers. All the morning he had done nothing else but grind down peppers on the stone, and now there they were in that concoction. Perhaps the old man expected me to refuse, or at least that I would be taken by surprise; instead I forced myself to eat calmly and to hide the nausea, and still more the tears, which the burning taste of the spice produced. I saw that I had won, because Johannes forgot to eat and spent his time watching me, to see the effect of the pepper in my face. I put all my pride into that task. And for the first time the eyes of Johannes betrayed curiosity, the curiosity of the dynamiter who is quite sure he has lit the fuse and would like to know why on earth the bomb does not explode. It was my first victory and I managed to exploit it by eating in silence. Johannes could not contain himself, and with a visible effort asked me if I liked the food. I replied that it was good, briefly, without adding anything further. Johannes began to eat again; I read unexpected disappointment on his face, and a little later he gave in. "Isn't it very highly spiced?" he asked hesitatingly.

"Spiced?" I looked at him with surprise, trying to see what he was referring to and then concluded: "It is exactly right." I can say that from that moment Johannes began to respect me, indeed to fear me, and I no longer had to go round him in circles beating my boots and talking at the top of my voice. When I looked at him he now confined himself to pretending not to see me, but he was no longer insolent, even if he deliberately avoided addressing me, perhaps in order not to be forced to call me by my rank.

But apart from Johannes and his stubbornness, which I felt that I was more and more in a position to deal with, my stay in the village did not appear as easy as it had originally. On the morning of the eighth day—perhaps at that moment the tramp was weighing anchor or saluting the city—I noticed that I had no more cigarettes and searched in vain with my finger in the empty packet. The stock from Massaua was finished. Or else Johannes had taken a part. I had a good look in my pack. Nothing there. Patiently I began to look in the clearing for the stub ends which I had thrown away with such improvidence, and collected a dozen. I was preparing to tear a blank page from the bible when I remembered that some of her letters were now illegible. These relics could no longer say anything to me, being so washed out and blurred—so they were there as simple sheets of paper which I must use. I said this to myself while I was making cigarette papers out of the first page, perhaps in order to calm the extremely sharp attack of remorse that hampered my hand. "Forgive me, darling," I said at last. Johannes turned round and looked at me as he always did when he heard me speak.

The airmail paper went very well; so I made the first cigarette, but towards evening I was back where I had started from. Now I would suffer from lack of tobacco, too; nor could Johannes give me any, since I had never seen him smoke. And if he did have tobacco? Would he not use it to humiliate me further?

The solitude increased my discomfort, adding to its sadness. I went up and down through the clearing; I did not dare to go down the hill for I calculated that the limits of my safety ran along its edge. The supply mule also went up and down; sometimes it trotted and appeared in better fettle, perhaps it would get well. This hypothesis contributed to my sadness. In fact my sympathy for the beast had originated in the spectacle of its condition. That day when it ran off carrying my things away I had hesitated to fire because I considered it to be already condemned, but now that it seemed to mean to pick up again I envied it, feeling that I was a thousand times worse off than it; for it was at least discovering the consolations of liberty.

I often sat under the shade of a tree looking towards the table-land and the valley, which changed colour from the grey of dawn to the violet of sunset. Perhaps because of the solitude and the sad thoughts which disturbed me the valley now seemed far bigger to me, at times even immense, and I reckoned that there must be at least seven kilometres from edge to edge. Even if I saw it to be vaster, the two sides appeared more and more clear and bright, and I could have counted the trees and the rocks on them. However much I strained my eyes I never saw any more trucks pass; and perhaps I could not see them because the road climbed up behind the spur which in fact shut in the view.

No one ever passed in the valley, and this seemed to me to be a good sign; the village was therefore absolutely right off the beaten track, at the end of a path that led nowhere. In the one direction there was the bridge, in the other the tributary. Perhaps there must be other huts a few kilometres away, and that explained how Johannes had found the eggs. But it must be a case of a village still more wretched—if that were possible—than Johannes'. Perhaps a village inhabited by a single hen. I smiled at the idea, promising myself to ask Johannes to take me there to make the acquaintance of my benefactress. But my thoughts were not always so happy. My mind—sluggish during the first days—now began to awaken and to picture my condition and the dangers that rendered it more precarious. Since my arrival at the village I had, on purpose, thought no more of my illness, although every so often this feigned indifference was suddenly upset. There still remained a dull dread which I could not conceal from myself. When the calm and rest made the days seem interminable I realised that despair would get the better of me if I did not satisfy all my curiosity by reading the whole book. I did not want to read it, it repelled me since it was a book in which was written, worse than in the eyes of Johannes or in the liveliness of the mule, my condemnation. However, overcoming my repugnance, I read and learned that the various disturbances afflicting me lately were all of them symptoms of the disease.

I read slowly, trying to understand the scientific terms, trying to arrive at a conclusion. The conclusion was that I could treat myself, there were a lot of treatments I could take, but none of them would cure me with certainty. I could even get better, there had been cases of complete cure; and ten years later wake up one morning with my hand slightly changed, a different colour, slightly different. And touching it I would once more feel that it did not belong to me. I could hope to lull the disease to sleep, not to kill it. There would remain the solitude.

I was reading when I saw Johannes; he, too, was sitting on the edge of the clearing. He was looking at the valley. It was the first time I had seen him engaged in looking at the valley, and I was surprised at it. I considered that Johannes was insensible to views and perhaps incapable of seeing them; his primitive eye was certainly not wont to coordinate the various elements so as to make of them a picture worthy of attention. He could see a tree, a hut, the table-land, the river, the bush, but certainly not consider them as part of a landscape. His vision was rudimentary, casting aside whatever was superfluous, and yet now he was looking at the valley, and I saw that he *saw* the whole of it and that his gaze halted slowly on *everything*, considering it. A painter would not have looked otherwise.

Sometimes he blinked his eyes or bent forward the upper part of his body, but immediately he would resume his immobility. I was so disturbed by it that when Johannes turned to look at me, shaking his head, I could not make the least gesture nor even take my gaze off him. Suddenly I thought that I must ask him about Mariam, if she was really ill. I took the opportunity when Johannes, turning his eyes, let them rest on me, considering my person, I suppose, as part of the landscape. I said that I liked the place and since he did not reply—yes, I had overestimated his aesthetic judgment—I asked him if he had lived here long.

"A year." And he made a gesture almost as if he wanted to cast behind him the memory of times which were now past and useless.

"And did many people live with you?"

"There were nine of us," he answered. I let a silence pass, to dispel his distrust, and then asked him nonchalantly: "How many women?"

Johannes did not take his eyes from the valley and answered: "Two."

I feared that if I did not speak right away Johannes would guess the aim of my conversation. He had charmed himself into look-ing at the valley and once more it seemed to me that he saw it. I asked: "Were they killed, too?"

"Yes, killed," he said.

"So neither of them was saved?"

"Neither of them."

I sat down close to Johannes, shaking my head to make him see my sympathy. Then hesitatingly, because I felt that he was lost in his unwonted contemplation, I said: "Elias often spoke to me of a young woman, of a certain Mariam." I said the name lightly as one says the name of a person one knows very well. And I added: "Wasn't she from this village?"

Johannes scarcely looked at me: "No," he said, "she was not from this village."

Why did he deny it so openly? Perhaps it hurt him to admit that Mariam had run off before the massacre without saying anything, to go up on to the table-land, towards the good life. I saw Johannes again in the streets of the little town, stopping on the threshold of the open houses, and I remembered his eyes searching in the darkness of the room. "Funny," I said, "I thought she was from this village because Elias always talked about her to me and ..."

"She was not from this village," Johannes interrupted with a voice so calm as to give no grounds for supposing it was a fiction. Had he told the truth? Perhaps his stay in the little town and his useless wandering through the open houses had had another aim—I could not imagine what, but a very different aim. Perhaps Elias often met Mariam—who lived in the village with the hen—and these meetings had been sufficient to make him believe what was not true. He had said that he was her brother? All right, but here they are all brothers. Don't the sisters come up to offer you their timid complicity? Or else Elias had lied, innocently, as children lie.

"Perhaps she was from a neighbouring village?" I asked.

"I don't know," replied Johannes. Suddenly he added: "I did not know her."

It was difficult to gather anything from the old man's gaze. He was looking at the valley now and his falsehood was giving me a new tranquillity. *I could even believe that Mariam had never existed.*

The old man did not even suspect what calm his falsehood, which almost absolved me, was giving me. If he denied the existence of Mariam I, too, could deny her. But her sores remained. Yet that Mariam had ceased to exist, although the old man's falsehood was obvious, was a relief to me. But I was back where I had started from. I would never know anything about her, except that she was afraid of crocodiles, that she often sang—and I could imagine her melancholy chants as she looked over the countryside—and that she laughed, too, as she had laughed that night in my arms. And I was staying in the village, serving my sentence for her, a step from her grave, near the other tombs, waiting—but in no hurry; twenty, thirty, sixty years—to have a grave of my own. For the time being I had a hut and my sores—that was the indispensable beginning.

I rose to my feet with a start. "Very well," I said aloud, "there remain the comforts of religion, *vivens iterum Deo.*" And I laughed. Johannes looked at me, frowning, without understanding.

"*Vivens iterum Deo,*" I repeated, shouting. Since Johannes continued to stare at me I went off towards some other trees and stood there looking at the valley darkening under its implacable sunset.

4

When night had fallen I waited in vain for sleep. The sky was thick with stars, and at intervals in that silence I heard—or seemed to hear—the rush of the tributary. The crocodile was there—perhaps very old, if it never ventured down to the bridge where the drivers sometimes bathed. Seen from above it could look like a rotting trunk abandoning itself to the current, and instead it was a crocodile that knew the history of that valley and even a little of the story of the world, because the river had dug away for centuries before its eyes. "In any case," I thought, "it will outlive me." Who knew if one day I would not go to offer it my sores?

There, I would never manage to overcome my horror of the night in this country when the moon seems to roll through the dark and below me I heard hell yawn in the howls of the wild beasts. I had patched up one of the huts—I wondered if it were Mariam's—had put my pack in it, but I stayed there against my will. In front of the entrance, almost from an invincible super-stition, I kept the fire burning until the dawn. I told myself that it would be useful if I wanted to prepare some coffee, but it was merely fear that counselled me to have that fire. Fear of Jo-hannes, too. And of that grave which I had always before my eyes. It was the first thing I saw on waking.

So I had got myself a hut, but I did not yet dare to sleep in it; I preferred to go to bed in the open, although the night in these parts did not ever tempt one to stay outside. It was a different sky, and the light was simply night, closed in and without a chink, without the barking of dogs, without the comforting noises of life continuing, the snatch of song from the drunk on his way home, the screech of the tram. Only the hyena and the jackals, hysterical and very distant, as if they wanted to increase the solitude with their voices, offering it something to set against it, a measure. Sometimes the terrifying sobbing of a night bird alighted by chance in the trees of the clearing and refusing to be chased away. But the darkness was preferable to the hut, which might have worse surprises in store for me. That night I lay down near the fire and lay looking at the stars; they were very bright, but they weighed upon me and were too numerous for me to be able to discover the constellations and recognise them.

I thought that this was the solitude that awaited me. This was the empty and implacable solitude, the night I would have to face since I had decided not to interrupt it. It did not frighten me. What frightened me more was the hope rising within me, timidly at first, more insolent every day, because it was the sign that I would suffer more once I was out of that valley where my disease went unnoticed. It frightened me to think that I wanted to survive at any cost, and that I was already laying the blame for this decision on her, on my wife. Yes, the blame: I did not know what else to call it. I had decided to live for her, magnanimously; I loved and wanted to see her again; but I was no longer sure— now that the first impulse to rejoin her had died down—that she wanted to live with me, go on loving me. As for asking her for protection, with each day I was led more and more to think that it was only childish fear that had suggested it to me. Was I not perhaps getting the cards mixed up, was I not confusing my will to live with the need to see her and be near her? She was not my aim at all, but a point of reference, the most familiar, and there-fore it came naturally to me to attribute to her an importance she did not possess. Now I wanted to involve her, in the name of a love I would do better to forbid myself instead of feeding it with the daily reading of her letters, or with memories of our life together—one year and then the parting—with the memory of a year seemingly packed with things done, with words spoken and heard, with gestures.

In my note-book I had noted the days of the year, each one in a little compartment, trying then to remember the events I marked down at the side. Not the big events, but those that fixed themselves in the memory from within—events one cannot eas-ily anchor to a day or an hour because we simply do not know that they are taking their place there and outstripping all the others with an intangible significance of their own. That parting at dawn, or her hand against the wall of the room. When had I seen that hand? There, I remembered the month but was still uncertain of the day. And I could not settle whether it was in August or September that she jumped into the water without taking off her clothes, beckoning to me to follow her.

And her photograph still smiled as if nothing had happened! I looked at it for a long time, for hours, until the image lost all definition and I could see only two eyes, a nose, a mouth; features that seemed to me to belong to a face already lost. Here, too, perhaps I was reversing the situation: she was alive and I tried to believe that she was dead to bring her back to me.

If I looked up from that piece of cardboard I saw Johannes making adjustments to his poles, and from the way in which he was using his knife, with unexpected anger, I gathered that he was passing judgment on me.

My vocabulary had grown very poor and would become poorer; a few words for all the actions that were allowed me. To eat, to sleep, to look, to hope. But, to eat with a stomach that rebels, to sleep with dreams more gloomy than waking, to look at things I could not touch, to hope for healing that would not come. All the other words cancelled for ever. Could I impose such a poor vocabulary on her who threw herself into the water without taking off her clothes and made me a sign to follow her? Could she sacrifice herself at my side, renouncing her sudden mad pranks, for which I loved her? Would I see her grow old and ugly beside me, trying to smile? Would I hear her humming, to make me believe in her calm? The years would be of three hundred and sixty-five days and three hundred and sixty-five nights, all to be lived through with open eyes; and I would not hear her sobs, stifled in her room, which I would never enter. What right had I to impose on her a prison more odious than my own?

She would come into my room and say: "Your hand is better today," or else: "I have brought you a nice book," or: "What if we were to consult another doctor?" That would be if everything went well. Then there was the hospital—if I ended up in a hospital—full of students who come now and again to have a look and smoke cigarettes to overcome their nausea and are still too young to feign polite indifference.

Twelve days had now passed since the steamer sailed, and at this moment she was re-reading my letter, pondering the reason for those desperate sentences. I had been a fool to write to her, and on this occasion, too, had confused my need for protection with her anxiety to have news. I had not written to her again and I would not be able to write for many days to come. And her old letters no longer gave me any comfort since I knew that they were addressed to someone else whom she knew, not to me, the unknown being. What would I have still in common with the young man who left Naples two years before and to whom she had waved through her tears, breathless, despairing, careless even of exposing her grief thus to a patriotic and noisy crowd? I had told her to have the garden put right, to get certain things and to sell others; and we wrote to each other of a child whom we were going to wait for and take forward with us into life, of a child who would have all our defects and our virtues, or else only our defects, seeing that it is experience that teaches us our virtues and it is useless to anticipate them.

Our union, proclaimed in a church, had been broken in the courtyard of another church at the sight of the hands of the two girls. Like a relentless creditor I would have to enforce the marriage contract, demand her assistance and force her to have some sort of pity on my misfortunes. I could not ask her to live with me. Or would I live in the garage, in the kennel, provided I could look at her through the window-panes?

While I was thinking these thoughts a noise made me spring to my feet, because by this time even the shadows frightened me. It was only the mule approaching, attracted by the fire or looking for company. It stretched itself out clumsily, and when I began to stroke its back it moved its head, rubbing it happily against the ground. It knew nothing of my suffering and left me alone. "My dear," I said to it, "things are not going at all well. In fact, give me some advice. I have done one thing and another in order to see her again, and where has it got me? To where I will not see her again. I have committed the most stupid and childish crimes to enter paradise, and now here I am in this kind of hell, asking myself whether I have done well or ill. I'm not crying over the past, but I should like to know if it is fair that mules should have to peg out where two paths join, when Africa is so big. There's something else I should like to know: all that I have done, did I do it for her or for myself? That's all I want to know."

The mule went on rubbing itself, and from Johannes' hut there came a low muttering, the muttering of a room-mate who has to get up at five in the morning and cannot understand the insomnia of others. I fell silent and lay beside the mule, leaning my head on its back.

She would not abandon me, that I could swear to, and would perhaps even find what to say to diminish the importance of what I had done and what I could no longer do. In her tranquillity I would even recover my innocence; but one day she would wake up unable to watch me go under with such excessive slowness. And then? Well, all our moments of happiness seemed absurd; I could see that they were the courtesies of the hangman who puts off time, talking about the weather to the condemned man, and asking pardon if he ties him too tight. There were moments which no longer belonged to me, and I must no longer recall them. It was no use remembering that beach, the first time we found that we loved each other, and the silk of her skin and the tired look of her eyes at dawn.

My desire to see her again was so humble that even these thoughts comforted me; however I took the note-book, tore out the pages where I had marked the days of that year and threw them into the fire. I watched the pages as they curled up, already repenting my resolution—I would draw the little compartments again, that was all—when, far off in the valley, I heard the sound of a truck. "Come on," I said to the mule, "let's go and have a look."

The distance made the noise seem no louder than Johannes' snoring. It was climbing up to the table-land just as a bluebottle always climbs up to the top of the window-pane to look for the way out. It was an insistent and well-defined noise, but not strong. I thought of the major, of my unsuccessful joke, of his ironical salute—which had, however, moved me. That was the noise of life; the truck was climbing and ignoring me and other trucks would climb towards the table-land and ignore me. They could not help me any more.

I reached the edge of the clearing and gazed into the darkness of the valley which drew barely any light from the vault of the sky. I could see nothing, and the noise went farther away until it disappeared. Then, on the hillside, I saw the light of the lamps of a truck climbing. Against the dark wall they seemed like a match struck by a nightwalker looking for the keyhole. The light moved slowly and climbed up the hillside, still searching, then turned the corner and disappeared. There remained only the noise as before, often growing so weak that it disappeared, then coming back stronger and, at times, almost close at hand. I heard the gears being changed. Then the noise trailed away, or rather disappeared suddenly. Perhaps the truck had reached the table-land and was now running towards the coast.

I was left alone without even the noise, and returned in haste to the hut. I could not sleep. I took my jacket from the pack and turned the pockets out to look for a few threads of tobacco among the debris. Instead, I found in the little pocket, two tickets for a cinema in Naples. We had gone there the evening before we parted.

Then the lump in my throat melted, and kissing those pieces of paper, most poignant of all my mementoes, I let the tears run down my face. A fit of trembling seized me and relieved me. She, too, that evening, in the darkness of the hall, had wept on my shoulder. I seized the jacket and held the sleeve to my mouth, kissing it, and stifling my sobs. It was a useless precaution, Johannes had wakened and was muttering to himself, in fact he had begun to speak in his own language and was sure to be cursing me because I had broken his sleep.

I got up, picked up a dry branch and walked over to his hut; Johannes went on speaking; I began to beat the stick against my boot. Johannes fell silent.

I threw away the branch, walked over to the fire and stretched myself face down on the jacket thinking of her.

The next day I decided that I must go away. I saw that these ten days had been sufficient to make a coward of me and make the journey to Massaua appear not only full of dangers but useless. Perhaps all the thoughts of the preceding night had been suggested to me by nothing more or less than cowardice, and if I stayed longer in that village I would always discover excuses for putting off my departure until I believed it to be impossible. I would say I could not leave *for her sake*, just as before I had said the opposite. The day I arrived at this conclusion all the crimes committed would have been committed in vain. I would have to stay in the village for ever; or else wait to be discovered there by a carabiniere patrol; or else force myself to the first post, up there on the edge of the table-land, and anticipate capture by giving myself up.

Since I rejected the latter hypothesis I had to consider the possibility of staying in the village. All right, I could not stay there. Johannes had already shown that he could not bear my presence; his surly behaviour on the previous night was meant only as a foretaste of what he had in reserve for the future, when neither the stick beaten against my boots nor the revolver would frighten him. I must go away; by staying I ran the risk of weakening myself to the point where I could not stand a single lap of the journey, and yet I knew that the first lap, the hardest, must be made in a single day. I decided that I would leave the following day; the sun was already high. I need not worry about the baggage, which was always ready; I would go off without even saying goodbye to Johannes, so as not to offer him a victory on a plate. I had surprised him by my contempt. "Perhaps," I thought, "my unexpected departure will deal him a blow, and he will be sorry that he forced me to it."

I unfolded the map and once more measured the distance from the village to A. Fifty kilometres as the crow flies—let's say sixty, in short, twelve hours' march at a good pace, giving oneself only an hour's rest: the whole day. Perhaps I would stick it, and arriving at A. would knock at the door of some hospitable house, and why not Rahabat's house with its gramophone? No, not Rahabat; the major might come in. However, one house is as good as another. I must only not give way to the temptation to walk up and down pretending to myself that I was not caught, and to the temptation—the very strong one—to jump on to a truck, saying: "They won't stop this particular one."

If I succeeded in not giving way to these two temptations I would reach Massaua. And I was already rejoicing, for the idea of seeing a house again, a street and someone who was not Johannes was going to my head. I paced up and down the clearing, happy, because once more I had overcome my depression, and felt the desire to fight rise within me. But how wretched the village seemed to me that day—completely inpermanent, already devoured by ants, and, when Johannes was dead, a jackals' lair. Perhaps they were waiting impatiently for the old man to die to settle down on that hill and exist in the glorious smell of decomposing corpses wafted to them from the remotest distances. "Yes," I said, "a real chance for these wonderful beasts, this odoriferous vantage-point, when this fellow Johannes decides to bury his insolence."

When I saw Johannes coming towards the hut with the usual tin brimming with water I could not contain myself and said I was leaving. I had the stick in my hand, the one I had beaten against my boots, and I waved it merrily, giving him the news as if a long-awaited telegram had authorised me to leave this hated spot. He walked on, bowing his head politely—the lesson of the night had had its effect—then went so far as to smile and turned, pointing towards the plain. I was consulting the map when I heard him behind me, and had to put it back in my pocket so that he would not see the route already traced from there to Massaua. But perhaps he could not read a map and did not even imagine that these blue and reddish marks meant the sea and the land—his land. He seemed very glad and began to tell me all he knew about the plain as he had in the first days. Counting on his nose with his fingers he listed the five points where I would find water if I decided to leave the river. He repeated the names of the spots which all began with the word *mai*—in these parts every well or spring is indicated by this word which in fact means water—and did not seem satisfied until I had noted them in my book. He repeated them and wanted me to repeat them after him, these names. And finally, to make sure that I remembered them, he began to interrogate me. And said "Mai . . . ?" persisting until I pronounced the name of the place correctly. Suddenly he finished by saying: "Pleasant journey." He said it without irony, which was foreign to him, and went off as if I were leaving that moment.

Immediately afterwards Johannes became once more the intolerable old man of the early days. Having completed what he conceived to be his duty—to show the road to the parting guest—he wanted to show me that he had forgotten nothing of the night before. Now, for example, he was walking up and down the clearing muttering and with his eyes on the ground looking for something—the stick I had beaten against my boots. When he had found it he took hold of it and broke it ostentatiously, throwing it on the fire, but without ceasing to mutter. This childish gesture made me smile. "Johannes' anger," I thought, "is as short as the time he has left to live. If he cannot refrain from certain foolish protests it means to say that he is a weak creature. It's better so—by breaking that stick he has got rid of his ill-will, in the manner of children who hit the corner of the table where they bumped their heads. Now he thinks he has won and the illusion will make him bearable for the whole day, for our last hours spent together." And yet as I said this I felt that Johannes was capable of the most calculated vendettas; the hardness of those eyes suggested that his ingenuous outburst served only to hide a treacherous manoeuvre. When I called him, he stood looking at me suspiciously, and when he saw that I was smiling he advanced timIdly. "Johannes," I said, "tomorrow morning I shall leave the village, but first I want to thank you, and I think you will be pleased to accept this." So saying I handed him a fifty-lire note.

He looked at it in amazement; it was perhaps the largest sum he had ever seen, and he made to hand it back, terrified. I had to place the note in his fingers, but he remained looking at me, incapable of grasping it, and after a little it fell to the ground. I laughed and picked up the note and once more handed it to

Johannes. But now he shook his head and held out the note to me as if he were rejecting the price of betrayal or of silence. I saw that he was agitated, overcome perhaps by the mirage of ownership; but he could not accept, he would never have dared. He took advantage of my astonishment to hurry off and hide in the hut from which he emerged only to cook his food.

This time he appeared more sullen than usual; he threw me glances filled with such deep hatred that I became more and more thankful that I had to leave him. I sought in vain to interpret the reason for his refusal, until I said to myself that I could look for it in the mound in the clearing—that is, in the fact that I was allied with those who had helped to fill it. That was it, his looks were the same as on the day when I had found him busy filling the grave. "He has not forgotten," I said, "and he will never forget. It is a fine thing for me to ask him to put aside his hatred at the sight of a bank-note when he will never have an opportunity to spend it because this miserable earth and a solitary hen and the wretched animal that provides his hashes suffice to sustain him. He is a wise man, and like all wise men he detests money because he is suspicious of its lure. He wants to avoid temptation. In this desert! Or he only wants to show that I am his conqueror but not his friend—a man who can sell him things but not give them to him."

So my offer offended Johannes profoundly. Throughout the day he avoided looking at me and addressing me, and when it was evening I saw him going off towards the tributary with his petrol can. "It is an unusual time to go to the river," I thought, but did not attach more importance to the matter than it deserved. Perhaps the mule—profiting by Johannes' inattention or distraction—had drunk the water and now the old man was going patiently to refill the tin. He would come back. He could not at that hour face the road to the table-land at the risk of finding himself lost at night in the bush. To while away the time of waiting I prepared for my last night in the village, and boiled all the coffee that remained to me so as to mix it with the water in my water-bottle. It would come in handy on the way. I also decided to lighten the pack of everything superfluous—but there was very little to throw away. Since the provisions had long been finished, I was left with a few underclothes, the blanket, the packet of letters, the Bible, toilet necessities and the money. I put a large piece of bread in as well—I could make it myself now, and Johannes had sold me part of his flour—and tied the straps.

An hour later—the sun had already set—Johannes had not returned. The mule—now that I thought of it—had also disappeared with Johannes; so they had left me alone. That evening the sky seemed to be veiled by a sudden murkiness; I would not even have starlight. I began to lose patience, and having gone a good way along the path I called loudly on Johannes—two, three, ten times. But no one replied apart from the melancholy night birds; they were already beginning—even before the jackals—to consider the village as their future dwelling, and attracted by the silence, were staking the first claims. No one answered, and then I went back to the village thinking that perhaps Johannes had returned in the meantime. I told myself that his absence was of no importance to me so long as it did not mean the denunciation I feared.

I spent a long time, sleepless, by the fire, with my shoulders leaning against the hut. I thought that Johannes had perhaps gone to the neighbouring village, the egg village, and had stayed there overtaken by nightfall. But when I thought it over I had to exclude that possibility. I remembered that Johannes had gone off with the petrol can—a sign that he wanted to fetch water, so he must have stayed at the river; but what doing? Why had he dragged the mule along with him if he had only to go to the river? Certainly not to make the lazy beast carry the container. Well then? But it's clear Johannes pretended to go to the stream and at this minute is trotting along the short cut; in fact has arrived at the post and is telling the story of an officer who has been hanging about his village for ten days and keeps on talking of going to the plains but never goes away. I began to curse the old man who had played his cards so as to make my flight impossible. I could not set out before the dawn, and at dawn the hill would already be watched by a patrol. I recognised the cunning of the primitive man who trusts to the night to set his traps. "Well," I said, "you deserve it." Bursting with anger I looked at my watch; but it still stood at six—it had stopped. "Here we are," I said. It was a gloomy omen and it increased my ill-temper.

Another theory came to trouble me. Perhaps Johannes was drowned. And the mule must have remained on the bank, surprised by the swift scene unfolded before its eyes, incapable of grasping its meaning, incapable of helping the poor old man.

I started to my feet and took a great brand from the fire. Lighting my way with it—I waved it to keep it alight—I went further along the path, shouting to keep up my courage; the shadows had grown terrifyingly and I found the path with difficulty. I kept calling the name of the old man, not because I hoped for an answer, but to frighten the animals, who were certainly in the habit of going to the river at that hour to drink. The path was descending; it became rough and plunged down into darkness. The brand lit up a few paces before me, but prevented me from seeing the valley and the watercourse. When I reckoned that I had gone down the path a good way I said that there was no point in going on, that Johannes could not have been drowned and that the mule had not stayed on the bank. I would have heard it neighing. There was no one down there; I could not catch the slightest rustle except that of the water against the branches.

Supposing the mule had been eaten by a crocodile? I had to make sure; I climbed farther down, and shortly felt that I was on the bank, but I could see nothing. Only the louder rushing of the water told me that I was on the bank. I waved the brand over my head and saw nothing, although I guessed where the water ran in the dark. I lowered it and discovered the traces of the mule's hooves, but no sign of a struggle and no sign of blood. There were some long traces on the sand as if made by a harrow, but regular ones, not disorderly. No sign of a struggle. I cheered up, but not for long; that meant that Johannes was on the table-land. "Johannes!" I called again, but only the rushing of the water answered; and then I ran back along the path, scrambling up it a little too quickly. A few hundred yards on I bumped into the petrol can. It was empty and almost hidden in a bush. So Johannes had got as far as this. I noticed that the path forked, and I went a few yards along the unknown path still calling the old man's name. After a few yards the path ended in a clearing much smaller than the one in the village. Still waving the brand I saw that the clearing was closed at the other end by a circular hut, plastered and covered with straw. It was a very well-made hut, but completely abandoned. There was no door, and I did not dare to enter; I merely called Johannes again for some time, and then went back towards the clearing and reached it when the brand was out, and the fire, too. There were not even any embers, and I had to relight it anew. Within myself I cursed the old man for disappearing without a word to me, thus forestalling what I had intended to do myself—that is, to go away at dawn without saying goodbye.

"Try to sleep now," I said. There is no need to add that I did not succeed and lay awake alive to every noise, with my revolver in my hands, ready to fire at the shadows, at all shadows. Before my eyes was the mound, I had to look at it because I would never have dared to turn my back to it. I felt so exposed that I went into the hut, but immediately left it, still more uneasy, telling myself that after all I preferred to see, I wanted to see. And then thought of the curiosity that kills soldiers in battle when fear makes them put up their heads because they want to see everything, at least to see the enemy, not to feel him there in front of them without being able to see him. I called Johannes again, shouting until my throat refused to utter the least cry or even the least rattle. I sat leaning against the hut bathed in sweat from head to foot, and several times the revolver slipped from my hands. I picked it up again and finally left it on the ground, incapable of holding it. I felt that it was useless.

I was sitting thus, completely bemused, when to comfort me there stole an almost imperceptible gentle perfume. I imagine the sweat had revived her perfume on the sleeve of the tunic, the perfume left there when she wept on my shoulder in the dark cinema. It was a gentle, distant perfume, perhaps that of cyclamen, although I do not know the perfume of that flower. But its gentleness was such that the first association was an image of cyclamen, of a delicate bunch of cyclamens. But it was distant and I wondered if the valley might contain yet one more surprise in the shape of a bed of these delicate flowers. I sniffed at the tunic, but that was not where it came from. I did not remember her using such a perfume, so naive and so faint. Yet it gave me heart, taking me back to my childhood years. Where had I smelt that perfume? It was no longer a question of the ignoble odour that had overwhelmed me on other occasions but had not returned to perturb me. No, this was gentle and elusive, although I should still put it down to the supper I had missed.

Very soon the perfume disappeared and I remained alone. I feared I would be afraid, but what had I to be afraid of? There was no reason for fear, I kept telling myself. I stared into the dark and saw nothing: therefore I must not be afraid. Nothing appeared, not even the slightest shadow, and the tops of the trees did not stand out against the vault of the sky: the darkness was total and uniform. I could have said that I was blindfolded if my eyes had not distinguished depth in that darkness. And I did not hear the slightest sound, not even the nibbling of a mouse or the sigh of a mole. That night not even the jackals were howling, and the laughter of the hyena was long in beginning. "Is it possible?" I said. "Are there no more corpses in this valley? Are cyclamens flowering in their stead?" Even the birds were sleeping, none of them was grumbling or sobbing, and not even the ticking of the watch broke the silence. I wound it. Some grain of sand must surely have filtered into the works, because it was not going. I gazed at the embers of the fire, but the surrounding darkness was too much and I could not have left the hut, granted that I had managed to rise to my feet; I felt that the clearing would have thrust me back. Then I tried to laugh at my fear, I took a stick and began to beat it against the hut, singing. Then I recited aloud something which I had learned during my first years at school—a French rhyme of which the first line was: *"Une montre à moi? Quel bonheur!"* I was amazed that I still knew it, and kept on repeating it over and over again until the verses appeared meaningless to me.

But I had succeeded in calming myself, and no longer trembled. All through the night I repeated that poetry, and only at dawn noticed that I had a fever and was perhaps delirious. It was useless to think of setting out, the pack was ready but I would not have been capable even of lifting it. I cursed my fear, now that the shadows were vanishing and the clearing was reappearing, and I cursed Johannes. In fact I was busy cursing him when I saw him on the back of the mule coming from the path that led to the tributary. I could not restrain myself, I ran to meet him and saw that he was smoking a cigarette.

I was so disturbed at this that I asked no questions. Nor did Johannes, but barely greeted me, went into his hut and came out shortly afterwards to light the fire and prepare some beverage for himself in the tin. He seemed in the best of humours, speaking often to the mule and even giving it a piece of bread.

He had brought some eggs and a little sack of flour—perhaps he had been to the village, and there must be a path I did not know which led there. But that cigarette? He had asked for it from some soldier, or else they had given it to him in the same village—unless it was a question of a mere stub-end jealously preserved. From the way in which he held the cigarette between his lips it was clear that it was the first time. He was wasting it! When he had finished he ostentatiouly threw the fag-end towards me, but I do not think he meant to do it on purpose. Yet I ground down the butt-end in a rage, and with even more rage stormed at my puerile gesture. "Watch out," I said, "you are hitting the leg of the table."

5

Now I preferred to sleep by day and stay awake at night. I fell asleep towards dawn and my sleep lasted until the late afternoon. I slept in the hut, and to the voices I heard in the confused dreams of the midday heat there were joined the real voices of Johannes and the mule. From the time that I shut myself in the hut until I came out the old man talked steadily—it was his way of keeping himself company. At times, with unexpected coquetry, he spoke my language; he did not say anything very important, for the most part limiting himself to describing what he was doing at the moment. For example he would say: "Johannes is now taking the water and putting it on the fire," or else: "Now I will begin to cut the poles," and so on—brief sentences which reached me like welcome messages because they meant that Johannes had not gone away and that all was in order in the clearing.

At times, on the other hand, he spoke rapidly in his own language, and I was certain that he was addressing himself to the mule, although I found it difficult to imagine the gist of his speeches. I know that he spoke to the mule; and almost always his words ended with the noise of a pole hitting the animal's back, but they were friendly blows followed immediately by the mule's trotting to the far end of the clearing and then back again. And Johannes began over again. But this chatter did not annoy me, or at least I had learned to appreciate it; and as I dozed I often made guesses at what Johannes was doing or saying and never made a mistake. I should add that Johannes showed himself to be sensible of my forebearance—the fact that he did not see me on the clearing any more from morning to evening immersed in my painful thoughts certainly made my presence in the village more acceptable to him. A tacit truce had been established between us—I refrained from threatening him or asserting my authority; he had laid aside his insolence. If I addressed him he answered politely, and it was often he who began the conversation. In fact after that night he had offered to get eggs and flour for me for a ridiculous sum, and I—mindful of the first refusal—had not attempted to make him accept more.

On the afternoon of the twelfth day I went away from the clearing towards the circular hut I had caught sight of along the path leading to the tributary. Johannes watched me go away without saying anything, and shortly afterwards I was in front of the hut. It seemed better constructed than the others in the clearing. To enter it one had to climb up three steps of beaten earth. The floor was not on a level with the path and that was sufficient to keep out roaming animals or the ants which abounded there. The walls, thin but covered with whitewash, and the conical roof of straw made the hut look like a shooting lodge. The door was missing, but I suppose they must have taken it away, because the hinges were still there. The interior was circular, too; it measured perhaps six yards in diameter and seemed to be still clean; but it did not contain any furniture—not even of a rudimentary kind. On the floor there were some dusty pieces of pottery and that was all—no bed and not even a stool. I was wondering how on earth Johannes had not preferred this hut to the others in the clearing: it offered many advantages, apart from the fact that it was situated near the river—you had only to go down the steep path to find yourself on the bank. And the constant shade of the trees surrounding the little square—they were thick green trees—made even the interior dark; an inestimable advantage this in a spot where the sun never grants a truce.

I understood Johannes' reluctance better when, looking closer, I found above the door a stain, or something that looked like a picture. I lit a match and held it above my head; yes, it was a picture, a very simple one and a very common one in these parts—an archangel killing a dragon. The painter had done his best, but not being very sure, I suppose, what a dragon was, had given it the form of a crocodile. So Johannes had not lived in that hut because it was really a church or a votive chapel. But there was no trace of an altar, and nothing that could lead one to consider the place sacred except the picture. At last I came to the conclusion that it was not a church or a chapel—the picture would, in that case, have been in front of the door, visible from the outside as well.

I gave a last look at the archangel and was just going to step out when Johannes appeared on the threshold. He was smiling at me, glad that I should admire the hut, which to him must seem a wonderful structure. He pointed to the walls, he rapped them with his knuckles to let me hear that they gave out a noise, and meantime assured himself that everything was in order inside—I mean to say that he looked round with the attention of a servant showing the guest his room. Perhaps he wanted me to come and live there so as not to have me in his way all day. Not knowing how to respond to his enthusiasm, I praised the way it had been built and asked why he did not live in it. He answered that the hut was not his; and this was certainly the answer I least expected. I had by now lost the concept of property, and had never wondered if the African huts belonged to someone or whether they were provided by nature, included in the landscape, permanent properties at the disposal of us transitory mortals. From that I deduced that I was occupying my own hut illegally—in fact it had always seemed to me superfluous to ask Johannes for permission to occupy it. I told him smiling what I was thinking, and Johannes laughed heartily. No, I could stay in the hut, of course I could stay! But then why did he make such subtle distinctions? Why was it all right in the one hut and not in this? "Johannes," I said, "could I come and live in this hut?" He seemed annoyed at the question and answered that it was not his and he could not dispose of it. Of course I could move into it if I thought necessary, I had every right to, but he could not dispose of it. "Whose hut is it?" I asked. "Whose can it be," I thought, "if not the priest's—the one I saw in the bush along with Johannes? That's something that would explain the presence of this wretched painting."

Johannes hesitated, then said that it belonged to someone who was no longer in the village and would perhaps come back. And as he said these words he looked at me fixedly, bringing his head—or so it seemed to me—towards me. All right, I thought, it is Mariam's hut. "And this person," I asked, "lived alone?" He said yes. Why did this person live alone? This Johannes did not know or did not wish to say. No, he did not wish to say.

I climbed the steps again and lit another match to have a last look at the picture. Under the crocodile, this time, I found a small scroll with some words traced in Coptic script. "What does this mean?" I asked. The old man took the match-box from my hand, lit a couple, read it over, half-closed his eyes and translated laboriously. I did not wholly understand and had to make him repeat the words, and finally understood only too well; and at that moment I knew that this was my hut and that I would live there for ever.

At this thought such despair overcame me that I ran back to the clearing, and that miserable, abominable clearing seemed to me a marvellous sunbathed garden. The presence of the mule, the light that played on the trees and etched the distant mountains and the edge of the table-land, making them seem close at hand, the patched and rickety huts, the grass-grown mound, Johannes' crackling fire and the smoking pots—in short everything seemed to me to sing the praises of life. Never did a castaway on his raft, waking after nights of uneasy seas on the sands of a beach among ladies and their escorts, among doctors and photographers urgently summoned, experience so delightful a sensation of coming back to life as I did in that clearing. No, I would never leave the village to retire to the sinister hut that awaited me. When the mule passed within range of me I gave its nose a long caress; and my tears prevented me from seeing what Johannes was doing. Nothing out of the ordinary—he was whittling his poles.

"No one can stop me from staying here," I said to the mule, and, gratified by my caresses, it rubbed itself against my shoulder. So as not to give way to depression I decided to prepare my breakfast and began to make a flour paste. But shortly, unable to resist, I ran to Johannes: "Who is it that used to live in that hut?"

Johannes looked at me, pursing his lips, and stopped hacking at the wood. And seeing that he hesitated, I repeated the question once, twice, three times. I waved my doughy hands under his nose, ready to slap him if he did not reply. "Whose is that hut?" I shouted at last.

And Johannes replied: "A priest's."

My anger suddenly boiled over: "And where is he now?"

Johannes looked really surprised that I did not know where the priest was. Then with the hand that held the knife he said: "There," and pointed to the mound.

When he had taken up his work again I went back to mix the flour and looked at the mound—a slight hope was buoying me up, but I suddenly remembered what Johannes had said: that the person would come back. There, he had contradicted himself. He had lied so as not to have to admit the existence of Mariam. Or else he admitted that I was leprous and that that hut belonged to me by right but did not wish to admit the existence of Mariam.

"Johannes," I said, "when will he come back?"

He looked at me smiling, shook his head and said that he did not know himself, that no one could tell. And I was back where I had started, always back where I had started.

6

I marked the days with my pen-knife on the pole of the hut—there were eighteen notches. Another six notches marked the days passed since the beginning of my leave, and when there were forty-six notches—because over and above the month I counted the days of the hypothetical voyage to Italy, there and back—I would have to consider myself a deserter—another charge. But before that day I would really leave the village for Massaua, where no tramp skipper would deny me a passage now that I had so much money at my disposal. I counted it often; there were seventy thousand lire, and I kept them in the pack well shut up among my toilet things to prevent any mouse—I had seen a lot of big ones wandering about the hut—from eating them. I did not trust the supply mule either—it was always ready to eat something or other.

The supply mule was getting fat, obviously as a result of the free life it now led. It was no longer the moribund beast I had met on the path three weeks before—I saw that it was livelier, always busy swishing its flanks vigorously with its yellowish tail. I had taken off its chain a long time ago; now it even kept its neck erect and the coat began to grow shiny and the skin to stretch— the opposite case to mine, for I felt that I was growing thinner. It was a curious animal and I believe that it considered me to be an intruder, even more strongly than Johannes, with whom it had now succeeded in establishing a prudent degree of cordiality. When Johannes went down to the stream with his petrol can the mule followed him. It happened sometimes that Johannes went off without telling it—and I believe he did it out of vanity— and at once the beast struck up a clumsy trot, disappearing among the trees in the footsteps of its host, deaf to my calls. I suppose that Johannes provided it with food, hence this unbounded affection.

When Johannes took up his never-ending task of whittling poles, the mule would stop eating bark and go and watch, until finally it became too inquisitive, and Johannes would chase it off with the usual well-aimed blow on the back. Yet they liked each other, and more than once I was disturbed by an inexplicable feeling very akin to jealousy. Once the mule pushed its distrust of me so far as to refuse a piece of bread I offered it and immediately afterwards took a beating from the old man with complete docility. So thinking that its soldier must have accustomed it to such treatment, one day I tried beating it, too; but I was forced to admit that it might easily turn nasty. So I was surprised when, on the afternoon of the twenty-first day, the mule came to rub itself against my shoulder and lay down near the hut, paying no attention to Johannes who muttered words certainly incomprehensible to it.

I was tired of looking at the valley from the edge of the clearing. I decided that day to venture as far as the torrent and perhaps as far as the short cut, or perhaps even as far as the road, to see a truck—just to see it. I made a sign to the mule to get up, took my blanket, arranged it on the animal's back, and improvised reins with the chain and the cord. The mule let me do what I liked and finally took me on its back—accepting my suggestion of a stroll. In fact it looked as if it had wanted to ask for one. It walked quickly and only every so often halted to pull up some bush less dry than the others. Yet when I arrived at the torrent I was already tired of the walk, and beginning to see its dangers. I could not trust either the mule or my nostalgia for the roads where the trucks ran. I got down from the mule and it drank at a pool, the same in which Mariam had washed herself that day.

Every time my thoughts turned to Mariam I had to suppress a qualm of regret. I had gone as far, one day, as to congratulate myself on having killed her, thus sparing her the fate of the other inhabitants of the village; now I reproached myself for even that posthumous pity. "And then," I said, "they would not have killed her. She, too, would have gone with Elias and with the old man of the tribe to the table-land that day, since the old man had not gone to the little town merely to look for her. She would have gone there, too. If he had gone there solely for her the young men would not have played and danced that morning as they passed through the bush. "So," I said, "let us strike out the second proposition and say simply that I am glad I killed her. She had already killed me, and but for that ill-omened—or rather fortunate—beast her crime would have gone unpunished."

So I was glad I had killed her. And I no longer remembered the long lament that had escaped from her when I took aim, that heart-broken lament torn from her by fear and incredulity.

I went up to the tomb and barely recognised it; the wind had levelled the ground and carried away some of the bushes. No suspicious odour. I recognised it by the stones. In front of these stones all my hatred vanished and I found myself remembering the various moments of that day, her soft and elusive body, swelling and then dwindling in my arms, the thick blood beating in her throat and breast. And the hand laid modestly on her lips when I made her laugh at my drawings. From that blood and that hand had come all my misfortunes, and others would yet come—how many I could not imagine.

I saw her coming along the path, smiling and distant, and I even felt that she was innocent. Then I sought in my memory to find how else I could have caught the infection, but found no other way. Mariam had been the first and the last. I had not touched any native clothing except her dress, the dress I had accurately wrapped round the scratch, and I had been only twice in that woman Rahabat's house as a harmless visitor; and it was a house inhabited by healthy and even clean persons; yet beside her grave I could not succeed in dispelling the suspicion that Mariam was innocent—although everything accused her—and thus in dispelling the hope that my illness was imaginary. If Johannes had only spoken! But I no longer hoped for anything from that old man. And then, weren't there my blotches, my sore; wasn't there one hut better than the others and a verse which an unknown hand had dedicated to me, reminding me that I still lived in God. "Come," I said, "your doubts are too unbridled altogether," and I sat down near the tomb.

Although I sniffed I could smell nothing. No—the sweetish stenches that once had tormented me had been solely a product of my unsettled imagination. There was no vendetta on the part of Mariam because my crime did not exist. We must forgive one another. She was dead, I was spending my leave in that filthy valley—the leave for the sake of which I had put her out of her agony; if I am not mistaken, that was the essence of her vendetta. She had added the sores, the hut she had lived in; undoubtedly a better hut than the others.

"Dear Mariam," I said, "if I had not decided to go away one of these days—perhaps on Monday—I would willingly stay in it; and it would be handy for me to be near the river, I would be able to wash my sores without taking water from the old man. Among these gloomy trees I would enjoy a shade very similar to that which fell on your eyelids when I arranged the turban on your face."

I was speaking aloud, and the mule came to rub itself on my back. "I admit," I went on, "that your life had some value if in return you offer me what I never asked from you—hospitality. Yet it does not seem to me that the life of a person whom one meets accidentally—yes, accidentally—the life of a person who seemed more than a tree and something less than a woman is worth so much. Don't let us forget that you were naked and formed part of the landscape. In fact you were there to give it proportion."

The mule was getting bored, it was shaking its head and kicking its heels. It wanted to remind me that it was tired of wasting time, while at this moment Johannes was sure to be cutting his poles and muttering over our absence or over his.

I rose to my feet. "You must not have any regrets," I concluded, "the doctor at the camp would not have come, he did not look like a person who leaves his bed for the bush at five in the morning."

The mule struck me with its head, almost knocking me down. I could not help feeling glad it remembered me and I spoke to it for a long time, calling it names. It was a good opportunity for speaking. Then I jumped on to its back. It began to trot towards the hill and we arrived there almost at a run. I sat in front of my hut, and once more my thoughts turned to Mariam, almost with tenderness, I remembered her modest sleep and the gentle weight of her limbs. I thought of them until Johannes came up to me. He came slowly, obviously turning over in his mind what to say, but within a few steps of the hut he halted and went towards the edge of the clearing. After looking at the valley for a good long time he came back and sat down on the mound and then asked suddenly: "Where have you been?"

I did not even answer. I looked at him with annoyance so that he might understand that I did not owe him any kind of explanation, and that if I had been weak enough to furnish one on the first day I would now rebuff his curiosity. I could go away at once, I had got my strength back, and he must keep his distance.

Johannes did not insist, and with listless steps returned to his work. He was working with unusual vigour; he raised his arm high and struck accurately, without bemusing himself by looking at the objects in the clearing; certainly my mute reply had upset him and now he was venting his annoyance. In a few minutes he was tired, and rested; and, this time without looking at me, in a low voice repeated his question.

"Johannes, it has nothing to do with you," I said politely, although the lie made me laugh. But I could not tell him that I had been at the grave of the person who would "come back," and whom he was waiting for. In fact if he was barely able to tolerate my presence in the village, I imagine it was simply because he was waiting for Mariam to return.

Johannes seemed satisfied with my reply and went on working, but, as usual, hitting the poles in a tired manner, looking about him, amusing himself with the mule, shouting the usual phrases at it. Only many days later would I appreciate the treachery of his question. I smiled instead, seeing Johannes lose himself in his interminable work, and, hunting through my pack, took out the Bible and began to read at random. I read a page of Proverbs and two pages of Ecclesiastes and then a few more pages of Proverbs. I noticed, as I read, that these verses acquired new life in harmony with my surroundings: with those huts, with this lean Nature. And with Johannes, this prophet without a people, who had in his bones the truth of these sentences without knowing one them. Johannes was a sage and did not even know it. He had banished the world from him and lived beside his dead without fearing the fall of evening, waiting, rather, for its shadows which led him back to other dearer shades.

That was his strength—the strength to stay with his dead and to live his last days with them. He did not take it upon himself as a penance in order to merit paradise, but for the sake of remaining in good company. It had seemed to him absurd to deprive the village of the persons who had inhabited it and with whom he had spent his happiest days. His memories were in the keeping of the clearing, and in the morning, when he woke, his first glance, too, was at the mound. During the day he rearranged the fallen stones, let the plants grow on it without worrying if the mule nibbled at them afterwards. He was not a caretaker.

I thought that I had lost this strength of his, nor could I find it again, and I thought of the squalid cemeteries of our cities where we bury those who a day before had our own eyes and our own smile, burying them so hastily that they are for ever estranged from us—poor corruptible matter. Johannes rose from his couch and, although I had never seen him in an attitude of prayer, he prayed for his dead. That muttering which I heard at dawn coming from his hut was prayer. Often he sat on the mound and went on sharpening his never-ending poles.

I did not dare to imagine the last days of Johannes in that deserted village when I had gone. He would die of hunger, incapable of procuring his food, and his unburied body would be a meal for the mice, too. The very thought made me hasten my departure and fix an earlier date for it. I would go away in five or six days. Poor Johannes, I said. But perhaps Johannes had got beyond the age for death.

I would go away. I was an interloper among these corpses. I was—if anything—another kind of corpse, I still panted after life. Therefore the village was against me, just like the rest of the valley. Even the verses I read were directed against me, they accused me with the persistence and the cruelty of simple words which have suddenly acquired new meaning. I was an assassin, a sick man, a man struck down by divine wrath. And I still followed after vanity. I was also a fugitive, and for Johannes an enemy. That was why Johannes remained silent and gave himself insolent airs. He was waiting for me to leave the spot, for me to see once and for all that my presence offended him, the trees, the huts, the dead. If I stayed much longer something deep down in his nature would force him to the act which he himself feared—to cut my throat. With the same knife he used for preparing the stakes and cutting the grass. For a moment he would forget the respect due to me, the speech and the example of his venerated officers, and would cut my throat, perhaps with my head turned towards the east, on the village tomb. I would barely feel his hand on my throat, that iron hand eaten by rust. It would have been pointless to explain to him that I had to live, to go back to her and once more see her tear-drowned smile. Johannes would not allow himself to be deflected by such a personal excuse.

"All right," I went on, "let him cut my throat. All my misfortunes will be cancelled by a single blow. But is it possible that Johannes, if he has decided to avenge himself, will do so craftily, following the example of his surroundings? And why exclude the possibility that Johannes was incapable of crime, that he was a holy anchorite? A saint," I concluded, "to whom the Italian Government does not give his paltry pension in vain?"

He came up to me, sat down on his heels and with a voice that was almost affectionate repeated: "Where have you been?"

Anger brimmed in my eyes. "Johannes," I said trembling, "do not forget who I am." Then he rose slowly and sketched a quick military salute.

7

There were too many birds in the trees surrounding the hut. Their incessant muttering even prevented me from waking, plunged me into troubled waking dreams from which I emerged exhausted. They were unpleasant birds of a dark colour, like ravens, but more agile and of a less lugubrious nature, inclined in fact to company. They often came into the hut, and sometimes I had to chase them away with blows from my stick. They took little heed of my cries. Yes, that was a disadvantage, but from every other point of view it was the best hut. At night there was even a fresh breeze. Besides, these unpleasant birds were really good company. When despair overtook me and, stretched out on the pavement, I sought escape from my sorrow by sobbing they would appear on the threshold in little groups, looking at me sideways, like hens. They drew near and I would willingly have accepted their sympathy if the rank odour they gave off had not invariably obliged me to forgo it. I had to chase them away. And keep the pack shut because they liked stealing from it.

I asked myself whether this was resignation, this barren waiting, counting the days like the beads of a rosary, knowing that they do not belong to us, but are days which we must live through because they seem to us to be better than nothing.

Raising my eyes to the ceiling I often looked at the gloomy picture above the arch of the door, and I repeated to myself the words of the scroll—the scroll that condemned me with such unction. The archangel had the round and stupid face the native artists invariably give to their models. Instead of watching the dragon he was transfixing he was looking straight in front of him, or rather he was looking at me. From whatever point of view I looked at the picture the round eyes of the archangel stared at me. There was nothing strange about that. But these eyes were unbearable because of the idiotic faith which they expressed. The dragon—that ridiculous crocodile—had curled up under the lance-thrust and the archangel was not paying the least attention to it, being wholly occupied by a much more elementary thought. Perhaps he was not thinking about anything; he knew of his victory beforehand and did not derive the least satisfaction from it. It was not a fight but an execution, a way of proving the toughness of the lance and the skill of the horse. "It's too easy," I thought, "one doesn't kill a dragon every day. If this is meant to be an allegory, all right. But let the archangel try to kill the invisible dragons pullulating in my blood and in these cursed sores. Against these minute dragons a lance is of no avail, only time kills them, but it kills their bearers, too." That day there came over me once more sorrow at the sad fate reserved for me. My eyes filled with tears, and I was about to give way to my disordered emotions when through my leaden lashes I saw a shadow coming along the path. I could not move. Perhaps I did not want to move or was too tired to try. Under the dark dome the shadow could scarcely distinguish me.

"Good day, lieutenant," it said when it had reached the steps.

I started up and in the opening of the door saw a little dark outline against the dark of the leaves. Elias. He stood there with his chest stuck out, his right hand at his brow, his mouth expanded in its broadest smile, his eyes bright with joy. "Elias," I said, and my first impulse was to embrace him like a long-lost brother; I was able to restrain myself in time; but I was happy, and that I did not wish to conceal. I jumped to my feet and began to shower him with questions, not even allowing him time to reply. Overcome by this unexpected welcome, Elias looked at me diffidently and even with astonishment, wondering above all what could be the reason for my presence in his village. I saw that he was thinking this as soon as we were in the clearing. He avoided looking at me, embarrassed at seeing me reduced to such a state, with my long beard, my shirt in tatters and without my badges of rank. I had thrown away my tie ages ago. And my helmet, which I could no longer find—it must have been eaten by the supply mule.

Elias, on the other hand, was well dressed in his altered tunic. On his head he boasted a military cap and on his wrist a watch—a sign, this, that his profits were mounting. I asked him how long it was since he had seen the smuggler. "I saw him yesterday," he replied.

"Where, Elias?" He pointed to the edge of the table-land with his hand. "There," he said. He added that they were all there, on the edge of the table-land, in the old camp; they had been there a week. Was this then the awaited, the longed-for move? "Some mystery over counter-orders," I thought, and smiled. But I imagined their distress. "Are you with them?"

He shook his head with pride. He was free, independent, he travelled on his own account, and was beginning to experience the first joys of undistributed profits. For a moment I envied him, and that sureness of his—the sureness of a made man—even piqued me. He now spoke Italian almost fluently without always using the infinitive, mixing into it words from all the dialects. While he spoke, Johannes was searching in the child's haversack; he took something from it which he slipped into his toga, the

rest he barely glanced at with contempt, without taking anything. He left the haversack on the ground and I saw him go back
to his hut.

Elias remained standing, he did not even take off his tunic
although the heat was unbearable. He remained standing like the
city cousin who comes home between trains and observes the
scenes of his youth with amazement and distaste, panting to
resume his place among the people of his new daily life. He did
not take off his tunic simply in order to show that he was staying
only long enough for a courtesy visit; and he would leave us,
Johannes and myself, as one leaves old relations who remember
too much about one's infancy and know nothing about one's
present life, and so one does not know how to answer their
awkward questions, uncertain whether to leave them in their
ignorance or to upset the opinion they have of one. He had come
to visit the old man, perhaps to bring him a little money, a little
bread, and that mysterious object which Johannes had hastened
to hide in his hut. Now he would go away, happy to leave the
desolate surroundings of his birth place; for it had nothing to
offer him now except unmerited imprisonment and its attendant
sufferings. He remained standing and was already searching for
the words to say goodbye, so as to go away and reach the table-
land with his haversack. "Have you any cigarettes?" I asked.

"No, they're finished," he answered. He was sorry, but like a
tradesman who softens his refusals with a polite smile. Another
time, his smile said. "What have you in your haversack?" I asked,
hoping to buy something from him; and thus I obtained tins of
fruit and jam. He did not want to take my money; but seemed
pleased when I forced him to. "And not even one cigarette?" I
said.

"No, lieutenant." I asked if he would come back, and when. He
shrugged, it did not depend on him but on how things worked
out. There are drivers who don't mind, who let the children
climb up and others who won't; carabinieri who laugh and others who whip your legs; soldiers who buy stuff and others who
yell out as soon as you ask them a question. He would go back

to Asmara and there replenish his stock. Then he would come back, in a week, a month, two years. Or perhaps never.

Johannes left us alone; he did not seem even to have noticed the arrival of the child, and was now saying something to the mule which annoyed it. When the child went up to him I saw Johannes caress his head but without looking at him.

I thought of sending a note to the smuggler; but after having thought it over decided that it was not prudent to trust anyone. Suppose the smuggler cannot keep the secret, entrusts it to his closest friend and the same evening speaks of it in Asmara. No, no note. Then I decided to write to my wife and went back to the hut. Elias followed me.

Flocks of birds had invaded the hut, and it was not easy to chase them away; they persisted in staying there even after I had taken the stick and struck at them blindly. They rose up to the ceiling where I could not reach them and then there they were back on the floor which they had already fouled. One could not see in the hut and I was forced to return to the clearing to write. I took a sheet of paper, trying to touch it as little as possible. But I could not find words and the letter now began to appear unnecessary. What would I say? And yet I could not let slip such a chance. I would write to her, yes, in five or six days, once I had left the village, but it was as well to take advantage of the child's visit. When I tried to write, I found that the ink in my pen had dried up and I had to add a little water; these fading lines would increase her apprehension, I thought. I repeated what I had written in Massaua. But as I handed the letter to Elias I thought that direct post to her would be censored and that I had therefore given clues to whoever was looking for me. Probably in a month or two, since I had given no sign of life, someone would put forward the theory that I had committed suicide. "A ruined man," they would say. "He did what we would have done in his place." But I could not leave her without news of me, so I decided to write to her mother over a false signature. She would understand.

The child was going away along the path towards the hill and

I alone stood looking at him; Johannes had withdrawn into his hut to avoid the sun that beat on the clearing. The child went away happily, skipping; and when he turned round gave a great wave of his hand, as one man to another. He began to skip again; he had reached the path through the bush when I called to him. "Wait for me," I cried. I ran along the path. "Give me back the letter."

He searched in the haversack, showing no surprise, not even when he saw me tear it up. "Listen, Elias," I said. I sat down, inviting him to sit too. I made a long confused speech to him. He must remember this—I was not in the village. He had not seen me. He knew nothing about me. When I had finished, he nodded his head and I discovered something new in his eyes—not so much curiosity to know what had happened to me as the conviction that I was now a weak and defenceless creature. My men no longer obeyed me, he thought. I had been beaten, deprived of authority, and he could allow himself to protect me and to listen to my entreaties as one man to another. He betrayed his thoughts by a long whimper.

"You will not tell anyone that you have seen me?"

"No, no one."

"And could you not come back tomorrow with some cigarettes?"

He made me entreat him. Not tomorrow. Not the day after tomorrow either. He felt that he had acquired some importance in my eyes but his victory actually left him indifferent. He counted on his fingers. "In four days' time," he replied.

"Four days." I rose to my feet. "I'll wait for you," I said. He went off, but this time without skipping, master of the path, a little David who had overcome the giant and was now going back to his business.

I went back to the slope and stood looking at the table-land, thinking with consuming tenderness of my friends up there and then of the "rackets" with my name, now buried among the quartermaster's papers. The edge of the table-land seemed farther away than ever—the edge of the table-land which it was given to Elias to reach and would have been given to the mule to reach, had it not persisted in its devotion to these parts and to its surly old man.

After the visit to Mariam's grave Johannes had not addressed another word to me, and we had lived together for four days, ignoring each other. I had even tried to make him speak; he had always replied with nods and with short, scarcely mumbled words, but without ill-feeling, so that there had descended between us the indifference of castaways who no longer hope for aid and watch each other dying. I often tried to learn the reason why he had insisted on asking me where I had been that day. He obviously could not know of my sojourn at Mariam's tomb; his curiosity was therefore inadmissible. If I had as much as answered him, I would have appeared more contemptible in his eyes than the mule now grazing on the mound in the clearing. I did not regret, therefore, having snubbed him even if I now saw myself forced to mourn our brief and not particularly pleasant conversations of the early days. Even if I did have to go to the stream to fill the tin now that I had taken up quarters in the round hut. Besides, it was a comfort to me to stand on the bank and watch the water run past. But Johannes wandered about the clearing without seeing me, and did not feel the least need—as I did—to seize the slight excuses for making conversation life offered us. His natural state was now solitude, and perhaps the incident had given him the chance of falling back into it and of punishing me in the only way he knew to be effective. He kept away from the village for hours, and the mule followed him. They did not go up on to the table-land or to the bridge, of that I was certain; I always took the trouble to follow them for a good way without letting myself be seen. Perhaps they went to rest in the bush, leaving me for whole afternoons in a state of anxiety I often felt inclined to terminate by taking flight. But each time that I brought myself to the point of preparing the pack I found some new argument and gradually calmed myself down. I now spoke to myself aloud. I gave myself joking advice and even laughed, and perhaps these futile asides prevented me from go-

ing mad or from running to the first post, there on the edge of
the table-land, and saying: "Here I am."

When Johannes came back from his wanderings I felt better
and went back to my hut.

Now the old man was standing right in front of my hut watching me return. He was looking at me, there was no doubt about
it. I thought that this unusual attitude was traceable to the return
of Elias and to the fact that he wanted to speak to me about the
boy, taking the opportunity to make peace between us. I hastened my steps to reach him. I waited for him to speak first, but
he did not speak. When I smiled at him—I wanted to cross the
threshold of the hut and chase away the birds—he made a quick
grimace and shrugged. I was incapable of climbing the first step
and looked at Johannes. He was standing up, leaning with both
hands on his long stick like a lancer resting; and he kept staring
at me. In that darkness I could scarcely see his yellowish, watery
eyes. He did not seem in the least taken aback by my surprise, on
the contrary, he was more insolent than ever; and suddenly he
winked at me. The darkness may have deceived me, but he
winked an eye and not to chase away a fly. He went on to wink
at me once, twice, three times.

"Johannes," I shouted, "stop it."

The sound of my voice shook him. I saw him shake as if struck
by a sudden fever. Then he let out a crazy cry, a cry which froze
my blood; it was the cry which he had had on his tongue for
long—for centuries. He raised the stick, grasped it with both
hands and hurled himself on me. I had barely time to prevent his
splitting open my skull. The blow grazed my shoulder; Johannes
fell to the ground, dragged down by his own rush, and the stick
broke. He got up with a bound and then I fled on to the clearing.
I heard him at my heels, yelling; I picked up a stick and used it
to keep the old man at bay. Suddenly he, too, picked up a stake—I
could not prevent him—and was upon me. I defended myself,
but his yells, the yells of a warrior insulting and defying death,
took all my courage from me. Thus I had seen his brothers rush
the machine-guns with less solid sticks in hand. And the machine-

guns had not always stopped them. All my powers of defence were giving way in face of that maniac, and then I realised that if I confined myself to defence I would end the day in the stream. I began to yell, too; they were yells which arose from my deep-seated fear; they terrified me but gave me new and intoxicating strength. When Johannes struck me on the shoulder for the second time—and the pain made me catch my breath—I was upon him and brought the stake down on his head with all my power. He halted, stunned, then collapsed suddenly; his yell became a lament and then was silenced. I thought I had killed him and began to shake, bewildered, stammering. I called his name several times.

A moment later Johannes was on his feet, pale, taller than I had ever seen him. A stream of thick blood flowed over his face from a wound on his brow. Then I threw away the stake to show him that I did not mean to strike him and that I had been forced to do so by his threats alone. He looked at me, panting, his eyes filthy with blood. Staggering a little he went off towards the edge of the clearing and ran on to the path. "Johannes," I cried.

He did not listen to me but quickened his pace. Then I had to catch up with him; he obviously intended to go and denounce me and I could not let him go. I seized him by the shoulder and besought him to turn back. Hysterical laughter came from his mouth and racked his breast; with dry, gnarled fists he attempted to strike me in the face and I had to seize his wrists, but I found them stronger than my hands and was about to let go my grip when he collapsed on the ground, still laughing. I bent down to help him and a strong smell of cognac repelled me—he was drunk, and now that blinding sun was completing the job. He went on laughing and shouting and kicking, but always more feebly until he fell asleep. I could not leave him on the sun-baked path and had to load him on to my shoulders, climb up the hill again and deposit him on his wretched bed, first removing a bottle he had drained.

The wound on his brow was not deep. I washed it and scat-tered on it the few drops of cognac which had remained in the bottle. Johannes now slept profoundly, and from time to time I heard him laugh.

8

It was hearing him laugh—a harsh, prolonged laugh very like the one the wind brought from afar at night—that made me decide to kill him.

Johannes slept until the afternoon, and the whole time I stayed in his hut and watched over him. The wound was not worrying, but when Johannes woke up and saw that I was smiling at him he made to rise and began to call me names. I made him lie down again and held out the tin full of water. While he drank he did not take his eyes from my face, and when he had emptied the tin he thanked me.

With the exasperated energy of the awakening drunk he wanted to get up at all costs, but I forced him to stay in his hut and prepared his supper. It did not worry me to touch his dishes or his bread, my leprosy would overtake him, if ever, in the grave—not before. I opened a tin of jam and he devoured it; he made me treat him like a sick child. If I went away I suddenly heard his voice calling me. He called me "lieutenant." Perhaps this sudden change was largely due to my defence—that and the blow I now regretted having given him, but which Johannes himself could not refrain from admiring. Now he gazed at me with smiling respect, unless his behaviour was dictated by the revolver at my side.

He seemed, then, to have unexpectedly become my friend, but I could not trust this change, for it was certain to conceal some unpleasant trap—the next day, pretending to go to the river, he would smile and take the road to the table-land. He was not the kind of man to forgive me. The way he exploited my remorse to get himself waited upon confirmed this.

I waited, therefore, for him to fall asleep again and prepared a litter by twining fresh boughs between his poles. I would have to carry the corpse to the stream to hide every trace, although no one, except Elias, would ever ask what had become of the old man. Who would listen to a child? Indeed even Elias would not have wondered at the disappearance of the old man. And I could not surrender the advantage I had gained over my pursuers. Half an hour later the litter was ready and I looked at my revolver to see that it was all right. I was about to go up to the hut when I realised that I would not fire. I could not fire—and not because of repugnance but from impotence. Having failed with the doctor and then with the major I felt myself incapable of facing the test again. Several times I tried to enter Johannes' hut, and always left it discouraged. The target was there, his eyes closed, scarcely breathing; he would not even have moved his head, and yet my hand refused to pull the trigger. I stayed on the threshold, impatiently, telling myself that that useless old man could upset my whole plan of embarkation, and that therefore I had to kill him. "Yes," I said, "kill him. But I won't succeed." I began to walk up and down in the clearing trying to convince myself with arguments which I appreciated but which took away more and more of my strength. "I understand," I said, "but I won't do it." And I answered: "Come on, you must try, don't let it get you down." Alter an hour of similar unnerving meditations I arrived at a compromise. I would not kill him but only threaten him—I would make him understand that I was ready to kill him if he tried to betray me. Pleased with my resolution I undid the litter. But what could death matter to Johannes? Any threat would only strengthen his resolve. It was best not to give him pretexts with my foolish threats. "Perhaps he will really forget," I concluded.

Towards evening I at last decided that I would leave the village next day—that was the sure way to assuage the old man's desire for revenge. I would go away, leaving the mule—it would be difficult I thought to persuade the beast to follow me—and a lot of money. Johannes, who was capable of refusing five hundred lire, would hesitate before five thousand. He would find himself suddenly rich and would offer me the other cheek, forgive me.

That night I slept near the old man's hut to watch him. I had prepared the pack ready to leave at dawn, but when dawn came I saw that I was leaving against my will and that I would not easily find the energy to leave the village although I detested it. Twenty-six days had now gone by and the hill seemed to be the safest place—I had committed the error of hunted animals who dig themselves in and are unable to leave their lair, in which they prefer to die rather than tempt fate by leaving it. "I must go away," I repeated looking at the trees which now seemed my friends, the surroundings slowly emerging from the shadow of night, those huts where I could still find shelter. "If I do not go away today it is a sign that I do not want to try any more and that I really want to end my life in this spot."

So I put the pack on my back, took the money from my pocket, and went into Johannes' hut. He was awake, he had heard me preparing the pack and had also heard my soliloquies. Now he was waiting for me, quite composedly on his bed. "Goodbye, Johannes," I said. I left the money on a stool and announced that I was not taking the mule away. Let him keep it. As I had foreseen Johannes looked at the money, counted it and hid it among the folds of his garment. He seemed satisfied. But he did not thank me, he sat scarcely looking at me, then he held out his hand to me. When I shook it I felt that it was burning. "Are you ill, Johannes?" I asked.

"No," he replied. And added: "No, sir." His voice was weak, suddenly the voice of a defenceless old man. I sat on the stool near the couch and did not know what to do. I had to do something before going away; and then I uncovered his wound: nothing serious, in a few days it would have closed up. I cleaned it again carefully; but by the light already entering the hut I saw that Johannes was pale; there was an ashen veil over his sunbaked face. Perhaps it was only caused by that sudden drunken bout. I made him swallow two aspirin tablets and left the tube on his stool. It was the tube I had asked for that day from the lazy doctor; and I had kept it in my pack as a pledge of a friendship born under an unlucky star; and it was right that it should stay with Johannes, my implacable enemy. "Goodbye, Johannes," 1 repeated with an attempt to sound cheerful; and almost to calm my apprehension—I was always abandoning someone in misfortune—I told him that he would get better that day. I added to the gifts a box of jam. Now I could go away.

Instead I stayed. "Elias will come back in three days," I said, "and then I will leave Johannes. Without taking into consideration," I added, "the fact that Elias will bring the cigarettes and that will save me from looking for them in the villages or from asking for them from any soldiers I meet. That means far fewer suspicions left along my route." That is what I thought; but in reality it was Johannes' look when, having crossed the threshold, I turned to salute him for the last time, that held me back. It was a glance that had already struck me; at that precise moment—I had never gone deeply into the question—I knew that Johannes was Mariam's father. I had never asked myself what Johannes meant to Mariam and now I knew it. I had always rejected the idea that Elias was Johannes' son and now everything was clear. His looks had deceived me. But the day before in that furious struggle I had proved that Johannes' age was only a hypothesis of mine. I had fixed it as I watched him burying his dead. That day he was very old, the oldest person I have ever seen, indeed the most ancient.

I remained, and Johannes got better in three days, and in these three days one may say that we became friends, or at least I had that illusion.

9

On the morning of the fourth day after Elias' visit I was standing on the edge of the clearing waiting to see the child appear down there among foliage of the bush when Johannes called me. He was still very weak and courteously pointed to the empty petrol tin; he wanted to indicate that I should go and fill it, and I went. I was greatly excited that morning because Elias was coming. I blamed myself for not having fixed the time of his next visit with him; I would therefore spend the whole day waiting for him and

I could not rely upon his sense of time. Four or five days—it was all the same to Elias. In fact four days or four months. He did possess a watch, but only out of vanity and to let his young friends hear its ticking. He would come, heaven knows when, merry and without the least suspicion that he was late. And he would bring a crumpled packet or else two cigarettes, or only one stuffed behind his ear. I was becoming more and more annoyed at not having fixed anything, leaving it to his whim to decide. To calm myself, when I was on the bank and I had filled the can, I undressed and entered the water.

I swam close to the bank and quickly got out; I did not want to run any risk on that particular day, but the bathe revived me and I decided that I mustn't think Elias was so stupid. While I was lingering over putting on my clothes again I saw the water boil ten yards from the bank. A second later I had seized the revolver and aimed at the crocodile, for there is no doubt that is what it was. I took aim, but hesitated to fire; I knew that my bullets would scarcely graze the monster's armour and only if I hit it in the eye could I kill it. I held myself ready for flight back to the path, abandoning the can which would have been an embarrassment to me. However, the turbulence died away and I saw no sign of the crocodile. "It was a mistake," I thought; then I added that I had not made a mistake and that perhaps the crocodile had not seen me. It is a well-known fact that these animals see less well in the water than when they are on dry land. I waited on, and, without daring to confess it to myself, I wanted the crocodile to appear; I wanted to see it. Of course if it had appeared, I would have run away; but I wanted to see it, and it was not fear that suggested this singular wish to me nor yet scientific curiosity. It was solely the desire to see it and to fire the whole magazine at it. And then run off.

I began to call it names. Thus, I thought, the savages goad the reluctant game. I ordered it to show itself. Why was it running away? Did it want to take advantage of my departure—it was now fixed—to get away with things? So it knew that I was going away next day? I would like to take her back its well-cured skin.

I spoke out loud saying this and other similar foolish things, getting more and more excited. When I saw the water boil again, I fled in that direction, cursing; but perhaps it was only a passing eddy. The seven shots raised tiny sprays. Not content I took a big stone and hurled it into the water. "Take that!" I shouted. There-after, somewhat calmer, I took the can and climbed up to the clearing again; and once more anxiety over Elias' non-arrival overcame me. It was no use waiting on the brow of the hill; I went back to the round hut and amused myself by reloading the gun. Unfortunately I had wasted seven shots and had only one magazine left. But I would never need to use it, I said.

That day the birds were chary about entering the hut and as soon as I shouted went outside without having to be told twice. I spat on one of them that stood looking at me with one claw raised and its head on one side, and I saw it go almost mad and lose itself in the straw of the roof, fluttering its wings to clean them, unable to find the way out. "They have learned to know me," I thought. The trouble is that these natives do not hunt and the birds form deplorable habits and think one has to put up with their confidences for all eternity. "I'm not dead yet," I shouted, "and perhaps I will eat you first." With such cries I tried to calm myself. The bird found the way out and let something drop— something which it had certainly found in the pack; a piece of iron, a nut. I could not leave the pack open a minute. I picked up the nut and remembered the major. He had wished me a good holiday. And he had won that particular game. But the holiday was coming to an end, and now I congratulated myself on my prudence. "At Massaua the trap's sprung," I said.

I took the nut and threw it on the ground several times, pre-tending it was a dice, and called the points out loud. "Major, I will win," I ended up, laughing. But I became sad again when I remembered that even if I got back to Italy there were too many courts-martial waiting for me. Too many courts-martial and the hospital. And would she come to visit me? Would she bring books, oranges, tobacco? And each time an excuse for going away sooner? Or would she not come at all? One solitude is as good as another after all. I would hear my bedfellows mutter, instead of the dark-coloured birds. Instead of Johannes, an equally implacable doctor. Instead of Elias, who gets mixed up between four days and four months, an orderly who does not listen for the bell. Instead of an archangel, a priest who points out the joys of paradise. Instead of a river, a tramline.

I was in this depressed state when I once more smelt the delicate scent of cyclamens. It was an almost imperceptible and intermittent scent. In fact, the more I sniffed the more I had to admit that it was a mere impression I had. "Perhaps it comes from these trees," I thought. But the trees round the hut did not flower, insensible to the spring, and I do not think that the birds would have liked them to flower. In my waking sleep the perfume persisted, but vanished as my eyelids grew heavier, and in it I discerned a soupçon of withered cyclamen, a single old cyclamen withered in the bunch. "That's right," I thought, "my imagination is playing me false. I am tired, exhausted, and that makes me sensitive to the faintest odours in this village. I am getting the sense of smell of a wild animal." And I laughed. "Perhaps," I went on, "with time I will bay the moon, or hear a mole breathe two kilometres away." Yet I could not explain why I persisted in telling myself that it was a cyclamen, that perfume, if I did not remember ever smelling cyclamens. "It must be some flower of the bush," I concluded. But I noticed that the perfume was particularly persistent in the neighbourhood of my pack. I smelled the pack and then I remembered. I had put it in the major's truck among the other goods; he was carrying, among other things, the wretched scents so prized by the natives and which the merchant was selling in the square at A. Yes, now I remembered that during the journey from Massaua to D. that perfume had, in fact, almost overwhelmed me. A broken bottle, and the pack had been steeped in it. "All is explained," I said. And I was just falling asleep when I saw Johannes coming towards the hut running as fast as his weakness permitted. "Elias has come," I thought. When he was at the door Johannes coldly announced to me that the carabinieri had arrived.

He had spoken in a low voice and I thought that the carabinieri were already in the clearing. I did not know what to do.
I rose and first of all slipped on my tunic, I did not wish to be
found in that deplorable state. I buttoned it in haste, fastened my
belt and looked for my comb in my pack. Only then did I remember to ask Johannes where the carabinieri were. He replied
that perhaps they were coming up the hill path, for when he had
seen them they were still three hundred yards away. "Fool," I
thought. I took the pack and decided to flee. Suddenly I remembered the mule. If the carabinieri found a supply mule there the
old man would be accused of theft, and to exonerate himself
would show them my lair. "The mule," I cried. Johannes looked
at me for a moment without understanding, then ran towards the
clearing. I waited for him, trembling, at the fork in the path; and
in a little while the mule arrived, trotting along without a care.
In fact it stopped to graze, but Johannes gave it such a blow on
the back that it stopped suddenly and let itself be led to the
stream. While we were disappearing down the path the carabinieri were passing in front of the mound and I had time to see
them through the trees. I recognised their badges and saw that
they carried their carbines not slung but in their hands, so they
were ready to fire. And in front of them went Elias.

"Young bastard," I said, and went down the path pushing the
now docile mule on ahead. I was almost tempted to climb back
again and, before leaving the village with the carabinieri, to give
that child a well-deserved lesson. I had been stupid enough to
tell him not to mention a word to anyone about my presence in
the village in such a way that if he had not understood anything
before I had made him understand everything. And I had asked
him to bring back cigarettes, too. Now I remembered his first
refusal and then the severe glance with which he had examined
me down there on the path through the bush, and finally the
decision, which I had suggested to him, to return. He had
counted the days with his fingers on his nose, just like the old
man. And I had waited, full of trust in the child, who even as he
went away was already contemplating my betrayal. He had not

forgotten, Elias, my cuff in the tent, and he, too, wanted his part in the vendetta, the most villainous part. Fortunately, I thought, there is Johannes. If he has forgiven me and if his friendship of these last days is sincere he will do everything to save me. But can I trust Johannes, the third member of the conspiracy, with his brow still bandaged through my fault?

I decided that I would cross the stream, pushing on into the bush, towards the mountains. I would spend the night in the bush and next day would follow the path as far as A. If the old man contradicted what Elias said, the carabinieri would in the end pay no attention to the child. I would go back to the table-land because it is not at all pleasant wandering about the bush.

Having reached the bank I jumped on to the back of the mule and forced it into the water. It moved unwillingly. It went in with its hind hooves and immediately withdrew them. I could not urge it on, nor beat it, fearing that it might whinny, and I had to get down. The bed of the river was not very wide and a few strokes would take me to the other bank. Not knowing what to do with the mule I had to carry the pack myself. I was so excited and had to be so quick that I paid no attention to the animal's nervousness. It kicked out, drew back and positively refused to enter the water. At that moment I was not thinking at all about the crocodile—I had taunted it in vain and it had gone out of my mind; I thought it must be imaginary, or as docile as the one in the picture. I pushed the mule again and it gave a quick jump back.

On the bank there was a young crocodile, not more than a couple of feet in length, perhaps less. It was a very young croc-odile, I suppose, but I never wondered afterwards how many months or years old it was. It was of a dirty green colour, with dirty white and yellow patches on the sides. It stood on the bank, motionless, the tip of its tail in the water as if it wanted to see that the temperature was right.

I slowly drew my revolver and pushed forward the safety catch—I would hit it. It was scarcely two yards away—motion-less. While I was taking aim I remembered the carabinieri up

there in the clearing. All the mule's panic seemed to be concentrated in its swishing tail; and its upper lip shook a little. It stared
at that unknown animal with an almost human fear and would
not move from the spot until it had learned what it was. I, too,
did not dare to move; so we stood motionless, waiting. For what?
What were we waiting for? I thought: "We are waiting for the
beast's father or mother."

It was time to go away. I did not dare to take my eyes off the
crocodile. I looked round out of the corner of my eye ready to
act at the least rustle. If the big crocodile appeared—the very old
one, the one that knew the whole history of the world—I would
not get away. Perhaps the mule would flee. Perhaps I, too, would
flee, or else I would remain there, nailed to the ground. It might
even not come from the water, but from the bank and cut us off.
Then, if I found the strength to move—and I doubted it—I would
have to throw myself into the water as far as possible from the
young crocodile and reach the other bank. And would the young
crocodile not plunge after me, merely from curiosity or in play?
Once in the water who would be able to resist his infant teeth?
Would I dare to touch it, that slimy, armour-plated little monster?

We did not move. The crocodile even kept the tip of its tail
still, a thing the mule did not succeed in doing. And now I
understood what these regular marks were that seemed to have
been made by a harrow. They were made by the beast; so it was
in the habit of venturing on to the bank here—its den was not far
off and so its parents, too, were in the neighbourhood.

What if the mule whinnied? Perhaps the crocodile would
move, and then I should have to do something. I do not know
how long we stayed there, motionless, looking at each other.
And finally the crocodile moved; it advanced towards me and
stopped, raising its head two paces away.

It was moving its head slowly, a prey to languid curiosity. It
did not take me for an enemy. I could easily see its sharp teeth,
the long jaws that closed from time to time with a sharp, regular
noise like a well-made lock. It stood still—and not even the mule

had dared to move—and its horrible flanks palpitated. Perhaps it, too, was wondering what was causing this delay. I even go so far as to suppose—I don't know the habits of such beasts and I have no wish to learn them now—to suppose that it wanted to play. If I had put out my hand to it it would have taken it off, but only in play. It was very young indeed, the river had not yet taught it anything, and I was the first man it had seen. Perhaps my height began to make it suspicious. I was able to go into all this later, at the time I was fascinated by the monster and wished only to rid myself of it. The excitement of the morning had shaken me deeply, giving me a new, nervous energy. Then seeing that that trustful dragon was not rushing at my legs I told myself that I must do something at once without losing time. It was still motionless, the crocodile, and was barely moving its jaws, but its eyes did not leave me for a minute. Nor did I dare to take my gaze away from it, fearing to break the truce. "Its curiosity," I thought, "will not always be of a contemplative nature. I must act, but how?" It was the crocodile itself that suggested how, by raising its head. Perhaps it intended to launch an attack. But it raised its head. I took two paces back without ever taking my gaze off it and let fly.

The beast took that terrible kick under the jaw. It spun over on its tail, described a rapid semi-circle and struck the water with its back. For a second I saw its belly taut with the effort, whitish, veined with putrid colours, and its paws drawn up. Then it disappeared in the foam, turned round, perhaps stunned or only surprised, and went off under water, swimming.

It went away. I, too, was surprised at its flight and slumped down on the bank, with my mind in a whirl. I began to massage my ankle and talked out loud to myself: I do not remember what I said—perhaps I thanked the archangel for his lesson and laughed. I did not think of crossing the river, nor did I notice Elias who was coming down the path calling to me. He was making rapid conspiratorial signs to me, but he was smiling. When he was close to me he said that the carabinieri had gone away, I could come up again.

Now, what followed that day is soon told. Back in the clearing, Elias opened the haversack and took out the cigarettes, tins of fruit and of meat. The first intoxicating cigarette even made me forget to ask Johannes why the carabinieri had come. I learned later they had come attracted by certain shots. It was I who had fired—at the imaginary crocodile. They had run across Elias and had wanted to accompany him, suspicious of this overdressed child with all that stuff in his haversack. But Elias had managed to keep quiet and the old man had behaved even better. His pension certificate had been read and admired.

The next morning, at dawn, I was preparing to leave the village. I had taken so much heart that I had decided to try it, even if the road to Massaua was a very long one. When I said goodbye to Johannes I was convinced that I would leave, but perhaps I made the mistake of asking him what he wanted me to leave to remember me by. Johannes, handing back the money, pointed to the watch and said: "That." He said it in such a voice that I had to lean against a tree; my knees gave way under me. It was impossible to deny it, and now the old man's hostility was becoming clear to me—from the first day when I had come upon him burying his dead. Johannes' eyes never left mine and, even more than my pallor, the instinctive gesture I made to hide the watch must have betrayed me: that watch which the woman must obviously have shown on her return to the village. When I could speak I said: "Let's go." And I left him alone before Mariam's grave. And I did not leave.

I did not leave because Johannes had admitted Mariam's existence; now he would talk about Mariam and would tell me if my faint hope was unfounded or not. When the next day—I did not see Johannes again all that day—I asked him what I wanted to know, the old man did not reply. Weeping I showed him my sores and then he shook his head. He looked at them for a long time. The same evening he applied the first disgusting poultice to my belly and hand. I accepted it, sobbing, but without faith—it was not possible, it could not be true that I would be cured. I sobbed so much that I remained in a bewildered state in the hut—the best hut of all—until the dawn. I did not think, I tried not to think. When the old man appeared each day with his disgusting poultices I turned away my face so as not to meet his eyes.

On the morning of the forty-first day I took the short cut towards the table-land; I was going to give myself up. There was no point in hiding now. The sores were healing, Johannes had not deceived me. *And yet the first picture in the book was my hand.*

Passing in front of Mariam's grave I saw that it was covered with a straw roof. The roof was supported by poles—the poles the old man had whittled with such ostentation.

SOME OBSCURE POINTS

1

W HEN I TOLD my story to the second lieutenant two days later he made no comment. He remained looking at the valley which was beginning to clear with the first light of dawn; he looked at the mountains opposite and said nothing. To tell the truth I was expecting some fine quotation. I could bet all the money I had in my pocket—including the stolen money—that true to his timid cynicism he would remember some of his authors. Or else I feared a gloss inspired by his boyish and irresponsible humour. Or something about the paradise one sometimes gains by the worst actions. Or else refusal to draw a moral from facts, which are subject to chance, and therefore refusal to look for a moral in the whole human game of chance. Instead he sat silent, motionless, looking at the valley. I feared that the story of my adventures had sent him to sleep, but he had not lain down and I saw the tip of his cigar light up from time to time. Perhaps he was thinking. Or else he found my story unconvincing and regretted the hours of lost sleep. Unless he was listening to the voices of the soldiers still singing with joy because it was the last night they had to spend on the edge of that valley. At reveille we would leave for the coast, to embark four days later. In a week, Italy.

I would leave with them. I had arrived two days before ready to say: "Here I am," and to follow the carabiniere officer who would lead me, I thought, to some fortress in the old colony. I renounced my accomplices, not glad to expiate my crime, but tired of waiting; and I found the camp in a hubbub over the order for repatriation. When the major learned that I had not "expended" my leave in Italy, he said that he would put me up for

C.B. Then he added that I would deserve it and went off so as not to laugh. Passing behind his tent I heard him telling the others my adventure. I was still the man with the tooth and of the gold rush. This time, instead of going to Italy, who knew what I had been up to? Perhaps a woman, the usual woman, and he laughed. So there was not even C.B. to be entered in my records.

There were no denunciations. There was only a letter from her, but I had not opened it yet. I am beginning to think that I shall have to abandon my last accomplice, too. For that face of hers with its moments of gravity I have killed a woman. The doctor from the workmen's camp would not have come. But I killed her just the same. I shall have to leave her. I used to think that her melancholy came from the experience of her heart and was both deeply thought and felt. Now I shall have to convince myself that there is in her only an organic emanation, a cold and fetid breath. Perhaps the same breath that tormented me once, reminding me of what I most feared. If she were to go into the water without taking off her clothes, beckoning to me to follow her, I would stay on the bank, unable to accept the laws of her feigned madness.

So no one was looking for me. The major from A. and the doctor least of all. I had arrived ready to say: "Here I am," and the carabiniere on guard had saluted me. No one paid any attention to me. The post orderly had to rummage in his tent; he could not find the letter. And I already felt that whether he found it or no was a matter of no importance. I have not opened it yet.

That night I was, however, amazed by the second lieutenant's silence. The soldiers did not stop singing; they were waiting for the dawn to make sure that there were no counter-orders about the sun's rising. Another four days and the trembling of the steamer's engines would set their minds at rest about everything. They would not even find the energy to wave to the crowd on the pier.

When, impatient to break the silence, I asked: "Well?" the second lieutenant replied that my story presented some obscure points. I was inclined to agree and then he added that they could be reduced to four: the woman's turban, the sores, the massacre in the village and the absence of a denunciation by the major from A.

"Yes," I repeated, thankful that he had not referred to the crocodile. I would have liked to add the doctor. But the doctor no longer appeared to me as an obscure point—was in fact only too clear. Can I really forgive him for not having forwarded a denunciation? Misanthropist that he was, he wanted to invite me to accept my status of "untouchable" but not to impose on me that of accused person. Perhaps he thought the sentence written on my hand—it was too carefully bandaged—was enough without adding to it others in the records of a court-martial. The weaker of us had won. I had attributed my feelings of resentment to him. I must deduce from them that—in his shoes—I would have forwarded a denunciation; and so our unexpected friendship was killed not by that shot that went wide of the mark but by my feeble imagination. Will I be able to forgive in him, then, this fault which shows my limitations?

"Yes," I repeated. And I thought: "In a few hours we will pass through A. and I will see him sitting among the eucalyptus of his grove, more unapproachable than ever, in the midst of the disorder which I will learn to appreciate." Then to break the silence I said: "The massacre in the village does not seem to me to be a point that needs to be cleared up. It is only too true that it happened and we know how."

"But we do not know why," answered the second lieutenant, "and it will be as well to try to imagine it. The massacre will seem clearer to you when you learn that the young violinist—the one you saw passing on his melancholy way through the bush and whom you found later hanged, meditating on his misadventure—went to the workmen's camp thinking that the woman had been taken there by some officer with a view to marriage. He went there to ask for her."

"Well?" I asked. (I was thinking that the second lieutenant had an incurable tendency towards complications.)

"Well," he went on, "the workmen in the camp—still looking

for an excuse for a bit of fun—led the boy to believe that the woman was really there shut up in a tent. Perhaps the doctor's? The result was that the boy mastered his jealousy—they avoid jealousy because they give things their true value—until the sun had set and perhaps the joke seemed too much to him. Then he struck a workman with his stick, irreparably destroying his certificate of submission."

"A workman?" I asked.

Almost as if anticipating me the second lieutenant replied: "Yes, and we can at least hope that it was the blond workman."

"And they hanged the youth for this?" I asked.

"No. Unfortunately the same night there was an attack on the camp; the brigands were repulsed; they carried away some stuff and left some corpses. The workmen unfortunately connected the attack with the youth's threats—in fact they thought it had been instigated by him. And the next day, unfortunately, the *zouaves* passed, more concerned to make an example than to open an inquiry. The suspicion was enough."

"I understand," I said, "and if I am not mistaken you would tend to make the responsibility for the massacre fall on my revolver shot. At this rate the future of Africa had been compromised by my revolver shot."

"No," said the second lieutenant, "but the massacre concluded a series of unfortunate circumstances begun by your revolver shot. And, in its turn, your revolver shot concludes another series of unfortunate circumstances. Which was the first of these? If we could know we would have the key to your story. Instead, as it is, they appear to us merely part of a game where everything depends on the fall of the dice. Which was the first unfortunate circumstance? The over-turned truck? The fork in the path hidden by the carcass? Your halt by the stream? Your fear? The stone which deflected the shot? The animal? Or the packets of sweets she sent you? Or simply your aching tooth? It would be worth knowing, at least, if it was a wisdom tooth."

"No," I said, "it was not a wisdom tooth."

"Well," he went on, "that's one comfort. But we are back where we began. Like every story in this world yours, too, defies analysis. Unless one wishes to admit that the 'unfortunate circumstances' followed you because they were part of your person. They obeyed you alone. Were you, in fact. But where were you to learn otherwise? How can we draw a moral from it? Here you are, having become a wise man instead of the superficial young man you were, and only by virtue of some act of murder you have committed without attaching the least importance to it. I congratulate you."

We were silent. The killing of Mariam now seemed to me an inevitable crime, but not for the reasons that had led me to commit it. More than a crime, in fact, it appeared to me like a crisis, an illness, which would protect me for ever by revealing me to myself. I now loved my victim and could only fear that she might leave me.

Beyond the bridge the jackals were howling again, although the first signs of day were appearing. Opposite, beyond the rim of the table-land, rose the dark mountains of the region where, at distances of a hundred or more kilometres one from the other, little convents shelter persons who go there in search of solitude. Probably a solitude different from that which saddens us in the cities, and forces us out into the streets, the cafés, the theatres, to draw comfort from warmth of humanity—humanity which is just as sad as we are. But can they live under that sky which shuts off the horizon like a curtain, and among these black basalt mountains, which in spring burst into flower?

"Let's go on," I said. "Now the turban."

"Let's go on," repeated the second lieutenant. He added that this point seemed to him difficult to explain. "Why did the woman have the turban if she was not infected and therefore *untouchable*?"

"I'd like to have it from you," I answered. "In fact if we do not solve this first question there is no use asking the second."

The second lieutenant nodded and announced that he would

put forward two hypotheses: "The first," he said, "is that you saw the turban *afterwards*, when in the courtyard of the church we went up to the two girls who really had one."

I burst out laughing, and he observed that this hypothesis ought not to surprise me. Perhaps I did not have a very clear conception of memory and the way it anticipated things? And he went on. The second hypothesis required a parallel. The woman had put on a turban to wash herself, but she knew that she was committing sacrilege, or at least an absurd act. Now could she dare—and here the second lieutenant stressed the words—in this country where certain lost qualities are still preserved which other people are losing—faith, above all, and respect for the forms of religion? "Let us try," he said, "to find a parallel. We go into one of our own houses and there is no one there to receive us. We go along the corridors and by mistake—yes, by mistake—go into the bathroom. There we surprise the mistress of the house, naked, busy washing herself. A very common sight. It is her form of narcissism, her way of passing the time. And on her head the lady in the bath has a priest's hat."

"That's it," I said. "But in what house will you see such an uncommon spectacle?"

The second lieutenant said in a low voice: "In an asylum." And I could not refrain from laughing. So Mariam was mad! It seemed to me useless to refute his hypothesis and I said: "Let's go on."

"Let's go on," repeated the second lieutenant. But we were silent. "In four days," I thought, "embarkation at Massaua." The soldiers would be drunk with sun and wine. Then the Red Sea, a hot and melancholy sea, and finally Port Said. There would remain with us as a last memory of Africa the huge advertisement for whisky at the entrance to the port. It is the first African monument one sees on arrival and the last when one leaves.

The second obscure point was the sores. When I pointed out that they could be caused by indigestion the second lieutenant shook his head. "Let's try, however," I said, "to find a rational explanation for them. Perhaps they were produced by blood poisoning. The fast in the village and Johannes' poultices cured them. To sum up, they are not an obscure point," I concluded, "although the first picture in the book was my hand."

The second lieutenant thought a long time before speaking, then said that he did not consider a native capable of curing sores caused by blood poisoning. "Leprosy sores, yes," he added. "Here we are in the realm of metaphysics, and Johannes accepts metaphysics. But other kinds of sores, no. He lets the 'signori' cure them; and this, fortunately, is the mark of their superiority."

"Well then?" I said.

"Well then, the sores cannot be discussed, they must be accepted." And because I smiled the second lieutenant said that we could even try a rational explanation, but in ten years' time. "No," I said quickly, "let's accept them without discussion." We laughed. From the camp there now came a hum of voices; the soldiers had stopped singing and were beginning to make themselves ready. The pots of coffee were boiling on the cookhouse fire.

"I should like to know," said the second lieutenant, "Lazarus' reply to people who asked him what he saw on the other side. Probably Lazarus, with his head still in the clouds, replied that he had not bothered about it." We were silent once more. Perhaps both of us were thinking of Johannes: thoughts such as come when one looks at a valley growing light in the smoky dawn of a day so much desired. I thought of Johannes, of his poultices, of his last salute on the brow of the hill.

2

"There's the major left," I said. And I added: "That's an obscure point I should like to cast light on. It is clear" (here I laughed) "that the major was afraid."

The mountains had emerged from the shadow, the sun struck athwart them, while the valley seemed to have fallen asleep, like a sufferer from insomnia who waits for the company of the sun or the swish of the brush on the pavement before deciding to rest. The howling of the wild beasts was no longer to be heard, and the night breeze was giving way to the oppressiveness of the morning. "There's the major left," I repeated.

The second lieutenant lit another cigar; then he said: "Yes, the major was frightened and gave up the idea of denunciation. Or perhaps he was not frightened and only put it off. It's difficult to say."

"He gave up the idea," I said. "How could he have accounted for his profits? He was frightened of losing them, that's all."

I saw the major again walking up and down the quay and looking at the packing-cases which had been unloaded with superhuman exertions by half-naked natives. He kept looking at them with those eyes of his that could not conceal a craftiness recently acquired. And he kept turning his glance—like a hyphen—to the bright blue truck resting in the sun near the bar.

"Too simple," said the second lieutenant. "In any case it will be as well if we satisfy ourselves with regard to this fear. Fear has infinite gradations and can be classified. There is the fear which lays hold of one beforehand, and is the fear of the wise and the prudent; the fear which . . . Am I boring you?"

"No," I said, "go on." (In actual fact I was thinking the second lieutenant has not only a tendency towards complications, they are a vice with him.)

"The fear," he went on, "which lays hold of one afterwards and is that of brave men; and there is, finally, the fear which lays hold of one while a thing is happening, and that is the fear that kills—as you have rightly observed—or that makes one a coward. Now I am very doubtful how to classify the major's fear. Are you quite sure that you took off the nut?"

"Here it is," I said, taking it from my pocket. The second lieutenant looked at the nut and made it jump up and down on the palm of his hand; he did not seem altogether convinced. I was thinking that I would be sorry to meet the major in Massaua. I could give him back the money, in fact I must give it back to him, but why meet him? He will not be able to recognise me, I concluded. I have a much longer beard than when I met him for the first time and he ordered me to shave.

The second lieutenant remained silent, so I asked him to go on. And with an effort—perhaps he was sleepy—he said: "This valley has two sides. We are on the rim of the north side, you took off this nut from the major's truck on the rim of the south side; up there, if I am not mistaken" (and the second lieutenant pointed to the opposite rim, now taking on a pink hue). "You were worried about the denunciation, so you considered that you had been beaten when you saw the truck on the road leading to the bridge, that is to say to the telephone at the post. Instead the major went on without telephoning."

"Of course," I said, "but why did he go on without telephoning? Perhaps the telephone was out of order and on the way the major looked at his situation carefully and finally gave up the idea of the denunciation. Fear laid hold of him beforehand, in short."

"That may be," said the second lieutenant, "but I find it difficult to believe that the major was afraid of being reported. No, if the major was in business he had to have flank protection, perhaps he was the lowest rung in a much bigger game." And he added: "Was he to be afraid of the denunciation of an officer who was guilty of theft and already being looked for for attempted homicide?"

"Perhaps," I said.

"No," replied the second lieutenant, "he would have had nothing to fear. It is true all the same that you were afraid of his denunciation and to make it impossible, you took off the nut, thinking thus to interfere in the major's destiny."

"Well then?" I asked.

"Then only one hypothesis is left to us. If he went over the bridge without telephoning—let's rule out that the telephone was out of order because it is a double line—we must suppose that he did not want to telephone, not even once he had reached the table-land. Or else we must suppose that he did not wish to denounce you. And that was not a decision he took when on his way; on the contrary, he took it when he was climbing back into his truck after his discussion with you. What would it have cost him, actually, to turn back? Or to refuse to go on? Would you have fired? No, you had to avoid any complications. So right from the start he gave up the idea of the denunciation. Without attaching any weight to the Massaua gossip he had already resigned himself to the idea of the robbery. Unconsciously resigned."

"We are back where we started," I said. "Why did he not want to denounce me?"

"I leave it to you to judge," replied the second lieutenant. "Out of pity, I imagine. Or perhaps because he took your advice to recoup his money by making another trip. But I rule out fear. The major cannot have felt fear."

He fell silent; it was then that I asked if the major was dead. I had already suspected something from his reticences, but the brief reply still surprised me. Indeed, I at first refused to believe it. Perhaps, I thought, this was the second lieutenant's macabre pretext for amusing himself at my expense. Only when he had repeated the phrase several times—being himself surprised that I did not accept the end which had been the major's lot—I had to give in. He was not joking. "The major," he said, "went over the bridge, but never reached the table-land." And he concluded: "So he cannot have felt fear, but only terror or surprise."

He was amusing himself, getting the most out of it, so as to bring that long night, the last night of our friendship, to an end without regrets. Seeing that I remained silent—I was recalling the major sitting on Mariam's bed, busy rubbing his white and womanly breast, and his face beaming in a smile of indubitable sympathy—the second lieutenant became suddenly serious and said I might not be to blame. There are a lot of things that make a truck go off the road; in fact Africa is full of over-turned trucks. We could easily find out the cause if I wanted. "If the bolt is in place," he concluded, "no one is to blame. Least of all the nut."

I did not answer. He had gone on without telephoning, but had not reached the table-land. Perhaps he had gone off the road for other reasons, after having repaired the damage. But who had taken off the nut? Perhaps myself? I, that insolent youth consult-

ing his watch on the side of the road, trembling at the thought
that the truck had not fallen over? I, who from the beginning had
reserved for myself a part in the major's history? "Well," I
thought, "the story of the major is finished, but mine has hardly
begun." The trumpet was sounding reveille and at the first notes
a cry burst from the soldiers. They were all up now, striking the
tents. They were shouting to hail the day of their departure,
amazed that it was true. Egged on by these cries the trumpeter
repeated the call, adding wrong notes and comic variations to it,
then came and repeated it on the edge of the valley. He wanted
everyone to hear reveille on the day for which he had waited
two long years.

"We can find out right away if you like," repeated the second
lieutenant.

And they all heard it but no one could move. They could not
move, the ones in the packing-cases under the hot sand of the
river. Nor the hanged men or the Abyssinian who points to heav-
en—and who knows whether he does not see something more
than his aeroplane up there. Nor could the woman move, although I know that the head moves under the turban when I take
aim. Nor could the major move either, now. No one could move
out of that valley, I thought, except myself. But my story was
scarcely beginning and the major had given up the idea of de-
nouncing me. Merely put it off. Why had he gone on without telephoning? For a second when we were in the cabin of the truck, he
put his hand on my shoulder and I felt a tired hand, a hand which
belied the cheerfulness of his face and his second youth.

The second lieutenant insisted: "We can see right away if the
bolt is in its place. Do you want to?"

I did not reply. Why should I reply? He was making it a me-
chanical matter. Should I go down into a ravine, perhaps the very
one that opened beneath us in order to examine a carcase, to
remove all doubt? Doubts give comfort, it is better to keep them.
And besides I preferred to look at the valley. Johannes must have
risen, perhaps he was going to the river followed by the mule. By
the by, I had forgotten to warn the supply mule not to go to the

forking of the ways when his great moment comes. It is difficult enough already to get out of this valley! But then it is easy to go back.

When the second lieutenant went off along the rim of the valley searching in the ravine and finally threw the nut and I heard that sharp sound of struck metal—or perhaps it was the silver he had in his pocket—I did not feel anything. The nut was in place. No one wins and it is an unmarked dice which has now been put back in its place. Everything was in place, no one was looking for me and my story was just beginning.

So I looked at the valley when the "fall in" sounded, and this time the trumpeter played it at the double. It was time to go, to postpone reflections until tomorrow, to say goodbye to those who were staying behind. Perhaps the soldiers were even now ready; I had to inspect the platoon and drink my coffee; but above all I had to go to that grave, which already I knew too well. I went to meet the second lieutenant and said: "We must go." Then I added: "It seems to me pointless to talk of crimes since no one is looking for me."

"Yes," be replied, "quite pointless."

"If no one is looking for me," I insisted, "we can go."

"Without another thought," he replied. "Our neighbours are too busy with their own crimes to worry about ours."

"And I take it," I said looking straight at him, "that no one will look for me ever."

"I am sure of it," he replied. "No one will look for you. We are all innocent."

"It's best like that," I said. "If no one denounced me, it's better like that. Yet, people have no right to be so generous."

"Take it or leave it," said the second lieutenant finally.

The trumpet repeated the call in haste. It seemed as if he were repeating it for us—the others must already be in their places, there was not the least noise to be heard. "It is a pretty comical trumpet for my Judgment Day," I said, "but every man has his own." I said it looking towards the valley which at that moment seemed to me to be indeed unique and immortal.

"Don't believe it," said the second lieutenant. "There will be no other trumpets. The only ones you will hear will be those, but only for a few more days, then they will give us leave."

"And yet," I said, "this valley...." But I did not go on. No, there is no point in quoting an author when we have made cigarette papers out of a page of his book. (Isn't that right, Johannes?)

I did not go on and we made our way towards the camp because the trucks were arriving. I walked along beside the second lieutenant and suddenly I smelled his perfume. Obviously he must put some expensive brand of brilliantine on his hair. A brilliantine with a delicate, childish perfume, but the heat was making it rancid. An extremely nasty kind of brilliantine, which the heat of the valley was making sickly-sweet, putrid with long-withered flowers, a poisonous odour. I hastened my step, but that stinking trail preceded me.